SECRETS

OF THE

OLD LADIES' CLUB

SECRETS

OF THE

OLD LADIES' CLUB

A NOVEL BY

NAN TUBRE

iUniverse, Inc.
Bloomington

SECRETS OF THE OLD LADIES' CLUB

iUniverse books may be ordered through booksellers or by contacting:

iUniverse
1663 Liberty Drive
Bloomington, IN 47403
www.iuniverse.com
1-800-Authors (1-800-288-4677)

ISBN: 978-1-4759-7512-3 (sc)
ISBN: 978-1-4759-7514-7 (hc)
ISBN: 978-1-4759-7513-0 (ebk)

Library of Congress Control Number: 2013902418

Printed in the United States of America

iUniverse rev. date: 02/11/2013

DEDICATION

This book is dedicated to every friend I have had or ever will have. I have heard it said that an author should write of what he or she knows. I happen to know about friends. The characters and events within this book are fictitious. However, if you are my friend and you see similarities between this story and your life, you have my permission to think of yourself as my inspiration. You probably were! Don't worry—names and other pertinent information were changed to protect the innocent *and* the guilty.

You know who you are!

P.S. I love you.

Acknowledgements

Telling this story has been #1 on my Bucket List for a long time. Now that it is in print, perhaps I can live in peace. On the other hand, I think there is another story rolling around in my head. Before I take that thought any further, I'd like to thank all the important people who helped me give birth to this book. It was a long labor.

My husband Pete, you are the love of my life. I am so glad I have you! I very much appreciate you for tolerating all of my 'phases'.

My boys, Russell, Michael, and David, I love you fiercely. You make me strong. Because of you, I could not give up on this project.

Now, on to #2 on my Bucket List: does anybody have a piano for sale?

Regina Whitmore: Before you can be the person God meant you to be, you have to learn to forgive yourself.

Donna Thompson: What 'golden years'? As far as I'm concerned, they are all golden years!

Stella Morgenstern-Taub: Growing old is nice but it doesn't hurt to be a little immature now and then.

Bethany Bertrand: Our bodies may grow old but our souls don't. They just grow.

Cicely Johnson: You can't accomplish anything if you give up.

When you get to be our age, don't be shocked that deep down inside you still feel the exact same way you did when you were young.

TABLE OF CONTENTS

PROLOGUE

PART I

It is impossible to see the sun actually set from a certain little sidewalk café in Paris. Regardless, five dear friends sharing two bistro tables close to the street were able to enjoy the luscious streaks of plum, pink and gold splashing across the sky. A French sunset was like no other in the world to these women. They loved it. They inhaled it and were mesmerized by it. They planned regular trips abroad to enjoy the magic spell it cast on them. The lovely wine accompaniment didn't hurt either. The combination was pleasurable and necessary for these women who have history together. Over the years, their lives intermingled in many ways, thereby generating envy among those outside their circle. They have witnessed the good and bad times of each other's lives. They actively participated in decisions, drastic and otherwise, that affected the bond they shared. They were loyal, dedicated, and honest with each other. Well, for the most part anyway.

Just as the sunset ushered in the night sky, the city's lights began to come alive and wrap around Paris like a luxurious mink stole. It was a beautiful night with warm, thick air dripping with the tantalizing aromas of chocolate, baked bread, and darkly roasted coffee. A wafting breeze whispered secrets of the sensuous scent of some delectable French perfume, entertaining those in its path with romantic notions.

"*Bonne anniversaries*, happy sixtieth birthday, Cicely Johnson! May you continue to live long and love often." Regina Whitmore raised her champagne glass with a toast to the woman sitting to her right. "You've been a good and true friend. You are our Sister and now that you have come of age, we welcome you to The Old Ladies' Club!"

"Here, here!" a chorus of jovial feminine voices followed as crystal glasses clinked together in celebration of the moment.

"Come on! You mean I am officially in the Club now? Ha! Thank you, ladies. That's the very reason I'm still hanging around with you girls," Cicely laughed, her delicious brown eyes watered and her smile was wide and bright. She loved this moment. What could be better, except of course, if her beloved husband was still alive? At this table in Paris, France no less, sat her most precious friends and she knew her proverbial cup was full. Next to her family, the women toasting her were more important than she thought anyone ever could be. Together, they had accomplished a great deal more than what society expected of ladies of their age. The individual efforts and talents each person brought to the group enabled them to be financially secure, as well as rich with emotional support, friendship and love. Life without them was unthinkable. Cicely looked around the table and considered each woman. Regina Whitmore; a Viet Nam war widow, mother of two, one surviving. Estelle Morgenstern-Taub, whom they call Stella, widowed once, divorced twice. Bethany Bertrand; now seventy-two, the oldest of the group, a widow with one son. Finally, Donna Thompson; divorced, mother of two, one surviving daughter.

The year was 2002. The Old Ladies' Club had traveled to France in the wake of 9/11, the most disastrous terrorist attack on U.S. soil. The whole world was in turmoil it seemed, and the American people were stressed practically to the breaking point. The Club gave serious consideration as to whether or not they should go abroad, but the consensus was to cast aside all warnings about Americans traveling and just go. Although security was beefed up more than they had ever witnessed, the trip overseas went as smoothly as it did every time they traveled together. There was an impression in some circles that many foreign populations were not very fond of America and her people, and that harsh American politics overshadowed all the good the United States stood for. The tight knit group, celebrating a birthday of one of their own, chose not to acknowledge any prejudice that might come their way. For them, at least, it was a time of celebration. Even so, with complete respectability, these women did honor their country and her service men and women, especially those patriots who have fallen, by attending Mass on this trip at the beautiful, gothic Notre Dame Cathedral. Although each member of the Club dealt with tragedies in her own way, in light of the combination of events in their country and in their lives, every day was a day to celebrate. And so they did.

PART II

THE BUSINESS

By the time the business formed in the year 2000, Cicely was nearly 60 years old, Regina was 67, Stella, fighting off 66 years, Donna closing in on 70 years old, and Bethany, a joyful 71 years old. In the months prior to the cross-continental birthday jaunt, Cicely decided she needed a project. It wasn't normal for her to be idle and it seemed that she had way too much time on her hands. She took a long time to consider what her options were; volunteer at the hospital, join the garden club, or maybe even give art lessons to youth after school. Nope. None of those activities sparked an interest for her. Deep in her heart, she had a passion and it was interior design. However, not just any ordinary interior design. No, Cicely wanted to leave a lasting impression, something she could be proud of, something she could do to help others. An idea began to blossom in her creative mind. Her children were grown now and had their own lives. What was holding her back? Her thoughts wandered to something of which she had longed dreamed. Why not start by remodeling her house? She could completely renovate the upstairs into an apartment and rent it out to someone who might need a helping hand. She already pictured in her mind how the finished project would look and she couldn't wait to put her plan on paper.

Cicely was a cautious woman, never one to go off half-cocked. It wasn't that she lacked impulsivity, rather, she was very sensible. Becoming a millionaire overnight will do that to a person. Being thrust into the role of steward for that kind of money invoked a deep sense of responsibility for the young widow. Involuntarily appointed, it was her job, and only hers, to see that the financial future of her family would never be in jeopardy. The idea of creating an income property out of her home would help insure that financial security. If it worked out, and the venture was successful, perhaps another moneymaking project would present itself. Who knew? Maybe she was on to something. Cecily had a firm confidence that her vision could turn into something big.

Once she finished the design, she presented it to her architect son, Alton. He knew their house better than anyone for it was within the walls of this old beauty that inspiration for his future career was acquired and developed. The old family home was a distinguished two-story dwelling with five bedrooms and three bathrooms. It was situated on an acre of land, which was a rather grand size property within the city limits of Ocean View. The house was very large, and it needed to be for the size of family Cicely and Jim Johnson planted there.

The gleam in his mother's eyes convinced Alton to review the house plan she drew in a lined three-hole spiral notebook. If this idea made her feel so happy, he would certainly give it his best attention. To his surprise, Alton began to see the sensibility of her drawings with every page he turned.

"Mom, this is good! Where did you get this idea?"

"Well, I watch a lot of TV," Cicely smiled proudly at her son. "I don't know, Alton, I just need a project. I need that project to be one I can share with you kids. I'm going to talk to all of you and make sure that anything I do to the house won't cause a rift with anyone, after all, it is the home you were all raised in."

"Mom, I don't think any of us would object at all. We are all financially sound. The only one of us who might need your help is Danny. And he's doing well at St. Catherine's."

"I know he is, honey. But I need to be sure he will still be taken care of after I'm not here anymore." Cicely stated.

"Mama," Alton's voice softened, "we wouldn't let Danny do without. We would all take care of him, you know that."

"Yes, I do. However, you all have your own lives and it wouldn't be fair for any of you to have to sacrifice for him. St. Catharine's is expensive. I think this project would help by making sure Danny will be independently secure for the rest of his life." Cicely explained. Alton went to work on his mother's plans and once they were ready, he presented them to her. She was thrilled with the results.

"It's amazing," she exclaimed. "I love this! Now, let's tell your brothers and sisters." They were able to schedule a meeting that every family member could match to their schedules. All members of the family whole-heartedly affirmed the concept of turning the upstairs of their old home place into an income property for the sake of their downs-syndrome brother. Cicely had never had a prouder moment for her children. They loved one another, just as she and their father taught them to.

Work started on a hot July day and continued throughout August. Finally, when the job was finished, family and friends gathered for a grand tour and open house. Beyond the front door, an elegant stairway ascended to the second floor, while a door to the right opened to the main floor living quarters. The change was quite remarkable. Not only did the upstairs apartment offer two bedrooms, a bath, and living room, it also housed a kitchen with full sized modern amenities such as a dishwasher, gas range, and refrigerator/freezer. The counter tops in the kitchen and bathroom weren't granite, as was the latest style trend, but, regardless, they were a highly acceptable, quality solid surface. The bathroom was large, and although the bedrooms weren't huge, they both had walk-in closets with plenty of storage. The living room was situated in the area where a bay window accented the front façade of the house, and the earth tone paint colors throughout gave the apartment a warm, welcoming atmosphere.

Few changes were required of the downstairs, which was now a ground floor apartment. By converting a formal parlor, the floor plan was redesigned to accommodate two bedrooms and two bathrooms, leaving the kitchen, formal dining room and casual living room without alteration.

The two apartments were allotted a separate lawn and patio situated on either side of the large house. The backyard became the common area. Cicely spent so many hours over the years working in her gardens that she couldn't conceive tearing it all out. "I'll share," she told her family. She took great pride in the little pond her husband built for her before he died. Long ago, the two of them planted banana trees and palms to give the space a tropical feel. She usually had her morning coffee on the deck beside this pond, as she fed the koi and goldfish. It was a tranquil place where she felt close to God and to her Jim.

Mother and son received plenty of accolades from family and friends at the open house they hosted. "Most impressive," they were told. "Incredible transformation," everyone agreed. Cicely caught the impressed look in the eyes of her four best friends and it was all too easy to guess what they were thinking. Over the course of the next week, one after the other of her friends approached her. To no one's surprise, they all had the same idea; buy properties and turn them for a profit. "After all," they told each other, "we've got the money to do it. We certainly have the time! It'll be fun!"

It was Stella's idea to call a meeting to discuss the concept. They unanimously agreed their involvement would be strictly a business venture. Friendship didn't count. Business was business. None of the women were as eager as Cecily had been to convert their homes into rental properties, but all had a fair amount to invest in other properties, some that would, perhaps, need a good deal of renovation. Bethany offered to talk to her son Jack who was an attorney, about the ins and outs of becoming a business. He helped them form the group and the consensus was to call their business The Old Ladies' Club, in honor of the humorous way they spoke of their collective friendship. They laughed over the chosen business name knowing full well that age didn't reflect or dictate the strength of a person, her general attitude, or tenderness of heart. These so-called senior citizens were vibrant and felt they were in the prime of their lives. Age meant nothing more than experience, a whole lifetime of experience.

Without the first moment of hesitation, the group was off on an adventure, a profitable one to be sure. At the first business meeting, they developed a plan by drafting a statement mapping out their ideas and what they wanted to accomplish. Donna told the group that she discussed their proposition with her daughter, who was a very successful realtor. Belinda would be quite the asset in finding properties to renovate. She had the inside track, so to speak, and said she was happy to lend a hand. Cicely offered to talk to two of her daughters who were designers and had superb taste and fashion sense. With them on board, designing a space that would be beautiful, as well as efficient, would not be a problem.

Regina quietly listened as Donna and Cicely gladly offered the services of their families. However, she wasn't about to offer the services of her only remaining child. She wouldn't have dared to ask Larry Jr. for anything. If the answer would be no, and without a doubt it would be, she couldn't take the shame of it.

A property was located in a part of Ocean View that was only slightly undesirable. The group met to discuss working in such an area.

"We should do it," Regina told the others. "We could make a difference in the neighborhood, don't you think?"

The house turned out to be a sprawling ranch style large enough to convert to a duplex apartment building. Thanks to Cicely's construction contractor son, work was able to start early and finish quickly. The crew was well paid for their efforts as they completed the details on the house, and it was ready in time for the Thanksgiving holidays. At the next business meeting, the subject of tenants was discussed. Again, Stella was the first to offer an option.

"Why don't we consider tenants who really need an affordable place to live, someone who deserves a break, like a single parent or an older couple?"

"That's a wonderful idea!" Bethany added. "Lord knows there are a lot of them around. This town has plenty of people who need a break."

"We've all been so blessed," Donna said. "I say we should share the blessings!"

"I agree. We ought to make this business all about helping people." Cicely said

"Let's do it anonymously," Regina hesitantly suggested. "If we give and take credit for giving, would we be accomplishing our goal? Shouldn't we make it a point to bless others with a helping hand and do it without being hailed for it?"

Barely a moment later, the suggestion was overwhelmingly adopted. The Old Ladies' Club was now, exclusively, a business designed to help people. If profit came their way the ladies would gladly accept it, but profit wasn't their main goal. With the sale of their first property, they were able to buy two more. Early on, they decided not to seek mortgage loans or remodeling expenditure loans, instead doing everything outright with their own personal money. By the third and fourth renovations, their investments were recouped and the company had its own bank account. The business expanded rapidly. Bethany's son, Jack, accepted the position as their business attorney and gave them legal establishment, changing from OLC to OLC, INC., LLC. They were incorporated. Anonymously.

I

WELCOME TO
THE OLD LADIES CLUB

Every person in the room watched as Regina entered on the arm of her son, Dr. Lawrence Whitmore, Jr. It wasn't her beauty that attracted their attention, although she was very lovely in a regal sort of way. She was wore a powder blue dress with matching jacket and navy blue pumps. Her short white hair was perfectly styled and she walked slowly with her head held high. In her left hand was a box of chocolates, assorted varieties. Her son was a handsome middle-aged man, very similar in appearance to herself, and he guided her gently by her right elbow through the room. His commanding presence had a way of mesmerizing the residents of Heritage Memories Retirement Village. He was tall and his gray pin-stripped suit perfectly complimented his wavy, prematurely silver hair. These old folks seldom had the opportunity to see the owner and proprietor of their residence in person. Yet, here he was in the flesh with his mother beside him, as well. Now, that was a sight and everybody already knew how it would end. Dr. Whitmore would show his mother to her apartment, pay a visit to the administrative offices to deliver a how-great-the-staff-is pep talk, and then he would disappear until the next time. The next time, whenever that would be. Afterwards, Regina would hold court in the dining room and recount the day's events. A few of the Village's residents would sit in attendance, feigning interest, while everyone else in the common dining room went about the business of selecting their supper entrees and sides dishes. She put on airs, everyone thought, just because her son owned the place. She's snooty, some said, especially after her boy takes her out for the day, which, they sympathized, doesn't happen very often.

Later, when she was in her own apartment, Regina sat at her petite Queen Anne lady's desk, opened her journal to a blank page, and made an entry.

"June 1st, 2008

Larry Jr. picked me up today and brought me to see my new great-granddaughter, Penny. I didn't even know Taylor was pregnant. I haven't seen them since last Christmas. The baby looks like me. I miss her already."

The door to Regina's apartment opened and Stella Morgenstern-Taub crossed the threshold, followed by the strong scent of her newest rose scented perfume and her tiny Yorkshire terrier, Camille. The orange and black African print caftan she wore swirled around her full figured body and settled with a poof of air as Stella plopped into the armchair next to Regina's antique writing desk. Camille jumped on Stella's lap and crawled around in circles until he found just the right spot on which to lie.

"Don't you ever knock?" Regina looked over the top of her reading glasses at her uninvited guest.

"Hell no, why would I do that?" Stella asked, smoothing her shoulder length salt and pepper hair. Regina and Stella had a long history together beginning over 30 years earlier when both ladies worked at Southeastern Bell. Regina was a long distance operator and Stella filled the role of information operator. Oh, she was sassy that one, Regina remembered. A person could hear Stella laughing and joking with customers from any point in the long room crowded with switchboards and buzzing voices.

"It's not like I don't know what you're doing. So how did it go today?" Stella began. "Did he take you out to eat? Did he part with any of his precious money to buy you a gift?" She ran her right ring finger along the garishly red line bordering her thin lips. For years, Regina tried to convince Stella that lining her lips with that bright color did not make her mouth look plump and youthful. "Who needs plump lips at our age?" she argued time and time again. Eventually, Stella's resistance convinced her to give up the effort.

Regina's eyes glanced at the journal on her desk. She closed the book softly and faced her friend with a sedate smile.

"It was fine, just fine. Yes, we went out to eat. He took me to the Piccadilly. Then, he took me to the hospital to introduce me to my new great-granddaughter. After that, he took me to Dillard's at the mall and bought me some new underwear. Do you need to see them?" Regina answered in a sweetly sarcastic manner.

"What'd you eat?" Stella asked as she picked through the box of chocolates sitting next to Regina's journal.

"What?" Regina furrowed her white brow, annoyed that Stella was helping herself to her candy.

"What'd you eat at the Piccadilly? Did you have the liver and onions? I love the liver and onions. Did you get one of those big cathead biscuits? I love those too. Oh, the carrot soufflé, yesss! And I always get a dessert when I go to the Piccadilly, which by the way, never happens unless I can bribe Cicely to take me," Stella rattled.

"Didn't you hear me? I told you I have a great granddaughter. Taylor had a baby. Doesn't that mean anything to you?"

"Of course, I heard you and I know what it means. It means we are getting old. I never thought that would happen, did you? Just look at us. Here we are living the grand life in a fancy-shmancy old folks home. It means that the years have just flown by." Stella waved her hand as though she was casually dismissing her life.

"You don't get it. I said I have a new *great* grandchild and I didn't even know my own granddaughter was pregnant! How could they not tell me something like that? Sometimes my son acts as if I don't exist!" Tears welled up in Regina's eyes.

"Is she married?"

"What? She's just a baby!"

"Is Taylor married? Maybe he didn't tell you because she isn't married." Stella reasoned.

While considering the possibility, Regina looked down at her seventy-six year old hands and pretended not to see the age spots dotting them.

"I don't know if she is married. Nobody said anything one way or the other. All they wanted to do was take generation photos, you know, my son, his niece and her baby, and me. Four generations." Regina felt somewhat relieved. The possibility of Stella's explanation seemed valid enough. Maybe that was why Larry Jr. didn't tell that she was going to be a great grandmother. Taylor must not be married. Good grief, what did they imagine she was going to say? Did they think she was going to disapprove or have a stroke? Regina was beginning to lose the numbness that stunned her heart with this sudden surprise.

"What'd you tell 'em?" Stella asked with a mouth full of candy.

"What?" Regina directed her attention back to her friend.

"What'd you tell 'em? Dammit, are you deaf?"

"I didn't tell them a thing, smarty. I just pretended to know all about it. And by the way, Estelle, it's not an old folk's home." She was beginning to loose her patience.

"Don't get your new panties in a knot, Gina. Now your whole family is going to think you've gone senile because they know they didn't tell you about the new baby! Just for your information, Missy, we live here and we are old. It's an old folk's home!" She dropped a half eaten chocolate back into the box. "Why do you let Junior give you this crappy candy anyway? Didn't I tell you they give me the fudgie shits?"

"PLEASE do not let your dog lift his leg on the way out," Regina ordered.

She wrinkled her nose at the still suffocating, undeniable scent of roses lingering in Stella's wake. Now that her friend was gone, she could get back to the business of feeling sorry for herself. Her thoughts turned toward her daughter and her heart ached. They were close, she and Renee', as close as a mother was and daughter could be. It wasn't right that Renee' had to grow up never knowing her father. Fortunately, her daughter was resilient and inordinately sensitive. Even as a child, the youngster was able to sense her mother's struggle with sadness and regret. Assuming the role of comforter became second nature for the girl. Her unexpected death was a monumental shock to everyone. It happened shortly after she gave birth to her daughter. The whole family gathered for the joyous occasion, congratulating the new father in front of the nursery window while on the other side of the glass, baby Taylor stretched her little arms and legs and pouted with a cherry red mouth. She had just returned to the nursery from her mother's breast and her tiny lips were still smacking for more. When the ecstatic family headed back to the new mother's room, they were met with a startling commotion. Emergency carts were being pushed into Renee''s room by frantic nurses. Several professional looking personnel were rushing in and out, and then finally, a distraught doctor delivered the news. A blood clot had lodged in Renee''s heart and took her life.

To an outside observer, it would appear that Renee'was the glue that bonded the family together. After she died, the family ties seemed to go to the grave with her. At least, for a time anyway, Regina had baby Taylor to buffer her grief. She did everything she could, as the child grew older, to help her son-in-law provide a warm loving home. Tragically, he too, died young. After a fatal car accident robbed Taylor of her only surviving parent, the fourteen year old went to live with Larry Jr. and his family. Her uncle was kind enough to help raise her, stepping in for father-daughter dances, graduations and so forth. If he ever resented having another mouth to feed, he never mentioned it. Although grateful for everything her son did, Regina was lonely for her family and she was sure that if her daughter were alive, she would not have to worry about such things. Larry Jr. and his family rarely had time for her. A person would think his wife would be thoughtful enough to schedule visits more frequently, especially with two children and a niece to consider, but as always, there seemed to be some sort of strain between them preventing that. The elder Mrs. Whitmore had no idea why; it just was. The real problem for her was that Taylor became just as inaccessible as the rest of Larry Jr.'s family.

Refusing to let those old memories depress her, Regina shook off the morose cloak beginning to settle across her shoulders. She took stock of her surroundings and counted her blessings. She had a nice apartment; two fair sized bedrooms, one bath, a decent sized living room with a flat screen TV, and an adjoining kitchenette, essentially, a small refrigerator, apartment size electric stove, and microwave. The kitchen design was charming, although not as large as she was used to. The oak cabinetry was adequate and was topped with gorgeous black granite that, in the right light, sparkled with nearly transparent flecks of silver. This executive suite had an independent phone line and cable, as well, and the décor was of her choosing. She surrounded herself with antiques and favorite pieces of quality furniture she collected over the years. Some pieces had been in her family for too many years to remember. Many of these treasures were too precious to part with; the family Bible, the well-aged likeness of her grandparents on their wedding day, her mother's silver jewelry box, and her father's old tobacco pipes still faintly smelling of the rich scent of aromatic imported tobacco forever embedded within walnut and mahogany bowls.

Heritage Memories Retirement Village was a great place to live. Because Larry Jr. and his best friend, Chad Sanders, built it, their mothers had the biggest apartments in the whole complex. These executive suites were more than accommodating and the remaining apartments were several notches above ordinary, as well. The Village, one could say, provided independent, as well as dependent, living at its finest. Residents could keep a cat or a small dog as long as they were able to care for the animal. If their apartment did not come with laundry hookups, community laundry facilities were available close by. They could join others for meals in the dining room, or choose to cook in their own apartment, provided their appliances didn't violate the health and safety policies of the Village. "Yeah, like a slow cooker would set off the fire alarm," Chad's mother Donna snickered after seeing her apartment for the first time.

The memory of Chad Thompson surfaced for a moment. Regina thought of him often and considered her best friend blessed to have a son like him. Donna's boy was a most charming fellow, redheaded like his dad, and very tender hearted. In fact, his sweet, innocent heart was the incentive behind building the retirement home. He and Larry Jr. were only eight years old when they came up with the idea. Back in those days, Regina, Donna, and their husbands, Big Larry and Tom, were the best of friends. The similarities between the two families were remarkable and celebrated. Both had sons the same age. Donna had a year old baby girl, Belinda, and the little tyke was just as comfortable at Regina's house as she was in her own crib. Some years later, Regina gave birth to Renee', and her joyful presence filled the ragged hole torn in their heats when Big Larry's jet went down in Viet Nam. After Donna and Tom divorced, the two women remained best friends and continued to stay close as though they were sisters. Their children would always view each other as family. The boys were especially close. Wherever one was, the other would be as well. They were practically inseparable.

Regina let herself get lost in the memories of that time in her life. She recalled when Larry Jr. and Chad first decided to build a home for their parents as they aged. The scenario was as clear in her mind's eye as it had been that very day. Both families had gathered around Donna's dining room table to look at the dozens of family photographs covering the lace tablecloth. Everyone was sharing their favorites with the group; especially the pictures that made them laugh, cry, or hide their faces behind their hands in embarrassment.

Regina remembered everyone looking at Chad as his freckled face reddened and the corners of his mouth drooped.

"Baby, what's the matter?" his mother asked, alarmed.

"I'm going to miss you, Mama," the boy told her, unable to hold back the tears.

"Well, darlin', where are you going?" Donna asked her son.

"I'm going to get married and move awayyy," he wailed. "Can we move in with you?" He threw his body into her lap and buried his face in her neck.

Donna tried not to laugh and managed to tell him, "Sure you can, baby, but I've got a feeling that once you get married, you won't want to live with your old mama."

Regina noticed blonde-headed Larry Jr. listening intently to the exchanged and could see his young heart hurt for his friend. Her son slung his scrawny arm around Chad's shoulders and told him "Don't worry. When we grow up, me and you will build an old folks home for our parents and we can visit them anytime we want to!"

Chad's face brightened and he exclaimed, "That's a great idea! Let's start saving for it now. Here's a quarter!"

"Whoa now! I'm not planning to get old any time soon!" Regina laughed along with everyone else at the table.

Surprisingly, the two boys never forgot their promise. They joked about it now and then over time, but deep down inside, everyone knew that one day, the old folk's home would become a reality. Even after the boys grew up and left their friendship behind, they still managed to make the dream come true. Larry Jr., the doctor, handled the money end and Chad, the contractor, provided the labor, both offering an equal investment of time, money, and other resources to the endeavor. It turned out to be far better than anyone else could have imagined. To their credit, the partnership they formed to complete the plan yielded a highly sought after, efficiently run, quality retirement village. Regina and Donna could not help but be proud of their sons' accomplishment. During the ribbon cutting ceremony, the mayor made a speech about what an asset the Village would be for the town of Ocean View, Florida. Larry Jr. and Chad were both present accepting accolades, but that was the last time anyone saw them in the same room together. Their mothers knew it would be. The men's history dictated it. The two women clung to the memory of their sons standing side by side just as they did when they were inseparable children. Framed eight by ten photos of the grown men shaking hands hung in their respective mother's apartment, a reminder of a time when their friendship was solid and enduring.

Over the years, Regina and Donna developed a skill that allowed them to pretend they didn't see certain things, essentially turning a blind eye, as the saying goes. Their husbands commonly referred to the habit as "selective awareness", but the practice was established purely out of the need not to know what was happening around them. Such was the case concerning the boys. Regina's critical eye couldn't help but notice her son's penchant for books and spending much of his time alone in his room. Larry Jr. wasn't the type of boy who followed the crowd as a rule; rather he marched to his own beat. He was kind of soft and pale, and spent an inordinate amount of time in front of the mirror staring at his hair, his arms, and his chest. When the first few manly hairs sprouted from his lip, he was at the sink with a razor nearly before they breached the skin. Donna's son, on the other hand, was big and beefy. He was into all the sports he could possibly enroll in and still manage to keep up in school. He had girls calling him almost daily, slyly hinting that they didn't have a date for Friday night or an upcoming dance. When the dark fuzz on his upper lip appeared, Chad wore it like a banner smeared across his face. He didn't shave until the last possible moment, and, only then, to avoid chewing on his fine mustache when he ate. As for Larry Jr., with his sensitivity and apparent lack of attraction to girls, Regina and Donna both assumed that he would go his own way. For many years, the boys never gave an indication that their differences mattered much as they grew up together. They remained best friends all through grade school and high school. They even went to the same college and roomed together. However, the idyllic friendship ended just before graduation when Larry Jr. was accepted for the following year at Tulane Medical School in Louisiana. Although Regina and Donna pretended not to know, the boys had a huge blow-up about it. The two young men barely spoke after that. Larry went on to medical school and Chad stayed at the University of Miami to complete his fourth year football scholarship. The final blow to their friendship came when Larry announced, just one year later, that he was getting married. The news took everyone by surprise, especially Chad, who suddenly joined the Army and applied for Officer's Training School. For years, the boys were estranged from each other, coming together only to plan and build Heritage Memories Retirement Village. Most of their dealings with each other were done with plenty of distance between them, thanks to the invention of the internet and the assistance of Fed-Ex delivery. It wasn't until many years later, after Chad came home to visit and brought his friend, Dan, did everyone realize what they naturally assumed all along was false. Chad was the one who was gay. Big, strong, beefy Chad. Sports guy Chad. Officer in the Army Chad. The one-every-school-girl wanted to date, Chad.

When the tide of all those yesterdays began to recede, Regina decided to join the others for bingo in the dining hall. Her memories made her very melancholy and she needed some laughter to get her through the night.

II

CICELY

Sixty-eight year old Cicely Johnson was considered the youngster of the tight knit group of friends at the Village. She still renewed her driver's license every year, as did the rest of the group, but she was the only one who owned a car, a cherry 2006 Bonneville that rode like a dream. She was more than happy to take it out for a spin upon request, and laughingly proclaimed that staying on the road was her specialty. She was a happy woman, youthful at heart, enjoying life beyond what some of her so-called friends considered she should. She didn't let her age stop her from doing exactly what she wanted. If fact, she couldn't see what all the fuss was about concerning the topic of aging. She felt better than she ever had in her life and was still spry and top of her game in mental acuity. Her business sense had not declined but actually sharpened over the years, enabling her to become part of a very wealthy group of investors. Her only concession to aging was to keep her lovely shoulder length hair dyed a beautiful shade of chestnut. She was relatively short, only 5'1", had a small bosom and wide hips, perfect for making babies as her husband, Jim, proudly told anyone who would listen. Apparently, he spoke the truth because she had six babies. It was a sign of being good Catholics, they were told. She had their first child only 10 months after they married, and four more followed in quick succession. The last baby was born in 1981 when she was forty years old. It was clear from the beginning that this baby was different. Little Danny had Down's syndrome. Nevertheless, to the doting parents, he was perfect and they were thankful for the opportunity to cherish another child. In the months that followed, the baby charmed them with his contagious smile and boundless love. That love, that sweetness about him bolstered his parents to collaborate with a team of expert professionals, whose objective was focused on teaching, guiding, and strengthening their son. Their combined efforts were fruitful and little Danny flourished under the careful planning and nourishment of his family's love. His sunny disposition and loving nature endeared everyone to him, especially his devoted parents.

The truth was Cicely loved all children. She had no brothers or sisters, but her husband's huge family inspired her to add that much more love to the world by procreating. Raising her family was the joy of her life. In the early years of their marriage, her husband was a logger and later became a respected and well-known lumber broker. He was a good provider and a man with common sense, a trait Cicely gave thanks for many times over through the years. Jim was only fifty-three years old in November 1994 when he died suddenly from a stroke. Shortly afterward, a phone call from his attorney gave Cicely the second shock of her life. She had become a millionaire overnight. Jim promised on their wedding day that he would always take care of her and he did, even after his death, with a more than generous life insurance policy. She would be able to finish raising her children with substantial enough means to enjoy a life without worrying where the next nickel would come from.

Signing a barrage of legal papers in her attorney's stuffy office was harder than the young widow thought it would be. Afterward, the weakness in her knees forced her to take a seat in the office's waiting area before she could leave. As the weight of Jim's death, and the provisions he left in place, overwhelmed her, she bravely attempted to maintain her dignity but, slowly, as one tear after another leaked from her eyes, she had to surrender her will to the emotions penetrating her heart and soul. Someone handed her a tissue, and looking up, she saw that it was a woman some years older, with long, full, black and silver hair. She was tall and beautiful with an ample figure. The woman extended a hand with brightly painted crimson fingernails perfectly matching the red piping detailing of the black Ann Taylor suit she wore.

"Hi, I'm Estelle Morgenstern-Taub. My friends call me Stella. I couldn't help but notice how upset you are. You poor dear! Are you here for a divorce, too?"

"No, I'm not. My husband just died." Cicely looked shocked at the statuesque woman's remark.

"Oh. Sorry about your husband," Stella said with sincerity. "I guess that's better than getting a divorce. Oh dear! I didn't mean it like that. I've been a widow and I've been divorced twice, and being a widow is a lot better. Oh gawd! I'm so sorry! I don't know what comes over me sometimes. Occasionally I get to prove how flexible I can be by putting both feet in my mouth at the same time! Please forget I said anything. I hope you will forgive me for being so crass." Stella turned toward the back of the room and found a solitary seat shoved in a corner. She awkwardly sat, facing away from the grieving woman.

Cicely, grateful that the stranger had at least offered a tissue along with the embarrassing gaffe, blotted her dripping eyes and tried to quell the emotion threatening to boil from her quaking insides. With characteristic determination, she managed to stand and approach the chair in the corner. Her hand trembled as she lightly touched the slumping shoulder of the red-faced woman.

"Lady, I don't know who you are, but I want to thank you for giving me a reason to laugh for the first time in weeks! You are a hoot!" Cicely laughed, her eyes glistening again.

Stella, still stinging from embarrassment, was unable to keep from laughing as well.

"Well, thanks for understanding. I just assumed a woman sitting in the waiting room of an attorney's office would be here for a divorce, especially if she is crying. Really, though, I hope you will forgive me for being so rude. No harm meant."

"None taken. By the way, I'm the Widow Johnson," she laughed as she took Stella's hand and shook it warmly. "Cicely Johnson, and I am so glad to meet you, Stella."

She really liked that woman Stella Taub. She found her to be funny and spontaneous, not at all like anyone she had ever known. The friendship took a little bit of the sting out of losing her husband, and for that, she was grateful. Without her beloved Jim, the world was a daunting place, especially with six half-grown children looking to her for strength. She felt fortunate that Stella had a wide circle of friends and was very happy to make them available to her as well. This, in itself, was a relief to the young widow and proved to be a treasure trove of help while adjusting to life without her husband. She would not be alone after all. Because of Stella, she had people upon whose shoulders she could cry, people who would help her see that the sun would continue to shine and joy could still be found.

Regina, Donna, and Stella's dearest friend, Bethany welcomed Cicely with open arms. They were a delightful crew and she was very pleased at how easily their friendship evolved. She was grateful for the experience and readily accepted the outreach of hands, as well as the advice her new friends were willing to share. To her delight, she found that this was not an ordinary group of women. They were not quilters, nor scrap-bookers, nor homemakers. These women were all single and self-sufficient. Their children were grown and more concerned with their own lives than that of their mothers. Cicely agreed that it was a win-win situation because none of them had to answer to anyone. They could travel as they so desired, stay out as late as they wanted to, and drink cocktails any time of the day or night if that was what they wanted to do. They all shared the opinion that it wasn't until after age fifty that life came into full bloom. It was the perfect decade for a woman to enjoy life for herself because she still felt young at that age, but had much more wisdom within her. True, her breasts might sag a bit, her waist might be thicker, and her feet might be flatter, but her shoulders, although a bit sloped, were still firmly in place, and the obstacles that might have held her back were either forgotten or forgiven. Losing one's partner during or before that time in life was grievous and difficult to bear, but that was one reason, Cicely decided, that God made men and women different from each other. Men are meant to protect, and women, to befriend. Women need one another, they depend on one another, and they love one another. Best friends are a must-have.

Years before coming to live at the Village with her friends, Cicely was introduced to another delightful past-time of the group: traveling. Her initiation came in early spring of 1995, a few months after Jim died. She was miserable and felt as though she had only just begun to grieve for him. Up until that point, the commotion concerning his life insurance, and what to do with it, consumed nearly all of her time. Now that the legalities were finished, her calendar was open and she wasn't as preoccupied. She dropped into a bottomless pit of depression. Her new friends recognized the signs and organized a trip with the intent to help her gain a good footing on shaky ground, a new perspective on life, so to speak. At the beginning of March, Stella informed her that the group had a habit of going south during the cold months.

"Go south? How much further south do we need to get? It's not like it's freezing in Florida this time of year," Cicely questioned.

Stella laughed, "Honey, once you get a taste of Jamaica, you will think Florida is what you Catholics call Purgatory!"

Under pressure from the other women in the group, she reluctantly arranged for her five older children to assume responsibility for fourteen-year-old Danny while she was out of town.

Stella's prophetic words were proven righteous as the group disembarked the small jet that flew them to Montego Bay. Stepping onto the tarmac, Cicely was certain she could feel the troubles of the real world actually slide right off her shoulders. It was a new and inviting sensation. The group entered the tiny airport and were immediately swarmed by young Jamaican men; "Take your bag, *mon*?" "Lady, do you need a taxi?" Their accents were melodious and pleasing to hear. She found herself charmed and captivated. Well aware of her inexperience in foreign travel, she made sure to imitate the actions of her travel companions, all while scurrying to keep up with them. Their luggage was gathered and placed in the back of an open-air bus occupied by their driver and a friendly man who introduced himself as Malcolm. He, as it turned out, was the hotel concierge and his job was to be as accommodating as possible for the travelers.

"Do you want a drink for the ride, *mon*? We have Pepsi and Red Stripe Beer, all delicious and good for you!" Malcolm joked.

"Malcolm, you haven't gotten any Coca Cola yet?" Stella batted her lashes at the handsome Jamaican and offered a sly grin.

"Oh my dear! It is so good to see you again! No, lady, we have no Coca Cola here. But I can get you anything else you want—anything," he promised with a wink.

"Well now, darling, I might need—oh, I don't know—something. Do you remember what I required the last time I was here?" She tilted her head and returned the wink.

"Quite well, my dear! Do not worry, for it will be in your room by this evening, the same as always!"

Cicely looked questioningly at Stella, who refused to meet her gaze.

"My Lord, have mercy!" exclaimed Bethany, as she held onto the glassless window frame on her side of the bus. "Not again! I told you smoking's not good for you. Especially those funny cigarettes. They'll only get you into trouble!"

Cicely's eyebrows shot up and the look on Regina's face confirmed her guess. The funny cigarettes Bethany referred to must be marijuana, she reasoned. She watched as Regina rolled her eyes and shook her head. She looked at Donna for her reaction, not expecting her amused smile and limp shrug. Her eyes swept toward Stella again.

"To each her own," Stella laughed. She had a tube of dark red lipstick in her hand and managed to maneuver her face just outside the open window to catch a glimpse of her reflection in the side view mirror. After she applied fresh lipstick, she pressed her lips together and retrieved a tissue from her pocket to blot them. "Get ready, girls, we have landed!"

The drive to the resort on the other side of the island proved to be a long and arduous one. Cecily held her breath as the bus driver barreled through narrow dirt roads, dodging stray animals, muddy potholes and precariously close pedestrians. Forty-five minutes after beginning the jolting ride, everyone in the group, except Bethany, was very glad to accept the offer of the Red Stripe beer, hoping the brew would settle their nerves and make the ride a bit easier to bear. However, the aftereffect of the libation quickly made itself known as all of the bus's inhabitants were becoming quite uncomfortable, regardless of what they were drinking. Cicely tried to tell Malcolm in a delicate way so as not to embarrass herself, that she and the others had the need for a restroom. The poor man tried, but was unable to understand what she meant. She then tried to talk to the driver and, although unsuccessful, her effort was no small feat as the bus rocked and bucked on the barely passable road. An impatient Stella, ignoring Malcolm altogether, thrust her face in front of the driver's and made certain Cicely's inquiry was interpreted accurately.

"She wants to know *how many bumps* till we get there!" Stella had to yell to be heard over the roar of the un-muffled engine.

"Ah, they have to *peeee, mon!*" Malcolm said to the driver. "*Irie*, lady. We come to a bat-troom soon!" the two men laughed, heads bobbing, smiles wide and bright. Moments later, squealing brakes slammed the bus to a stop in front of a roadside open-air bar topped with a thatched roof. All the passengers exited the bus and picked their way around the establishment's rickety tables and chairs to the two buildings in the back. The purpose of each building was illustrated by stick figures carved into the heavy wooden entrance doors. On one building, the door displayed a picture of a stick figure squatting with little dots streaming from her bottom to the fictitious ground. On the other building's door, another stick figure held a stick penis in his hand. The scene depicted droplets arching like a rainbow. Bethany leaned over and crooked her finger to beckon a wide-eyed Cicely closer to her.

"Don't be shocked. They tend to use a universal language here. Refreshingly honest, don't you think?" The amused woman nodded her head.

After the tourists re-boarded the bus and it was just about to pull away, the owner of the bar, a short, dark, burly looking man sporting a double barrel shotgun, came running to the road. He stepped in front of the bus with his shotgun resting on his shoulder. Startled by the move, several passengers gasped loudly and a few of them quickly raised their hands in the air, certain they were going to be robbed. Malcolm and the driver stepped out and calmly walked over to the bar owner. No one inside the bus could understand the words the men were saying as they stood in the middle of the muddy road waving their hands and shouting at one another. Finally, Malcolm returned and informed everyone that the bar owner was upset because the tourists used his bathrooms and, more importantly, his toilet paper, without purchasing a single drink. A rolling tide of relief washed over the bus's passengers. Furthermore, he told them, the driver would be kept off the bus until somebody purchased something. Quickly, a hefty donation was gathered and handed to Malcolm who, in turn, gave it to the bar owner. The demanding fellow said something in their native language and stepped behind his bar. He subtracted two six packs of Pepsi and handed them to Malcolm as something of an absurd offering for the more than generous donation. He then waved to the faces staring from the bus windows as if to say he was, after all, an honest man. Now that the debt was satisfied, he indicated the driver could rejoin the group while he casually returned to tending bar. Malcolm laughed, threw his arm around the shoulders of the relieved driver, and led him toward the rutted dirt road. A busload of grateful tourists welcomed them aboard with a hearty round of applause.

Clearly, Cicely mused, this vacation would prove to be quite an adventure.

Within another twenty minutes, the rattling bus arrived at its destination. The hotel provided the women with three rooms to share, all clean and crisp, and smelling of tropical flowers and sunshine. They were beautifully furnished and decorated in the distinct flavor and relaxing style one could expect on the island. Two of the rooms were large enough to fit two king sized beds, a sitting area, and an en suite. The third room was scaled down with only one king sized bed, but was large and equally as beautiful. The women had an unspoken understanding that Donna and Regina would room together, and Stella and Bethany would do the same. That left Cicely the single room, for which she was grateful. Their accommodations were at the end of a long corridor, which was open on both ends to the outside elements. A salty sea breeze drifted through the hallway, bringing with it the seductive sound of the ocean surf and the lazy call of a sea bird's invitation to join him on the beach. Outside, sun-drenched tourists lounged about a sparkling, pristine swimming pool, while others helped themselves to the generous banquet laid out under a large thatch-covered pergola. Island music floated in the air, enticing even the most serious minded person to simply release her tensions and glide along with it. Lilting, contagious laughter elicited smiles and coaxed one's curiosity to seek the source of such humor.

After unpacking most of her luggage, Cicely changed into a pair of white linen capris and a sleeveless taupe blouse with a white floral print. She tucked her shoulder length auburn hair into a sporty white canvas sun hat and slid her feet into a pair of seashell pink flip-flops. As she walked down the breezeway corridor toward the beach, she could smell the salient ocean and hear the waves roar as they reached for the beach. Outside, the sand reflected the sun, and nearly blinded her as she emerged from the open end of the long hallway. Cicely realized that it was a good thing she remembered to bring sunglasses and she quickly pulled them from her straw bag. The beach was littered in both directions with dozens of lounge chairs of all styles. She spotted Bethany in one of them and watched for a moment as her friend adjusted her chair to sit up slightly, giving her a better view of the panoramic ocean. She noted with amusement that the woman was wearing a bright pink flowered bathing suit and a floppy, wide-brimmed straw hat. Her body was slim and well proportioned, with a nicely sized bust, tiny waist, and long, lean legs.

"Darling suit, Bethany," Cicely complimented as she settled herself into the lounge chair next to her friend.

"It's funny, isn't it? Did you imagine that I would be brave enough to wear one of these rubber band messes in public! I wouldn't wear it in public at home, but I do like the fact that my rear end seems to disappear when I put it on," Bethany chuckled. "I simply love sitting on the beach like this. It's practically the only reason I come, you know. The sun is so warm and lovely here, don't you think? Oh, and healing, as well. Every time I come here, the first thing I want to do is get into a bathing suit and get on the beach. It feels so wonderful, like God is waiting for me here. Do you know what I mean?" The serenity in Bethany's eyes was glowing through her dark sunglasses.

Cicely nodded and looked toward the ocean in front of her. She felt the sea breeze sensuously caressing her skin and loosening a few strands of hair from beneath her hat. She felt soothed and relaxed. From the smell of the ocean and the lazy, lapping sound it made against the sand, to the perfume of brightly colored, exotic flowering bushes nearby, Cicely knew exactly what Bethany meant. Indeed, the sky was a deeper blue, the water a sharp cerulean, and the white sands looked like hot salty clouds.

"It is wonderful," she agreed, feeling the words were inadequate. A shadow fell across the two and, looking up, they saw a tall man whose long mahogany hair was twisted into locks that covered his entire head, and hung between his thick, broad shoulders to the middle of his back. He was dressed completely in white; shirt, pants, as well as shoes. His wide smile was genuine and his handsome eyes were alive with laughter. With a rich accent and animated expression, he asked the patrons if they would like something to eat or drink. Bethany surprised Cicely once again.

"Something with rum in it, Sir. And a little coconut. Pineapple, too. And one of those tiny umbrellas, please." she ordered. "And, if you don't mind, bring my friend here the same. This is her first time here. She needs to know how delightful those little umbrellas are."

"As you wish, Madame," said the man, broadening his white smile. By the time he returned with their drinks, Cicely's body had conformed to the lounge chair and she felt as though she was pleasantly melting in the Caribbean sun. She took a sip of the drink and let the delicious flavors of tropical fruit and sweet dark rum bathe her taste buds and burn its way down her throat.

"Oh my, this is delicious!" Cicely exclaimed and reached into her pocket to offer the waiter a tip.

"No, no, Madame. It is not necessary at this time. It is a pleasure for me to serve you," the young Jamaican said while bowing his head and turning to go.

"It's customary to settle up at the end of the trip," Bethany explained. "And I advise you not to partake of too many of these delicious concoctions. They have a way of making a person forget her religion!"

Cicely saw Regina, Donna, and Stella emerge from the breezeway connecting their rooms. As they joined the pair on the beach, Stella tossed a bright lime green and pink sundress onto Bethany's lap.

"Come on, put this on over your bathing suit," she demanded with a grin, "It's time to join the chow line! We're starving, and here you two are wasting time drinking rum in the sun!"

Much later, after sampling nearly every dish on the enormous buffet, all five friends were back on the beach stretched out in lounge chairs, watching a spectacular sunset.

"This is always my favorite part of the trip here," Donna told the group. "And after the sun sets I swear you can see every star in the heavens from right here at this spot on earth."

Everyone agreed that sunset was the best time of the day. Nevertheless, Cicely was caught up in the emotion of missing her late husband. Her heart began to ache and she felt tears sting her eyes.

"Must be the sand getting in my eyes," she said, trying to make an excuse for suddenly having to wipe her eyes with a tissue.

"It's not a problem, dear. Sand can be blamed for a lot of discomfort, if you know what I mean," said Stella, tugging at the hem of her Bermuda shorts. She reached into her pocket and removed a strange looking cigarette. Cicely's mouth dropped open when she realized that it was a marijuana joint. She said nothing as she watched her friend light it and take a long drag, afterwards holding her breath before exhaling. Then she passed it to Donna, who also took a long drag. From Donna, the joint passed to Regina. Finally, it came to Cicely, who hesitated to take it.

"This isn't Las Vegas, but the same rule applies. What happens in Jamaica stays in Jamaica," Regina explained. "Toke it if you want to. We never do this anywhere else but here. Bethany never touches the stuff and Donna and I don't either except for the first night here. The only reason we do it is that Stella insists and calls us cowards if we don't smoke with her. It's her way of challenging us. It doesn't take much to make her happy, so we do it. Kind of reminds us of the sixties, you know? I know you remember the sixties! Now, that was a decade, wasn't it?"

Before long, Cicely felt as though she didn't have a care in the world. She was comfortable and content, moderately high, and only slightly alarmed that she wasn't entirely in control of all her faculties. The sky above them was crowded with stars and the women had a wonderful time watching the tiny spheres shooting across the sky from time to time. They tried to count them but each failed effort resulted in gales of laughter. Finally, far into the night, after the marijuana afterglow faded, they found their way across the white, ethereal, moonlit beach to their rooms. Cicely stumbled onto the giant bed, still fully dressed, and slept a deep, wonderful sleep. She awakened the next morning to see sunshine pouring through the window like liquid gold. Bethany was shaking her.

"Now you know why I don't smoke the stuff," Bethany informed her. "It's almost noon! You're wasting the day away! Get up!"

Cicely got up and quickly went to the bathroom. When she looked in the mirror, she saw at least half a dozen little paper umbrellas scattered in her hair on top of her head. Memories of drinking rum and dancing on the beach to rhythmic Jamaican melodies surfaced and Cicely felt her face burn. *My Lord, what would my kids think if they saw me now?* She thought.

The rest of the week passed too quickly. They enjoyed a jumble of entertainment from the resort's swinging nightclub, to the outdoor bar with the wildly popular drink aptly named 'upside-down Margarita', to the memorable nights on the beach. The activities seemed endless and were great fun. They rode donkeys, played tennis and golf, and had their breath taken away by the beauty of the ocean depths seen through the bottom of a glass bottom boat. They were able to join a shopping trip to Ochoa Rios to take advantage of the incredible bargains on gold and diamond jewelry, and they returned with many souvenirs. Cicely especially treasured one purchase in particular. It was a lovely pair of earrings. They dangled about an inch and a half from her earlobe and had five 18-karat gold stars suspended by tiny gold links from each French hook earring. When she saw them, she knew she had to have them. In her eyes, they represented a new beginning; five stars for the five friends. The stars would forever remind her of her first time on a Jamaican beach. Of course, besides the shopping excursion, there was a lot of dancing, dining, and drinking. The whole experience was a carefree exercise in having fun.

On the fifth morning of their vacation, Cicely let Regina and Donna talk her into snorkeling in the clear shallow water fairly close to shore. To her amazement, it was a magical ride to an oceanic wonderland. Scores of colorful tropical fish she had only before seen in aquariums flitted about and even allowed themselves to be touched. To her horror, she discovered their venture had carried them to the other side of the beach resort. They surfaced in front of a sign reading:

"CAUTION: NUDE BEACH.
CLOTHING IS NOT AN OPTION"

It was true. Every person within sight was completely naked, nor were they covered in any way. Her snorkeling buddies laughed as she clasped her hand over her mouth in disbelief. They were about to hastily exit the beach when they heard a familiar voice.

"Hey girls! Did you come down to join me?" There was Stella, in all her glory, not wearing a stitch except a large straw hat and a pair of sunglasses. "Come on, we'll make room for you," she said as she nudged the gentleman beside her. "This is Johnny and his wife

Pat. They offered to bring me here and, I must say, it's been quite liberating!"

The shocked look on Cicely's face prompted Regina to answer for the three of them. With a great deal of effort, she managed to nonchalantly wave hello to Stella's new acquaintances as though seeing a crowd of naked people lined up in beach chairs, drinking, and enjoying the sun was a normal, everyday occurrence.

"Thank you, dear, but we didn't bring enough sun block with us and I'm afraid I couldn't do without it! We will see you at dinner. Ta-Ta!" Discretely directing her eyes downward, she took Cicely by one hand and Donna by the other and guided them toward the direction of their resort. Once they were safely out of range, Regina turned to her friends and mischievously winked.

"Remember what I told you—what happens in Jamaica . . ."

"Stays in Jamaica!" the other two chorused.

"Well, this sure ain't Las Vegas, *mon*," Cicely added in her best Jamaican accent.

On the flight back to the mainland, Cicely tried to express her feelings about the trip to her friends.

"This was like no other vacation I've ever had!" she said. "I feel so relaxed and so alive!"

Stella looked at her with laughing eyes. "Mission accomplished, girls!"

III

BETHANY AND STELLA

To the members of the Old Ladies Club, residing at Heritage Memories Retirement Village was a chance to live closer to each other, but still have some privacy and alone time, should they need it. Because it was built by and belonged to their sons, Regina and Donna were the first two to move in. Stella moved in next, followed shortly by Bethany. A couple of years later, Cicely decided to sell her large home-turned-duplex and move into an apartment at the Village too. Fortunately, money wasn't an issue for any of them and, thanks to their business, they could well afford the amenities and conveniences these arrangements presented.

The construction of the Village was said to be the utmost in modern innovations stridently addressing any needs the older generation might have. It was designed to be a large establishment with a north facing porch extending across the entire front of the building. A line of a dozen or so rocking chairs, straight and clean, gave the appearance of a stern welcoming committee of white painted soldiers. At times, they host a passive figure, but mostly they remain empty, rocking alone in a gentle breeze. The front porch was never a favorite place for the residents of the Village to hang out. There were several other places of interest with much more to offer other than sitting on display for curious passers-by. A massive, automated front door leads to a huge rotunda centered between three wings extending south, east, and west. A beautiful and peacefully quiet welcoming area serves as passage to a hub of activity, the epicenter of the administration offices. The east-facing wing houses six large, elite two-bedroom apartments, each with French doors leading outside to private patios. The west wing consists of twelve smaller one-bedroom apartments, also with private, albeit smaller, patios. The center-most wing was built for residents who, for one reason or another, aren't independent enough to live in their own apartment. These sixteen rooms are private and equipped in much the same fashion as a hospital room. The inhabitants of the assisted living rooms on the south wing also have the option of using their own furniture and décor, thus providing a familiar atmosphere more reminiscent of home. Supplementary care is more accessible with the addition of visual and audio monitors as well as the same type call button installed in every apartment.

Various elegantly decorated common areas surround the rotunda, allowing plenty of room for the population to mingle and entertain. Among those areas is a staged auditorium doubling as a theater, a more than adequate library, game room complete with a pool table and piano, a charming, fair-sized, ecumenical chapel, and the cafeteria-style dining room. Each morning the tables are set with a fresh seasonal posy, which, in the evening, is replaced with a lit pillar candle and formal linens.

Another building, separate from the main, houses an exercise gym and a heated swimming pool equipped with water sensors that can alert personnel should an emergency arise. Adjacent to that facility is a large barbeque area complete with picnic tables, lawn chairs and umbrellas. A small pink and white building next door sports a huge faux pair of scissors on the roof, in addition to a small red and white barber pole beside the front door indicating the location of the beauty salon/barber shop. "Wonder what kind of damage they could do to us in there," Stella observed on her first tour of the place. A few steps from the salon is a charming gift shop famous for providing everything a retired person would need: deodorant, denture cleaner, various creams and lotions, and, of course, personal hygiene necessities. An abundant array of fresh flower arrangements fills a glass display case and, quite often, orders for special occasions are added. Darling gifts available for choosing include those suitable for grandchildren. The Village residents came to depend on the little gift shop for its easy accessibility and fairly inexpensive prices. According to most of them, it sure beat getting lost in one of those huge superstore centers.

It is in this little shop that one could usually find Bethany Bertrand, who by the year 2008 was an eighty year old, mocha skinned woman with surprising green eyes. As a woman of color, she preferred the term 'negro' as opposed to 'colored' or 'black.' Her choice of descriptive pronouns wasn't as much of a racial issue, she explained, as it was an issue of pride. Though many suspected Bethany was half-Caucasian, she embraced her Negro heritage with both arms and reveled in the fact that her ancestors had persevered and refused to 'take a seat in the back'. *I'm a human being just like anyone else. I've got feelings too,"* she said in response to the occasional slur she heard thrown about by certain unfeeling, ignorant individuals. She weathered the tumultuous civil rights era with her pride intact and, in fact, was held in high esteem from practically every person she met. Her character was strong enough to defy the constrictions of bigotry and ignorance.

Having been raised by a hard working single mother did nothing to impose a negative impact on Bethany. She had a warm home, plenty to eat, clothing on her back, and was able to go to school every day. Even in her little corner of the Bronx, Bethany knew she was blessed. More blessed, she was sure, than the little girl who lived in the row house next door. New York, in the 1930s and 1940s, was teeming with diverse cultures of every type. Italians, Irish, Chinese, Black, Puerto Rican, and more; all establishing their own neighborhoods and fashioning them to resemble their respective mother countries. Here and there, a neighborhood would spring up out of the bricked streets and lines of row houses to display a wide array of diverse nationalities. Such was the neighborhood in which Bethany was raised along side Estelle Morgenstern. They met toward the end of the Great Depression in 1939 when Bethany was only ten years old, and Estelle, a child of five. Their families became acquainted, at first, in passing at the front of their building, then by exchanging a few words now and again. There came a time when the Morgenstern's humbly asked Bethany's mother if her daughter could care for their little girl until they got home from work. Both parents had to work long hours in their family's store and they couldn't take Estelle with them. It was then that a life-long friendship began. The two youngsters were always together while their parents worked, so more often than not, young Bethany assumed the role of mother to little Stella. She took the child to school with her, brought her home, and fixed sandwiches for their supper. Many times, she had little Stella all tucked in and sleeping before her parents came home from work. The two families remained close for years, each filling the gap for the other. With times as they were, having help just a step away was important, so when World War II raged across oceans, both families felt secure in their multi-ethnic neighborhood. It wasn't until June of 1945 before everything changed and the Morgenstern family moved to a larger, much nicer neighborhood. The girls were devastated and vowed to stay in touch no matter what. By this time, Bethany was a young woman of sixteen and Stella, a precocious eleven year old. It certainly was an effort to honor that promise, but for the next several years, the two managed to keep their close-knit friendship active, in spite of the long distance between them.

When she was 18 years old, Bethany met and fell in love with a young Creole man from Louisiana named Jacques Bertrand II. He had caramel skin, thick, curly black hair and beautiful green eyes that, oddly enough, matched hers. His physique was tall, but solidly built, and stocky. He had a thick French accent that charmed young Bethany. On top of that, Jacques was extraordinarily intelligent and possessed a photographic memory. He could proudly offer an opinion or a fact on any issue; politics, mechanics, art, love. No subject daunted him. Only four years older than Bethany, he managed to excel in his education, affording him the privilege of early graduation from college. He was accepted at the New York State Institute of Applied Arts and Sciences in 1946 and found, early on, that the workings of the human body were his forte. Jacques applied, and was accepted, to the Tallahassee Branch of Florida State University Medical School, partially due to his excellent academic record, but more likely than not, because of his father's deep pocketbook and political connections, something Jacques abhorred but certainly appreciated when the time was right. Shortly after their wedding, the newlywed couple moved to Florida and looked forward to the future. The bride's mother joined them one year later to help with the care of their newborn son, Jacques III, whom they nicknamed Jack.

Not far from Tallahassee, the tiny town of Ocean View was tucked in the country, away from the problems of the big city. There was one opening for an intern at the county hospital and, luckily, Jacques earned the position. It was in this place that the Bertrand family chose to build their lives, family, and medical practice. To help with their finances, Bethany found work at a delightful little shop known as Ocean View Variety Store. While her mother tended to little Jack, she worked from nine in the morning to six at night stocking, arranging merchandise, cleaning, and running the register. It was a job she looked forward to and truly enjoyed. At the end of the day, when she was able to go home to her darling baby, husband and mother, she counted her blessings and, as was her habit, gave thanks to Almighty God for her life. Her work at the shop was so consistently good, she was promoted to manager after only two years. Then, when the owner passed away in 1955, Bethany and Jacques were able to purchase the store from his family. It remained a part of their lives for many years to come.

The gift shop at Heritage Memories Retirement Village reminded Bethany of the Ocean View Variety Store. She was drawn to it and was able to volunteer there for a few hours a week. It wasn't like a real job. No, it was more like just being able to do something useful. It gave her a purpose and something to look forward to. However, for quite some time she was bothered by a few minor, she thought, incidents that she couldn't explain. One such incident was that, without her knowledge or awareness, her bladder began to leak. At first, Bethany thought she must have sat in something damp. After she began to wake up between soaking wet sheets, she knew the incident wasn't some a minor issue. She was too ashamed to tell anyone, so she kept it to herself. Little did Bethany realize that several people were already aware of her incontinence. That sort of thing certainly wasn't something a person could hide very easily. Another issue was bothering her; for some odd reason she began confusing the past with the present. For example, she developed a tendency to answer the shop phone with "Good morning, Ocean View Variety Store". More than once, she argued with a potential customer over whether or not a particular item was for sale or could be ordered. Sometimes Bethany would wake up in the morning and her apartment didn't look familiar at all. She would search for clothes, dress herself, and quietly sit in a chair until Stella came to take her to the dining room for breakfast. Somehow, she always knew that Stella would come. Occasionally, she had her blouse on backwards, and sometimes her wet pants had to be changed before they could leave together. Nevertheless, Stella, her Stella, was always patient and helpful. She was the one constant in her life that never changed. Bethany might confuse this seventy-five year old Stella with a ten-year-old Stella, but she was still her Stella.

Breakfast in the dining room was usually a cheerful affair. The diners gathered early and greeted each other as they took the seats habitually claimed as their own. The breakfast tables had vases of bright, white daisies surrounded by salt & pepper shakers, bottles of hot sauce and steak sauce, and small cobalt blue dishes containing yellow pats of margarine. Most residents ate a substantial breakfast and supper, choosing to forgo a large lunch in favor of putting together a sandwich in the privacy of their own apartment. Nearly everyone took a nap after lunch, which gave the Village a quiet, undisturbed atmosphere. Mornings, the earlier the better, were a bustling affair at the Village.

The smell of fresh coffee, bacon, and hot buttered toast slithered from under the French doors of the dining room and invited early risers in. Bethany enjoyed the community atmosphere there and looked forward to going to breakfast. This morning, Stella had to awaken her so she could get ready, which was something very unusual. Once her face was washed and her clothing was on, they set out for the dining room. Stella, as always, had her little dog Camille tucked out of sight in her oversized purse. They chose their breakfast from the grill menu and joined Regina, Donna, and Cicely already at their table.

Cicely was always the happiest of the group in the mornings, sometimes maddeningly so. Today she announced that she would take a ride to Wal-Mart and invited the others to join her.

"What are you going for?" Donna asked for the group.

"I heard they got a great new nail salon at the front of the store and I want to get a pedicure. You know we can't get that here. Our salon only does manicures." Cicely informed her friends.

"I'm up for it," Stella said. "I think I want one of those fancy manicures where they use fake nails and make them look real. How do you think my hands would look dressed up like that?" she held up her bumpy arthritic fingers for every one to see.

"Really dear, don't you think you're a bit too old for that?" Bethany teased while keeping a straight face.

"*Dear*, you should think about getting your eyebrows waxed while we are out. Maybe you could buy one of those tiny eyebrow combs. I'd be willing to bet it'll help you see better!" Stella volleyed. The exchange gave everyone at the table a good laugh, including Bethany. She never let Stella's teasing goad her. In fact, Stella's sense of humor was one of the things she loved most about her.

"Hey, you're never too old for anything, right girls?" Stella laughed.

About that time, a shadow fell across their table and the women looked up to see tall, handsome Ralph Watkins ease past. They watched as he winked and whispered *"Stellaaaaa"* with a gravelly voice.

"Please tell me I didn't see that," Donna chuckled.

"Point made," Stella crowed, dropping a morsel of her jelly biscuit to the waiting Camille at her feet.

"Oh my heavenly Lord!" Cicely exclaimed and Regina shook her head.

"I think I'll get a manicure too," Bethany informed the group with a sly smile.

Mastering the aisles of Wal-Mart is no easy task for most older folks. Some of them carry canes or clutch the bar of a shopping cart to steady their stride and many of them use the motorized carts available at the door. Bethany was the only one of their group who needed to rely on one of those carts. She called it her Cadillac. Her navigation skills were precarious, at best, so Donna volunteered for the task of keeping Bethany from running over any people or displays. Before getting her settled into the cart, Stella pulled a thick towel from her bag and discretely covered the seat, thereby protecting the saddle, as she called it, just in case there was an unfortunate, decidedly damp, accident. Donna pretended not to notice as Bethany cast a grateful glance to Stella.

They scoured nearly every department of the huge store, taking their time, looking for bargains, and filling their shopping carts with merchandise they weren't apt to find at the little gift shop in the Village. On a whim, Donna added various items to her cart such as fresh chicken, sausage, onions, garlic and more. It was her intention to cook up a big pot of gumbo for the group. All of the friends agreed it was a wonderful idea as they had been gifted with Donna's culinary skills before, and gumbo was one of her best offerings. She was sure to purchase an insulated bag to keep all of their items cool until they were able to return home.

By the time they got to the checkout, their energy levels were beginning to wear down and they looked forward to having a seat in the new nail salon. They all decided that manicures, as well as pedicures, were the way to go, but Stella was the only one who requested the new acrylic nails. They giggled like teenage girls as the nail technicians bathed and groomed their hands and feet. Bethany's feet were especially ticklish, prompting Cicely to whisper in Stella's ear,

"Be sure to cover my car seat with that towel!"

Stella glanced around to see if Bethany noticed the exchange and she saw the older woman deep in conversation with a nail technician.

". . . So, you know why they invented those silly mechanical scooter chairs, don't you? It's a government conspiracy. Oh yes it is! Just look at how they're advertised straight to us, the oldest ones on Social Security. Everyone knows that old timers have a heck of a time driving. They keep getting in accidents and all. Why, even the cars on the street will run over you in a heartbeat! The government is trying to weed us out I'm telling you. Yes they are! That's why they advertise that Medicare will pay one hundred percent for one of those scooters. 'No out of pocket expense', they say. Every time one of us is knocked off in an accident, they're one up for the next generation. 'Spend a little—save a lot', that's what they think!"

Fortunately, the nail technician working on Bethany's knobby feet knew how to keep a customer satisfied. She bobbed her head in agreement with every word she heard, and kept her amusement to herself.

Later, after Donna's apartment was filled with the savory aroma bubbling from her deepest pot, the dinner guests arrived one by one with mouths watering in anticipation of the hot Cajun culinary delight. Bethany especially relished the dish because it reminded her of Jacques and his Creole background. As she always did, she took the opportunity to repeat her late husband's humorous response to the many accolades received for his expert gumbo-yielding talents. *"If it's a little salty, it's just the sweat off my brow!"* The story had been repeated so often over the years, no one bothered to roll their eyes anymore, but just accepted the eccentricities of their dear old friend.

Stella was the last to arrive and she was cradling an old familiar guitar in her arms. Bethany's face lit up when she saw it.

"Oh good! I was afraid you wouldn't bring your guitar because of your new fingernails!" she exclaimed.

"I thought about that already," Stella told her. "But the technician promised me these darn things will hold up to just about anything. We'll see!"

After supper, everyone sat comfortably in the living room, and Stella began to strum her guitar. Her newly acrylic-ed fingernails danced over the strings nimbly without the first arthritic hesitation. She coaxed a melody from the acoustic instrument that had them all nearly in tears. When she finished, her friends, not wanting the magic of the melody to dissipate, were silent for a moment before applauding. Then Stella looked at Bethany seated to her right, nodded her head ever so slightly and began to strum her instrument once more. Bethany, recognizing her queue, closed her eyes and barely, almost breathlessly, swayed in rhythm with Stella's music. She began singing a rendition of Peggy Lee's *Fever* that could challenge the professional singer's claim to talent. The years on Bethany's face seemed to drip into a puddle on the floor at her manicured feet as she responded to the soul of the song and became more animated. She flirted with lyrics, exaggerated movements, and coquettishly winked, her voice husky and fluid. She was no longer an octogenarian, but a passionate woman offering a fiery interpretation, one that would have made the songwriters, John Davenport and Eddie Cooley, proud.

"Never know how much I love you
Never know how much I care
When you put your arms around me
I get a fever that's so hard to bear," Bethany wrapped her slim arms around herself.

Throughout the performance, her friends added their vocals to hers, forgetting, just for the moment, that they were in a different place and time than they were when the song first became popular in the 1950's.

"Just like old times, Stella," Regina told her friend. "The two of you still have it!"

"Old times my ass, Regina!" Stella answered. "We never lost it! You know, that song reminds me of my first husband."

"What about your second and third husbands?" asked Bethany.

"No, not them, I didn't know either of them long enough to have a song for them," Stella declared.

IV

SURPRISES

"What the heck are you doing?" Regina roused herself and sat straight in the recliner. "Why on earth did you wake me from my nap? I was just getting to sleep good."

"Trust me, sister, you should be glad I did. You are about to have company. Let me get a comb. You've got a really bad case of chair-hair," Donna cautioned. She tried to fluff Regina's short white curls where they flattened against the back of the recliner, exposing the ever-present cowlick her friend spent years trying to control.

"Did you know you just about have a bald spot back here?"

"Oh, hush yourself! Who is coming? Larry Jr.? That would be something; two visits in three months—might be new record. I wonder what's wrong. I hardly every have company. Well, unless you count every knot-head who thinks they can just waltz in here without as much as a knock on the door!"

"You left the door unlocked again, so that makes you the knot-head, not me," Donna retorted. She handed the comb to Regina and flipped a long graying russet braid off her own shoulder. "And it's not Larry Jr. It's your granddaughter. The one who just had a baby. I saw her in the parking lot and she's on her way in. So stop jabbering and straighten yourself up! You don't want her to think you just lay around all day, do you?"

Regina was still trying to rearrange the back of her hair when a soft knock at the door interrupted the flurry of preparations. Donna beat her to the door before she could even turn around and opened it smiling as if she was expecting some one else.

"Why, Taylor, what a surprise!" Regina slipped in front of Donna and nudged her aside. "Come in here, Honey, and let me see you!"

After greeting 'Aunt' Donna with a kiss on the cheek, she dropped the diaper bag and backpack inside the door and reached for Regina. Her grandmother happily returned the hug, squeezing Taylor around the waist. She stepped back with surprise when she realized that there was a wriggling bundle packed inside the orange Aztec print sling tied across the young mother's body. With an expectant smile, Regina peeked inside the sling and met sleepy blue eyes framed by copper colored lashes. One dimpled baby hand wrangled the corner of a Winnie-the-Pooh blanket into a pacifier of sorts. The baby's other hand rhythmically grasped and released a tuft of feather-y curls sprouting from her head.

"Hey Gina! Look who I brought to see you!" Taylor unwrapped the infant from her cozy nest. The baby clung to her mother, not wanting to give up her comfort and warmth so easily.

"Oh Taylor! How wonderful to see you and the baby! Is everything all right? Did your uncle ask you to come?" Regina tried to stifle the feeling of anxiety manifested by the thought that something bad might have prompted the unexpected visit. After all, aside from seeing Taylor at the hospital when Penny was born, this was the first time their paths crossed in many months. The fact was they usually only saw each other at Christmas. The fault wasn't that Regina didn't try to connect. She did, quite often. In fact, much to the jealousy of her other grandchildren, she doted on Taylor from the time she was a tiny baby. Her heart tore at the certainty of the difficult life her granddaughter would have to face because she was motherless from birth. When the child was completely orphaned by the time she was a teenager, Regina did everything she could to stay active in her life. Something changed after the girl went to live with Larry Jr.'s family. As far as she could tell, it seemed her efforts to stay connected were unappreciated and unanswered. Stella, ever the blatantly honest friend, told her several times that there was only one thing any of her grandchildren wanted from her and that was her money. Regina hated to admit it, but in her heart, she knew it might be true. It was so sad to her, this loss of family ties. For years, she tried to figure out what she did to warrant being treated in such a way. Eventually she gave up trying and after she moved into the Village, she decided the checkbook was closed. Although she did keep the tradition of giving something special to each of them for Christmas, a gift of monetary substance was not included. From then on, Regina sent each of her grandchildren a nice, but empty, greeting card for birthdays and special occasions. She doubted they even noticed she made the effort, but to satisfy her own sense of grandmotherly obligation, she kept the routine without fail. Even in the days when she did lavish them with gifts and money, they never responded with as much as a single thank you card or phone call. She blamed Larry Jr.'s wife for that. A mother should see to it that her children were brought up with good manners. When Taylor's father was alive, he made sure the appropriate response was given in return. After he died and the young girl went to live with her uncle and his family, all of her proper etiquette training seemed to have been in vain.

Now here she was, smiling, standing in front of her grandmother. Taylor held the baby in front of her like a shiny new trophy. She gestured for Regina to hold her but the older woman seemed a little flustered and balked at taking the baby.

"C'mon Gina, she won't break, I promise. Nothing is wrong, I just wanted to come by to see you, and let you see your only great-grandchild. That's all, no strings attached," Taylor assured her.

Regina awkwardly took the baby in her arms and nuzzled her sweet face. Oh, the smell of a baby! That is one of those scents that become ingrained in a woman's memory. It was enough to bring Regina to tears. She felt Taylor's eyes on her and looked up to meet her gaze.

"Are you alright?" Taylor asked.

"Sure, I'm fine. I just haven't held a baby since you were born, that's all. Your daughter reminds me so much of your mother when she was a baby," Regina told Taylor.

"Penny looks like my mom did?" Taylor's voice was soft. "Do you have any pictures of her? That's why I wanted to talk to you, Gina. Since I had my baby, I haven't been able to get the thought of my mother out of my mind. How I wish she could be here to meet her own granddaughter! There is so much I need to ask you. Would it be alright if we talk about her?" She settled herself on the comfortable emerald brocade sofa adjacent to Regina.

"Oh Taylor, of course it's alright! I would love to tell you about her. She is still in my heart as if she never left this earth," Regina answered, grateful for the opportunity.

"She had red hair like Penny's when she was born, but it turned blonder as she got older until it was the exact color yours is now. We called her 'little Blondie'." She handed the baby back to Taylor and went to the bookshelves where she kept her photo albums. Pulling one of them out, she continued, "You've probably seen most of these pictures, haven't you?"

Taylor shook her head.

"No? Well, let's sit down and go over them and I'll tell you all about your mama." She handed an album edged in cream-colored grosgrain fabric and aging white lace to Taylor and took a seat beside her. Turning to the first page, she read the inscription:

"For my darling daughter,
Renee',
To be yours on your 21ˢᵗ birthday"

Tears unexpectedly stung Taylor's eyes but she smiled through them at her grandmother whose moist blue eyes mirrored hers. Page after page of the photo album left both women challenging emotions long since buried beneath years gone by. By the time the last page was turned, grandmother and granddaughter had stepped into uncharted territory and began to forge a bond with each other.

"What was he like?" Taylor asked.

"Who, my dear?"

"Your husband, my grandfather. Big Larry. What was he like?"

"Well, Taylor, Big Larry was something else! He had an incredible sense of humor and was always pulling pranks on me and Little Larry, making us laugh all the time. He was a good dancer. We used to go dancing all the time. Yes, Big Larry was something else alright." Regina let herself feel her husband's presence as she spoke.

"Mom was born before he got back from the war, wasn't she?" Taylor asked.

"Yes darling, she was born the night they told me he wasn't coming home," Regina answered. "I went into labor almost immediately after I was told he died. I couldn't think of anything else but the loss of my husband. There could have been a hurricane outside for all I knew. By the time I realized I was in labor, I nearly delivered by myself. Lucky for me, your mom was a small baby. Everybody said it was because I was so worried about Big Larry that she didn't get very big." Regina bowed her head as she told Taylor about that night. "But she was strong. Big Larry would have loved her no matter what."

"Was something wrong with her?" Taylor asked.

"Oh no, child, she was healthy, just so tiny. Big Larry never got to know her, that's all. I didn't know I was pregnant until after he left for Viet Nam, and I didn't hear from him for a long time. Unfortunately, I'm not sure if he ever got my letter telling him I was expecting a baby." Regina's face turned pink and, quickly, she added, "He was a very loving man. I was considered an older woman when I had her, you know. I was already thirty-six years old. Finding out I was pregnant at that age was quite a shock!"

Neither woman noticed when Donna left. She had slipped out quietly, leaving the two to pour over picture albums and memories.

Taylor's interest in old family photos generated a longing in Donna to review her own photo albums. She didn't look at them very often as it had a way of turning a beautiful, bright day into one of melancholy sadness. For the most part, her pictures were of happy times, but even seeing all of the happy faces therein didn't compensate for the heartbreak she felt every time she viewed an image of Chad's beaming face. She mourned the loss of her son deeply, as any mother would. At the time, not much was known about the deadly HIV virus. He contracted it from his long time partner, Dan. Apparently, Dan had been exposed to it some years before but by the time his symptoms manifested, it was too late. Chad was infected as well. They died within months of each other and were buried side by side, as they wished. Donna wasn't entirely comfortable with the fact that her son loved another man instead of a woman, but she was loyal to her son until his dying day. His father never accepted the fact his son was gay and, basically, disengaged himself from his son's life entirely. However, Donna could not bring herself to do such a thing. Chad was her child and not to be part of his life would have been inconceivable to her. It was comforting to know that Belinda took the news of her brother's sexual preference in stride. She was much more liberal than her mom and dad.

By the time Donna reached her apartment, she decided that she would not look at the pictures with a heavy heart. Today she would celebrate the good life she had been a part of, and the happiness it brought her. She took out her albums and poured over the pictures with a new attitude. Even seeing her ex-husband's likeness didn't foul her mood. The surprise and pain of their divorce had eased somewhat over time and the bitterness that could have evolved from it simply did not. That wasn't her way. She was more prone to set it aside and would not acknowledge those negative feelings ever existed. She chose to remember the early days with her husband instead. They were so happy together and so much in love. It was a shame that he decided to leave the family and move on. He never really gave her an adequate explanation, just that he felt he had to go. When Tom left, she and the children seldom heard from him. At some point, they heard he moved to North Carolina and opened a store there. After several years of separation, she finally gave up hope that he would return. She attained the divorce herself and, in the process, took back her maiden name, Thompson. It was time to move on and enjoy a new beginning. Donna set her pre-divorce album aside and replaced it with one she put together to document her career.

Getting a job was a decision she made soon after Tom left. A job would help keep her mind occupied and perhaps heal her heart as well. She went to work as an admissions clerk at the Ocean View Hospital until the opportunity to go to radiology school surfaced. At first, she was afraid she wouldn't be able to raise her kids while working and going to school. In the end, she decided that going to school was the one thing she could do for herself that would also benefit her family. Her priorities never changed. Her family always came first. Thankfully, she didn't have to worry about money. The divorce settlement provided very well for her. Tom never fought her on that. To her surprise, he responded favorably to all of her petitions. She enjoyed a long and productive career as a radiology technician but she knew when it was over, and she gladly retired at age fifty-five, never looking back. Working in the hospital had become very difficult for her, not to mention that a younger generation started filling the available job openings throughout the hospital. She could still keep up with the best of them, but years of seeing people in pain, witnessing the anguish of family members when their loved ones suffered, or detecting changes on a radiology exam that would alter a life forever, all took a toll on her. Wisely, she chose to leave before the probability of being considered archaic by the next group of younger technicians could manifest itself. Leaving the workforce was an easy adjustment, and Donna smiled as she compared the pictures of herself from when she first started working, to the day her department held a going away party for her. The strained expression she wore toward the last years she worked disappeared at the end.

When she closed her photo album and stirred herself from the land of memories, there was a knock on the door. She opened it to find Bethany standing there.

"Have you seen my Stella?" the octogenarian asked. "I seem to have misplaced her."

They located Stella in the chapel sitting alone with her eyes closed and her hands, palms up, raised waist high in front of her.

"What are you doing in here?" Donna poked Stella in the shoulder.

"Hallelujah, she's been saved!" Bethany exclaimed with uncharacteristic sarcasm.

"Shut up. What do you think I'm doing here?" Stella opened one eye and looked in the directions of her friends. "I'm praying. Jews pray. Didn't you know that? Our God was around before yours was. My people have been praying long before your people ever did." She opened both eyes and kept them aimed straight ahead, emphatically raising her hands a little higher.

"That's not fair! Our people came after yours. You know we have the keys to the kingdom of heaven and . . ." Bethany's staunch Baptist spirit sprang in defense.

"Don't let her get you going again, girl! You know Stella's just trying to irk you," Donna tried to head off the inevitable cross words edging their way onto her friend's pouting lips.

"You might as well give up," a twinkle of humor lightened Stella's voice as she pretended to be offended. She leaned toward her visitors for a closer look. "You've been in my apartment again, haven't you Beth?"

"Of course. I was looking for you. I didn't know you had to pray. In the chapel. In the *Christian* chapel! How'd you know I was in your place—did God tell you?" Bethany teased.

"You could say something like that," Stella answered. "I'll need this back, thank you very much." She gently moved Bethany's hair aside to access the clasp of a stunning string of buttery cream-colored pearls around her neck. A puzzled look briefly shadowed her friend's face.

"Nothing to worry about, dear. I know you would have returned it eventually. Let's go get something to eat," Stella put her arm around a relieved Bethany and guided her toward the dining room. Camille's tiny Yorkie nose suddenly popped out of the top the neon green shoulder bag hanging on Stella's arm.

"Come on, Sister Donna" she called over her shoulder tossing her mane of thick salt and pepper hair, "You're invited too!"

"I can*not* believe you took that dog into the chapel!" Bethany commented disapprovingly.

When they reached the dining room, they found Regina having supper with a guest. She introduced her granddaughter to her friends with a genuine smile quite unlike the hopeful one often pasted on her face when, on the rare occasion, Larry Jr. came to visit

"You remember Taylor, don't you? I know it's been a long time since you've seen her. Look how grown up she is! That little bundle there is my great granddaughter, Penny. Can you believe how beautiful she is?" Regina beamed. The baby cooed at the women fawning over her and waved her chubby arms at them. Bethany lifted her away from her mother and held her tenderly. Penny snuggled in the grandmotherly arms and sighed contentedly at her as she rocked back and forth.

Regina, noticing the suddenly pale face on Taylor, glanced over to the next table, and observed a couple with their dentures in hand, dipping them in and out of their water glasses before sloshing them back into their empty mouths. She looked back at Taylor who, by this time, seemed to be swallowing a hard lump in her throat.

"Sorry sweetheart, you'll have to get used to such things when visiting the dining room. Here in the Village, washing your dentures at the dinner table is perfectly acceptable etiquette! It isn't exactly appetizing but that's the way it is," she laughed.

"Your little darling has the brightest red hair and the cutest little mouth!" Bethany changed the subject.

"Yes, she looks just like my Renee' did when she was born," Regina informed everyone and Donna agreed.

"She was a beautiful child. Such a shame that she left us so soon," Donna said.

For a moment, a dark cloud hung in the air. Regina and Taylor became a bit misty eyed.

"You certainly gave her the right name, Taylor. She is as bright as a new penny!" Cicely declared, delicately breaching the somber moment.

"As much as I'd like to stay, ladies, I need to get my little one home," Taylor reached for the baby snuggled in Bethany's thin arms. With a disappointed look on her face, she relinquished the little one and made Taylor promise to bring her back for a visit soon. After the young mother managed to collect her infant, diaper bag, and back pack, she said her goodbyes and left, turning around one time to blow her grandmother as kiss.

As soon as she was out of sight, Stella turned to Regina and, completely disseminating the idyllic moment, demanded, "What the hell was that all about?"

"I'm not sure," Regina responded. "All I know is that she showed up and wanted to see old pictures and talk about her mom and dad. I'm glad she came. I'm not used to one of my Grands coming to visit for no particular reason at all. It was good to see her, don't you think?"

"Well, I'm glad for you, Regina." Cicely recognized the opportunity to bring a bit of news to the table. "It's good to see someone new around here. By the way, did ya'll know, there's a new resident moving in soon," Cicely changed the subject. "I saw him at the Administrator's office yesterday after I got back from the beauty shop. He's pretty good looking, too," she laughed. "I think he is going to live in the west wing. Do you know the apartment where old Bob Williams lived before his daughter took him home with her?"

"That's great—new blood!" Stella chimed. "I might be interested but only if he doesn't look like all the other old farts around here with suspenders pulling his pants up to his chin!" Everyone laughed, but even as they joked, Cicely had a pleased look on her face as though she had some secret expectation of the new tenant. Her smug look was not lost on any of the women sitting at the table.

V

GUESS WHO'S NOT COMING TO DINNER

E very Sunday morning, Village residents of various denominations gathered in the chapel for services. The first service was at 7 a.m. for those of the Catholic faith. The Protestant services began at 9:30 a.m., and most of the Catholics usually stayed over for that service as well. The optimal social factor was the reason for the double dose of the Word on Sundays. Even those who were not of the Christian faith occasionally came to one or the other service. Catholic, Protestant, Jewish, Buddhist, it made no difference to those in this close community. The tradition was a well-accepted practice at the Village and served the purpose of bringing people together in peace and harmony.

When she moved to the Village, Cicely was happy to offer her musical talents for Sunday morning services. For as long as she could remember, she sang in the church choir and she was delighted to be able continue the tradition. Her voice had a beautiful second soprano timbre, and she was equally as talented playing the piano. Usually, some of her family came to early Mass with her and afterwards, they would have breakfast in the dining room. Then she would rush back to the Chapel to add her beautiful voice to the Protestant choir.

Bethany also sang in the choir, but only for the Protestant service. Unfortunately, the older woman often fell asleep and missed a majority of the sermon, but for the most part, she managed to wake up in time to sing along with the rest of the choir.

After Sunday services were over, many residents customarily gathered in the game room to socialize with each other and any family members that might be visiting. Early one afternoon, Regina noticed that Cicely wasn't present as usual and assumed she had driven to the home of one of her children for Sunday dinner. She had a habit of doing so occasionally, but always told someone where she would be, so it seemed odd that no one knew where she was. *No matter*, Regina thought, *she would show up eventually*. She turned her attention to the domino game in front of her. Later that evening, by chance, she spotted Cicely coming in through the door from the parking lot. Regina hurried to catch up with her and linked arms as they strolled toward their apartments.

"Did you have dinner with your family today? Are they all doing well?" she inquired.

"No, as a matter of fact I didn't," Cicely answered. "Would you believe I had a date?" Her smile spread across her face from ear to ear, as she blushed.

"Well now, do tell! Is it somebody I know or someone from the outside world?"

Cicely squeezed her friend's arm a little. "You know that new resident I told you about? It turns out we have quite a lot in common. His name is Paul and he's seventy-eight years old, which I know is a little older than me but it isn't that much difference really, do you think? Anyway, he seems to like pretty much everything I do. Can you imagine? He likes dancing, and Italian food, and going to the movies. In fact, we just got back from the movies. I had to park the car. Did you see him come in?" Her bubbling enthusiasm was contagious.

"No, I didn't see anyone come in. I've been in the game room playing dominos with old man Stenson and his wife, all afternoon. It was fun, but I'm kind of brain sore now. How about you? What are you going to do?" Regina asked knowing full well what the answer would be.

"I'm going to say good night to my date! He's a lot more fun than dominos!" Cicely laughed, and practically flew toward the west wing. Regina watched her go with a pleased smile on her face.

The next morning at breakfast, Regina, Donna, Bethany, and Stella met at their usual time. Once again, the only one absent was Cicely. Regina relayed Cicely's exciting news to them and they all agreed it was a good thing. After all, she was younger than they were and the only reason she lived at the Village was that she didn't want to live alone or have to deal with maintaining a house and yard. She wisely chose not to intrude on her children's family lives, although every one of her six kids said it would never be an imposition to have her live with them. She liked to be independent and staying at the Village gave her that. Living in such a close proximity to her best friends was a definite added advantage.

It was later in the day before any of them saw her. Stella and Bethany were on their way from the exercise room when they bumped into her and her new friend.

"Stella, Bethany, this is Paul, our new resident," Cicely tried to calm the flamingo pink rising from her neck to her cheeks as she introduced him. Paul politely held his hand out for the ladies to shake and nodded his head slightly. He was tall, slightly bent at the waist, and smelled pleasantly of Old Spice aftershave lotion. He had two towels thrown across his shoulder and wore a loud orange and turquoise Hawaiian shirt over deep blue swim trunks.

"Have you lovely ladies been for a swim?" He smiled brightly.

"Good Lord gawd no! There's no telling what's in that pool! I heard that they had to fish a turd out of it the other day! I wouldn't dare go in there. Would you, Bethany?" Stella looked toward Bethany and winked.

"No, can't say that I would. One can never be sure what's in that water. They keep it full of chemicals, too. I tell you, after you get in that pool every inch of skin on your body gets a rash and starts itching 'till you just about want to go crazy," Bethany proclaimed.

Paul snorted and laughed aloud before he could stop himself. Cicely's embarrassment spilled over her face turning her pink cheeks to a full-blown fire engine red. Her hands fluttered up and down the buttons on her bathing suit cover up.

"I suggest we pass on the swim, Sugar." His eyes twinkled while he tried to mask his obvious amusement.

"Um . . . yeah, I think we'd better. Thanks for the heads up, Stella. Bethany, take care. We'll see ya'll later." Cicely stammered before leading Paul in the opposite direction.

"You are too stinkin' mean!" Bethany snickered, poking her friend in the ribs.

"Ha! Ain't that the truth!" confirmed a proud Stella.

The heat of the morning sun reflected off the concrete sidewalk as the pair turned toward the main building and hurried to Regina's apartment, eager to share their impression of the newest resident.

"He's real! We actually saw him. He calls her Sugar. That means he already has a pet name for her and you know what that leads to," Stella proclaimed. Bethany nodded in agreement with Stella's insinuation.

"Oh good grief, do you really think it's serious already? Come on, girls. Let's be real," Regina said.

"Let's be real about what?" Donna entered from the hallway and joined the trio. "What's going on?"

"We were just talking about Cicely," Bethany offered. "Her boyfriend is real and he's a looker too! He has real nice curly hair and he's tall and well dressed. He reminds me of my Jacques. Stella, do you remember Jacques? He was tall like that and had thick, curly hair. But his was black, not like Paul's hair."

"His name is Paul?" Donna asked.

"Yes, it is. We didn't catch his last name. You ought to see Cicely with him. What a hoot! I do believe that she's never dated anyone in her whole life other than her husband. It's no wonder she looked as nervous as a teenager! At least she found someone who doesn't look like he's been embalmed already," Stella chuckled.

"Yeah, she ought to take some lessons from you, huh? I bet you could teach her a thing or two about dating," Donna good naturedly pointed out.

Stella, who enjoyed being the object of attention, crowed "Don't you know it! The only bad thing is, at our age, foreplay begins with Ben Gay!"

The rest of the week passed with virtually no further sighting of the couple. Cicely showed up to join the other ladies for breakfast, but was not around for lunch or supper. When asked if Paul would be joining them for breakfast any time soon, she let it be known that he didn't like to eat a full breakfast. He preferred to start the day with a protein power smoothie with lots of good things in it like carrot juice and kelp. Afterward, he liked to work out at the gym.

"It's been quite a while already since you met him, right? Not all of us have had the pleasure of meeting him. When are you going to bring him around? If it wasn't for Stella and Bethany saying they actually saw him, I swear I wouldn't believe he was real!" complained Donna and Regina agreed with her.

"He's going to be at church this Sunday so I'll introduce him then. He said something about joining the choir too. Only he's not Catholic so he'll only be at the Protestant service. I can't wait 'till you hear him sing!" Cicely beamed.

"Looks like someone's been making beautiful music together!" Stella winked.

"That's the tall gentleman, isn't it? Tall like my Jacques with thick curly hair, but Jacques' hair was black, not like this man's. I miss my Jacques. When do you think he's going to come get me?" Bethany said, gazing into thin air with a far away look in her eyes. Her statement made everyone in the room pause and hold their breath.

"Bethany dear, Jacques isn't coming back, remember? We talked about this yesterday. Jacques is gone and you live here at the Village now." Stella took her friend's arm.

The mocha-skinned woman appeared startled when she heard what Stella said. Then, with a tug on the hem of her blouse, she seemed to right herself and come back to the present.

"Oh, that's right. Of course, I remember. Whew! Sometimes, I tell you, I get so turned around I don't know what I am doing!" Bethany looked tired. "I think I need to take a nap."

"Come on, dear. I'll go with you," Stella told her. Reaching into the pocket of Bethany's sweater, she retrieved a beautiful Rosewood ink pen and set it on the table in front of Regina. "We'll just leave Regina's pen here. You don't need to borrow it right now, Beth. I've got one you can have." Touching her index finger to her lips while catching Regina's eye, Stella steered a confused Bethany into the hallway and onward to her apartment.

"I knew Bethany was slipping but I didn't know how badly," Donna confided.

"I know, can you imagine? You never think it will happen to someone you've known for so long, then before you know it . . ." Cecily's demeanor and voice changed. "Do you think the same thing will happen to the rest of us?" she asked quietly.

"What about the business? Do you think she can still handle it?" questioned Donna.

Nobody knew the answer. It was obvious Bethany's episodes were increasing in frequency and the level of uncertainty it garnered was alarming.

Regina left the small group and walked back to her apartment. After letting herself in, her eyes went straight to a framed photograph on her bookshelf taken before their last trip to Paris. The faces smiling into the camera lens were oblivious to what the future would hold and perhaps it was better that way. *'It's hard'* she thought, *'to loose someone even when they are still physically here. It's like grieving their death before they even pass away.'* She knew it wasn't necessary to put into words how they all felt about Bethany's situation. Their concern was equally shared.

Sunday morning was filled with a great deal of anticipation. Today they would meet Cicely's new friend. To say that each woman took extra care in her appearance was an understatement. They dressed meticulously; donning their Sunday best, making sure each hair was in place, and retouching their lipstick before heading toward the chapel. Without a doubt, this was going to be a special day.

Regina and Donna met each other in the hallway and ran into Stella on the way out.

"You're going to services too?" They echoed each other's words.

"Why not? Do you seriously think I would miss this?" The amusement in Stella's eyes made them sparkle. She observed how well dressed her friends were and said, "Looks like I may be a little underdressed for the occasion!" She picked up the skirt of her flowing caftan and fluffed it out. "You should dress for comfort like me. Who knows how long we are going to be sitting there."

"Do you think so? Well, I wouldn't be caught dead wearing a dress with knee highs stockings," Donna giggled and pointed at her legs. Stella dropped the skirt of her dress and somehow managed to quell a look of embarrassment before she entered the chapel.

After services began, one by one of the ladies was seen turning around in her seat to look up to the choir loft. They craned their necks trying to see Cicely and her new friend, however, it was no use. No one could see the choir from the pews below.

Reverend Early, a young pastor from South Africa who immigrated to Ocean View some years ago, was the guest preacher. He gave a rousing sermon that mesmerized the congregation with every word. A robust man with a deep baritone voice, Reverend Early proclaimed the Word loudly and passionately. His face beamed and his large brown eyes sparkled and danced. He spoke with one hand raised, finger pointing to heaven. His other arm stretched toward the congregation as if embracing every person in attendance. Occasionally, someone would shout "AMEN!" furthering the preacher's ardor, but to a particular few, the sermon seemed far too long. While he preached, Regina, Donna and Stella squirmed as if they were sitting on an ant pile and were barely able to contain their lack of patience. Finally, with a thick accent Reverend Early made an announcement:

"Ladies and Gentlemen, we have a surprise for you this morning. There is one among you who has a talent he wants to give to the Lord. So, without further adieu, let us offer with him our praises to

God." The Reverend rocked back and forth on his feet as he spoke, keeping time with the rhythm of his South African accent.

Someone dimmed the lights as soft guitar music floated from the choir loft. Several people in the congregation looked at each other and nodded in appreciation. It wasn't often they heard an instrument other than the organ or piano played in church. Suddenly, the guitar strumming stopped for a full two seconds and a deep, manly voice began a dramatic rendition of a well-known hymn. The guitar resumed playing but this time the notes took on a decidedly jazzy effect. The musician played with enthusiasm, intermittently adding theatrical emphasis.

> "O Lord my God! When I in awesome wonder
> Consider all the works thy hands have made,
> I see the stars; I hear the rolling thunder,
> Thy pow'r throughout the universe—displayed,
> Then sings my soul, my Savior God to thee;
> How great thou art, how great thou art!
> Then sings my soul, my savior God to thee;
> How great thou art, how great thou art!"[1]

"Ladies, Elvis is in the building!" Stella said, leaning toward her friends' direction, entirely missing the look of stunned disbelief on their faces.

Donna's head snapped in the direction of Regina, who was holding a trembling hand over her mouth. Both of them looked as if they had seen a ghost and their eyes glistened with tears threatening to escape.

"It can't be!" Donna whispered.

"Do you think it's really him?" Regina whispered back.

The guitar music got louder and picked up tempo. The mystery voice began to boom the second verse. Donna's tears found a path down her cheeks and she quickly rose and left the chapel. Regina stayed seated, not knowing what else to do. Stella leaned toward her and asked, "Is she verklempt or was it something I said?"

"No, it's nothing you said, but I can tell you this—that man's name isn't Paul. It's Donna's ex-husband, Tom!"

"Donna's ex-husband has a Las Vegas act?" Stella quipped before Regina also left the room.

By the time Donna reached her apartment, numbness and disbelief turned into angry tears dripping off her chin. She slammed the entry door and threw herself on the bed. Every nerve in her body trembled. *Where the hell has he been? Why is he here?* Donna couldn't rationalize what was happening. She hadn't heard from Tom in years, and now, all of a sudden, he appeared out of nowhere. He had completely walked out on them, not even keeping in touch with his own daughter. Not at Christmas, not birthdays. Not one word in years. Going over it in her mind, Donna realized Cicely said his name was Paul. Of course! Paul was Tom's middle name. Thomas Paul! Donna didn't recall hearing Cicely say his last name. She couldn't have known who he was because Donna changed back to her maiden name when they divorced. *That dog! Sneaking in here under a different name. What was he thinking? That we would never find out?*

Back at the Chapel, Stella waited for Bethany to come down from the choir loft. By the time her friend joined her, she was sure the newest resident of Heritage Memories Retirement Village was going to be one big simmering pot of trouble. Cicely and Tom followed Bethany down the stairs.

"Stella, I'm sure you remember Paul Sanders. He's the soloist you heard this morning. Isn't he fantastic? I told him everybody would love his singing. I had to convince him to do it because he's kind of shy, you know," Cicely announced in a proud voice.

"Nice to see you again. Cicely speaks highly of you. Was it 'Tom' she said your name is?" Stella coolly asked.

Tom met her with a warm handshake. His expression never changed but his eyes told Stella he knew what she meant.

"No Stella, I said his name is *Paul,* not Tom. That's ok. Those names do kind of sound alike. Right, Paul?" Cicely had him by the arm. She noticed Tom and Stella had not broken their gaze.

"Is something wrong?" she asked.

"No Sugar, nothing's wrong. It's just that I think Stella and I might know some of the same people. Do we, Stella?" Tom asked.

"Yes, as a matter of fact, we do," Stella flatly stated.

"Um, isn't that nice," Cicely hesitated, sensing something was amiss. "Well, shall we go, Paul? We're going to my daughter's house for dinner today. So we'll catch you all later, ok?" Cicely, sensing tension, glanced nervously from person to person.

"You sang beautifully this morning. I could have sworn you were Elvis. I do hope you don't mind me teasing you. Have a good day, Tom . . . or Paul . . . or whatever your name is," Stella said, finally breaking her gaze with a wry smile and turning away.

"Stella, Bethany, I sincerely hope we will all be friends," Tom said as he left with Cicely.

On the way to the dining room, Bethany took Stella's arm and looked into her eyes. "I've known you for most of your life, Stella Morgenstern Taub. I know when something is not right and I want you to tell me what it is," Bethany whispered. "Do you know that man?"

"Bethany, I don't know him but I know *of* him," Stella confided. "He's Donna's ex-husband!"

"Oh my merciful heavens, what is he doing here? Does she know he's here?"

"Oh yes, she knows."

There were two things crystal clear at breakfast the next morning; one, the brilliant blue of the Florida sky, and two, the fact that even on a cloudless day, you can hear thunder roll. It came in the form of a very loud, high pitched exclamation, followed by a tone of exasperation, then one of indignation, and lastly, pure anger.

"What? I knew something was going on! How could he do such a thing to me! Oh my God, what have I done to Donna? I'm gonna kill him!"

Everyone in the dining room stopped doing what they were doing and looked toward the direction of the tirade. Across the room, Cicely jumped up from the table she shared with Stella and Bethany. Her face was contorted with surprise, anger, and heartbreaking pain. Everyone watched her leave the dining room with her short slipper-clad feet pounding the carpet. She was mad. She was very mad. If anyone stood in her path, they moved away as quickly as they could. The burning hot energy emitted from the angry little auburn haired woman could have parted the Red Sea at that point. Stella and Bethany looked at each other with eyes open wide and shuddered to think what was going to happen next. Moments later, they saw Cicely's Bonneville leaving the parking lot.

The news quickly reached Donna that Cicely had learned the identity of her new beau. Past anger renewed itself at the thought of her ex-husband hurting her dear friend. After a sleepless night, Donna paced the floor of her apartment, wondering what she should do. Should she confront Tom? Should she act as if it didn't matter that he was here? She decided to go to the horse's mouth, so to speak, and ask him what on earth he was thinking by moving into *her* territory.

She found him at the gym. He saw her as she entered and immediately stepped off the treadmill, found a bench, and motioned for her to join him there. Wiping the sweat off his face with a white towel, Tom patted the bench beside himself, indicating Donna could sit there. She, in turn, pointed to the door, wordlessly telling him to meet her outside. This was her turf and she wasn't giving him the pleasure of telling her what to do, no matter how small the request. She walked out of the door, sat in one of the lounge chairs on the veranda and waited for him. As he joined her, she pretended to be calm by greeting him with a steady stare. She tried to measure her words precisely.

"Well?"

"Well, what?" he asked

"What are you doing here and why now after all of these years?"

"All right, Donna, I knew this was coming but I have as much right to live here as you do. Chad was my son too when they built this place. The boys never said I couldn't live here."

"That's right, he was your son! He was the son you turned your back on, the son you denied! You left him when he needed you most and didn't even come to his funeral!" She could feel her jaws and the muscles of her neck tighten. "What are you doing here, Tom?" she said through clenched teeth.

"Look, I'm not trying to start anything. The truth is I needed some place to go. A lot has happened since I saw you last. Some of it, I am not so proud of. Don't get all heated up because I chose to come here. I talked to Larry Jr. and he gave his approval. I didn't get the greatest apartment, but at least, I have someplace to live."

"You went to Larry Jr.? Behind Regina's back? How could you?" Donna rose to her feet with frustration and fresh anger causing her knees to tremble.

"I know, I know," Tom raised his hand defensively. "I was going to talk to you about it first. I wasn't sure how you were going to take it. As a matter of fact, you're doing exactly what I thought you would. Maybe you have every right to feel like you do, I don't know. But please, give me a chance and I swear I won't get in the way or cause problems for you," he said in a low voice.

"*Maybe* I have every right to feel the way I do? *You think*? You listen to me! You walked out on us. You've been gone ever since. You missed seeing our family grow. You never even contacted your own daughter! Did you know she had twin sons? You completely turned your back on all of us! If you think you have to live here, fine. But you leave my family alone!" Donna couldn't soften the sharp edge in her voice. "What about Cicely? Why did you come here telling everyone your name is Paul? How did you plan to explain that? She's my friend! She deserves better than the likes of you!" she countered, spitting the words from her mouth.

"That's not fair! I like Cicely. I told her my name is Paul so she wouldn't know who I am until I had a chance to talk to you. After a couple of days, I couldn't find a way to break it to her. She's a good person and a lot of fun to be around. If it's going to cause problems,

I'll stay away from her, too. Whatever you want, Donna, whatever you want."

Donna wasn't prepared for Tom to stand up and walk away from her, but he did, proving to her that they were, indeed, on common ground. As he was leaving, he spoke over his shoulder to his ex-wife; "You look good for your age, Donna." Infuriated, she stomped in the opposite direction, ignoring the few people who witnessed the exchange. She had to find Regina.

By the time Donna got to Regina's apartment, she had run out of angry steam. Now she felt as though her sails were deflated and a terrible fatigue blanketed her body. She knocked on Regina's door. No answer. She knocked again. *Now, where could Regina have gone,* she wondered. There was no way she could have known that Regina had plans of her own, plans that concerned her, but didn't include her.

Dr. Larry Whitmore Jr. answered the phone in his office, spoke briefly with the caller, and told his nurse that he would have to leave for a few minutes on a personal matter.

"But Doctor," she said, "we've still got patients in the waiting room!"

"Tell them it's an emergency," the doctor said waving her off on his way out the back door to his office. The nurse threw her hands in the air with a frustrated sigh and braced herself to face the room full of patients sure to voice objections at the delay they would now have to endure.

A half hour later, Dr. Whitmore was standing in the employee's back parking lot of the Village.

"I got here as soon as I could. You said it was urgent, Mother. What's wrong? Are you sick?" he asked.

"Sick? No, I'm not sick. I just wanted to tell you that Tom Sanders is here!" Regina exclaimed.

"I know that. Is that what you think is so urgent?" he asked impatiently.

"Of course it's urgent! He's Donna's ex-husband. He can't stay here."

"I know who he is, Mother," Larry Jr. sighed. "He called me several months ago. We talked and I said he could move in as soon as we had an opening. When Mr. Williams moved home with his daughter, I gave him that apartment. It's only fair."

"Fair? You call that fair? Larry, do you realize what you've done? Donna will never have a moment's peace now that he's here!" Regina's voice wavered.

"Chad was his son and we built this place together. Tom deserves to live here as much as Donna does."

"No, he doesn't. He left his family long before the two of you built the Village."

"Mother, let me ask you something. Is it Donna's peace you're worried about or is it your own?" his eyes narrowed.

"Donna's, of course! What do you mean?" Regina eyed her son questioningly. He didn't answer but his look was one of contempt. For a brief moment, she stared at him, trying to analyze the meaning of his words, before turning on her heel to leave. Suddenly, she whirled around and faced him again.

"You know, Son, you used to call me Mommy. Now you only call me 'Mother'. That's kind of cold, don't you think?" and she walked away leaving her son red-faced and standing alone in the parking lot.

Just as Regina was rounding the corner on her way back to her apartment, she saw Donna knocking on her door and heard her whisper "Regina! Regina, are you there?"

Regina backed up so she wouldn't be seen. She couldn't bear seeing her friend right now. She waited until Donna stopped knocking and then listened for the apartment door across from hers to open and close. She peeked around the corner to make sure the hall was empty before slipping into her apartment. Once inside, she picked up her phone and punched in a number.

"Taylor, I need a huge favor," she told her granddaughter as soon as she answered. Twenty minutes later, Regina had her bag packed and was tossing it into the trunk of Taylor's car. She climbed into the front passenger seat and hugged her granddaughter.

"What's wrong?" the young woman asked with concern. From the car seat in the back, her baby was babbling and waving her hands in the air, grasping at imaginary playmates.

"Honey, if you don't mind, I just can't talk about it right now. I'm so sorry to put you out, but I need to get away from here!" Her eyes pleaded with Taylor.

"Not a problem, Gina. I'm here for you," assured the younger woman, and she pointed her car in the direction of her home.

Regina leaned her head back and closed her eyes. *I'm 76 years old and my life is one big soap opera,* she thought. For whatever reason over the years, she knew that the truth would come out and her secret would unravel her life. People would be hurt. She would be disgraced. She would lose her friends, maybe even her family.

Aware of the incredible drama his presence caused, Tom sat at his dinette table and dropped his head into his hands. What a mess. He knew that by showing up at the Village, he would create quite a stir but he had no choice. This was the only place he could go. He picked up one of several medicine bottles sitting on the table and popped a pill in his mouth. After he put that bottle down, he picked up the next one and did the same thing. After lining up all the bottles in front of him, he began filling his pill organizer. It was a lot of medicine for one person to take, and it seemed that lately his life had become one giant pill to swallow.

After watching Cicely storm out of the dining room, Stella and Bethany decided that, rather than deal with questioning stares from the other diners, they should have their afternoon cup of tea in their own quarters. They felt badly that they had to be the ones to reveal Tom's identity to Cicely, especially after seeing the surprise and pain in her eyes. Because they were still unnerved by the events of the morning, they decided to make a pot of chai latte. *We need something sweet and soothing after all the drama that's been going on around here*, they told each other.

"It seems like everybody's got their feathers ruffled." Bethany bluntly stated.

Stella agreed and confided in her friend, "Donna never has shared anything about her ex with me. All I know is he left. Never said a word or gave a reason. He just left. Their son died, and their daughter had to walk by herself down the isle when she got married, and he never had a thing to say about it. That's pretty low-down, if you ask me. Regina ought to make Larry Jr. kick Tom's ass to the curb!"

"Maybe so, but don't you think he ought to be able to explain why he's here before he gets crucified?"

"Bethany! How can you say that? Think about poor Donna! I tell you, that Tom has some chutzpah showing up here!"

"Estelle, he's old. We're all old. What can he do? Maybe he's looking for forgiveness. Maybe he made a mistake in life that he wants to make right. We've all made mistakes, haven't we? Hopefully we can have them reconciled before it's too late." Her expression grew kinder and quieter.

Surprised at her friend's words, Stella fidgeted uncomfortably. "Yes, you're right, Beth. We've all made mistakes. From your mouth to God's ear, may we reconcile our mistakes."

For Bethany, the short moment of clarity was over. She rocked in her chair silently for several minutes before stopping, and then asked Stella when her Jacques would be coming to get her. Stella had to wipe her eyes before telling her "It won't be long now." She watched Bethany settle herself comfortably and resume her rocking and reminding Stella of a time long ago when she was the only person to turn to. She winced at the painful memory and steadied herself against the flood of emotion she knew would consume her, as it always did when she allowed herself to relive that devastating time in her life.

Her memories transported her to a time when she was only 16 years old and had fallen madly in love with an Irish boy. His name was Matthew O'Neal and he was the most handsome boy she had ever seen. His sandy brown hair and emerald green eyes took her breath away. They adored each other and spent as much time together as they could without letting on to their parents how serious they were. The two teenagers even discussed marriage and planned for the day when they wouldn't have to sneak around to be with one another. Too bad they were impulsive and young and couldn't wait. Unfortunately, Mathew didn't count on becoming a father at the age of 18. When Stella told him the news, he did the one thing she never would have believed he would do. After not hearing from him for three days, she listened to her heart whisper that something was seriously wrong. She felt nauseous and sweaty as she walked the fourteen blocks to Matthew's house. Nervously, she climbed the stairs of the stoop and knocked on the door. When Mrs. O'Neal appeared, she didn't invite the young girl in but left her standing on the stoop as she coldly broke the news that Matthew went to live with an uncle in New Jersey. With the echo of a warning to never call again for Matthew, Stella stared at the door slammed in her face. Within an instant, anguish and fear overwhelmed her, and the pit of her stomach felt as though she had swallowed a block of ice. Her knees became wobbly and she abruptly sat down on the stairs and wondered if this is what it was like to faint. For the first time in her young life, Stella didn't know what to do and she was afraid. She couldn't tell her parents that she was in the family way. They would kill her. More importantly, to see the disappointment in their eyes was something Stella knew she could not bear. The broken-hearted girl had only one person she could turn to. She called Bethany.

After the initial shock of her news, Bethany wasted no time urging Stella to join her family in Florida. Getting permission from her parents was easy enough for the young girl. All she had to say was that she was interested in a career in medicine and wanted to check out the medical school in Tallahassee. Mr. and Mrs. Morgenstern trusted Bethany and Jacques, especially since Bethany's mother had joined them in Florida to help with the couple's new baby boy. Letting Stella go to Florida wasn't even an issue. They were proud of her for what they thought was a plan to follow in the footsteps of their friend and prestigious doctor Jacques Bertrand. She left with their blessing, and they never learned the truth about why she wanted to go. Bethany and her family opened their arms and their home for Stella, and comforted her knowing the path ahead would be very difficult, to say the least. Stella was adamant that she would give the baby up for adoption. Nothing anybody could say, or do, would change her mind. "I can't take care of a baby" was all she would say. She never wanted to be reminded of Matthew O'Neal again. Her heartbreak was devastating, but she took comfort knowing that Jacques agreed to be her doctor. Several months later, her labor started and the time to deliver was at hand. The pain wasn't intense at first but rapidly escalated to the most searing pain Stella had ever known. She labored for many hours and by the time her daughter finally presented herself, Stella was unconscious. Jacques told Bethany there was so much bleeding, he wasn't sure he could save her. They tended to her for three days before she opened her eyes, and when she did, her face was void of any emotion. Not once did she ask about her child. When Bethany told her that she had a daughter, Stella turned her face to the wall. She wouldn't even look at the baby. On the fourth day, the figure of a nun dressed in a long flowing black habit, darkened the doorway to her room. She was kind and gentle and spoke sweetly about finding a good home for her baby, and how happy some lucky couple would be to have such a beautiful little girl. The only words Stella spoke were small and painful. "Thank you" was all she could say before Sister Dominic silently took the infant away. Afterward, the young girl refused to talk about it. Keeping her promise to her parents, she did inquire at the medical school but soon told them that she was no longer interested in a job in the medical field. "It doesn't matter," she told them when they voiced their disappointment, "Bethany got me a job at the store where she works. If it's alright, I'd like to stay in Florida."

Stella roused herself from the memories that carried her away from the room where Bethany was slowly rocking back and forth. She ached just as she did all those years ago when she would sit in that very chair, rocking Bethany's son deep in the night when the house was quiet and the only light was from the moon shining through the window. No one was awake to hear her lullaby or to see how she desperately held the boy or the tears she cried for the loss of her baby girl.

VI

A REVELATION

Taylor showed her grandmother to the spare bedroom and propped the overnight bag on the cedar chest under the window.

"Gina, make yourself at home. I'll be back in a little bit. I have a little research to finish up at the library. If you want to, we can talk about what's going on when I get back. Ok?"

The delicate scent of lilacs invited Regina into the room and offered a calm and soothing atmosphere that she gladly welcomed. She answered Taylor with a nod, and then moved over to a twin bed opposite the sunny window. It was covered with a quilt that she recognized as one that Renee' made when she was a senior in high school. Regina marveled as she lifted the edge for a closer look and remembered her daughter painstakingly laboring over each stitch. The quilt was perfect and still looked as new and fresh as it did so many years ago. She knew that tonight when she was ready for bed, she would pull that quilt over herself and it would feel like Renee''s arms were wrapped around her. How she missed her daughter! She couldn't imagine how she would be able to tell Renee''s daughter what had driven her from her home.

After settling in, Regina wandered through the 1940s era cottage. Nice. The kitchen was a cheerful, lemony-yellow time capsule with red appliances and green laminate counter tops. The dining room was nothing more than a nook with a four-chair dinette set separating the kitchen from the living room. Beautifully aged hardwood floors stretched from the front door through every room in the house, except the bathroom, which was tiled with two-inch octagon white tiles and a spattering of an occasional black tile. There were two small bedrooms on opposite ends of the house. One was the bedroom she would be using and the larger one, of course, was Taylor's bedroom. Baby Penny's white crib was nestled in the corner on the far side her mother's double bed and Regina was glad to see that they slept in the same room, especially since Penny was still so little. They would be very close that way. Although Taylor herself had not grown up liking the girly-girl style, her daughter's crib wore a frilly pink and white dust ruffle with a comforter to match. A canopy of the same fresh pink gingham topped the crib, making for a perfectly coordinated ensemble fit for a little princess. At the foot of the crib stood a white wicker stand with four shelves holding the infant's clothing. Her dresses and diaper shirts were pastel and lacey, with ribbons, bows, and cute little flowers embroidered on them. Regina smiled as she touched the tiny clothes and remembered how she had dressed Taylor's mother in baby clothes such as these when she was born. If Renee' were still alive, she would have loved being Penny's grandmother. Her death was a shock to all of them and seemed to be the final catalyst that unwound the bond connecting everyone in the family. The simple truth was that Renee had been the glue holding the family together. Once she was gone, everything fell apart. Regina wasn't able to sustain a loving relationship with Larry Jr. by herself, and he seemed unwilling to meet her halfway. Whatever it was that kept them apart apparently was enough to build a wall between them that lasted for years.

In no part of the house did Regina see any evidence of a man living there. Curious, she thought, and odd that Taylor would become a single mother, especially since she knew well how it felt not to have a father. She hadn't asked about Penny's father. She hoped for the day when Taylor would tell her without any prompting.

Regina's heart was flooded with a new sense of respect for her granddaughter. She was only twenty years old and already making her way in the world without the safety net of her parent's love or support. She had already proven that she was very mature for her age. When she turned eighteen and her father's life insurance was released from the trust it had been held in, Taylor took the money and invested in herself. She was not only putting herself through college but she purchased this house as well. Granted, it wasn't very big or grand, but it was Taylor's outright and it was home for her. She dressed it modestly, effectively achieving a simple, elegant style.

Regina found her way around the kitchen and put together a pot of coffee. She was glad that Taylor's taste in fresh ground matched her own. *Nothing better than a good cup of coffee,* she thought. By the time it was finished brewing Taylor and Penny were home. Regina found the cups, sugar, and cream and set them out so they could enjoy a cup together.

"Thanks, Gina! I sure can use a cup." Taylor smiled. After getting Penny settled in her baby swing, she joined her grandmother at the dinette.

"So tell me, what's going on?" Her concerned eyes searched Regina's.

"I don't even know how to put it. First of all, Donna's ex-husband moved to the Village."

"No kidding? After all these years that old fart finally showed his face?" Taylor looked surprised but not shocked, at least, not as Regina had been shocked by Tom's arrival.

"Yes, he did, and without warning, I might add. Nobody knew he was coming, except, of course, Larry Jr. He knew all about it and didn't even consider what it would do it poor Donna." Regina said.

"Yeah, I can see where she would be upset. But what else is going on?" Taylor asked. She reached across the table and sympathetically laid her hand on her grandmother's arm.

"What do you mean, honey?" Regina's voice was guarded.

"What else has you so upset? There has to be something else. I'm sure you wouldn't get this upset unless there is more to it then you're saying. I mean, look at Uncle Larry. You two haven't been close for as long as I can remember so it shouldn't surprise you that he wouldn't consult you or anyone else about who lives in the Village."

"Seriously, Taylor, that's all there is," Regina insisted. "It's true your uncle and I haven't been close since your mom died, but that doesn't have anything to do with what's going on now. I've accepted that and moved on. He has his own family. That much is clear, but I haven't fallen into the category of not being able to take care of myself yet. What I can't accept is the fact that he has no regard for how this is affecting poor Donna. It's one thing to resent a parent, and something else to deliberately overlook the feelings of someone you've known all your life. I hate to say it, but I'm mortified at his behavior."

"I understand, but you shouldn't let what he does or doesn't do knock you off balance. You've known for years that he only thinks of himself and his family. It's as if they don't have room in their lives for anyone else. I mean, you practically don't exist to Aunt Sherry, and the girls. Really, although I should say in their defense, my cousins have air pockets where their brains are supposed to be. They blindly follow whatever their parents tell them. Sure, they're older than I am but they're like little clones of Aunt Sherry. If one of them ever had an original thought, it would be like a bubble popping in her head." Taylor chuckled at the thought.

"It must have been hard for you to live with them," said Regina, trying to change the subject.

"It was a lot to get used to. Somewhere along the way, I figured out that I didn't fit in with them. I guess that's why I was such a little trouble maker growing up. I'm not like them. It's not that I'm better than they are. I'm just different. Even though we lived under one roof, I can remember feeling lonely all the time, except when I came to visit you. That was the best time, Gina. I have memories of you teaching me to sew, knit, and bake cookies. I can almost smell chocolate chip cookies when I am around you. Did you know that? I didn't realize how much I've missed you until after I had my own daughter," Her voice softened. "You are the closest to my mother that I've ever known. That's why I came to the Village that day. I've missed you. I wanted to show you my baby girl and ask you to be a part of her life." Taylor covered Regina's hand with her own. "So whatever hurts you hurts me, too. You are welcome to make yourself at home Gina, but I think you need to let somebody know where you are. Your friends have got to be worried about you, to say nothing of Uncle Larry." Taylor reasoned.

"I'll call Stella and let her know. But your Uncle Larry? I'm sure he couldn't care less!" insisted Regina.

After a quick phone call to let Stella know that she was with Taylor, Regina joined her granddaughter and the baby in the living room. The sight of the two of them snuggled together warmed her heart. She took a seat next to Taylor on the sofa and reached for the baby. The little one willingly went into her arms and grabbed a fistful of white hair, sending both women into fits of laughter as they gently tried to untangle Penny's pudgy fingers.

"Taylor, I know it isn't fair for me to ask this, but what about Penny's father? I mean, I can see that you're not married, but I haven't heard you say a word about having a boyfriend, much less a husband." Regina gently asked.

"That's because I don't have much to say about Penny's father. He's a nice man but not someone I could have for a long-term relationship. He doesn't even live here. I've never told him about Penny."

"He doesn't know he has a daughter? Why? Surely you don't think that's right, do you?"

"Gina, just like you have some things you can't explain to me, I have some things I don't want to go into either. This is one of them. It's complicated. I'm sorry." Taylor's soft eyes were honest and apologetic.

"I guess that's only fair," Regina answered.

"I can handle this on my own. Penny is my life now. She's mine and only mine."

The next week seemed to fly by. While Taylor attended classes, Regina took it upon herself to keep the house clean and cook the evening meals for the little family. She had forgotten how good it felt to take care of someone else. Her granddaughter welcomed her help and enjoyed the time they spent together. They were bonding and it was good. One evening after supper, Taylor approached the subject of financial affairs with Regina. Just curious, she said, to know how she and her friends were able to fund everything they do, especially the many travels they took together.

"Oh honey, you would not believe it!" exclaimed Regina.

"I'm not trying to be nosey, and I know why you and Donna live at the Village, but what about your other three friends? I know that if Uncle Larry has anything to do with it, it has to be very expensive to live there. Does social security pay that much or are they just independently wealthy?" asked Taylor

"You could say we are all *dependently* wealthy. We have a partnership." began Regina cautiously. "A long time ago, before any of us came to live at the Village, Cicely decided to turn her house into an income property by renovating her second floor into an apartment. She didn't need the money, it's just that her children were all grown and married so she was looking for a project and that one seemed perfect for a start. It worked out well for her. She made a lot of money, which inspired us to pool our money together to buy several houses that needed to be renovated. We each made an equal investment and the partnership was born. We always sold for a profit. We've done quite well over the years."

"I never knew about this. What a wonderful idea! What about these days? The economy is on a down turn. I know it's a buyer's market because that's why I got my house so reasonably. Haven't your properties lost value?"

"Good Lord, no! Stella insisted on organizing monthly business meetings to discuss our investments, the economy, and all of that. It was somewhat hard for us because whenever we would get together, we wanted to visit and so forth. She put an end to that nonsense with a big brass bell she rang every time we got off track. Do you know how loud and annoying a clanging bell can be? It is awful, but it helps us stay focused. We make a good team. Some of the research we did warned us about the economy. You could say we saw it coming so we decided to stop selling properties and lean more toward leasing them. It's worked out so far. I mean, it's not as if we need the money but it's good for us. We decided a long time ago that because we are so blessed, we needed to give back. So, many of homes we have are rented for a very nominal amount. We don't advertise what we have available so an interested tenant will usually hear about a property from a friend, or a friend of a friend. You know what I mean. We try to help as many people as we can, especially if there are children involved. Anyway, we have an office staff that screens applicants and keeps the business end in order. Out of Cicely's six kids, four are on board with us. We employ them."

"Aren't you afraid some one is going to take advantage of you? How do you keep up with all of that?" a surprised Taylor asked.

"Oh, don't worry. Stella keeps everybody in line. In fact, she keeps all of us well informed and we each have the opportunity to add our two cents to the business any time we think we need to. And don't forget, we sign the paychecks. We have to know what's going on. We have a lawyer on board, too. Bethany's son. Jack got us incorporated and made everything legal. Cicely's kids are all paid employees, except Danny of course, and Cindy; she's still up in New York. Cicely's other two daughters are the designers, one of her sons is the architect, and the other is the construction contractor. Donna's daughter, you know her daughter Belinda, is our realtor. We've kept the business in the family, sort of."

"What does Uncle Larry think about all of this?"

"Darling, your Uncle Larry doesn't know a thing about it. He thinks we are all a bunch of senile old folks who don't have a lick of sense. Let him think it, we don't care. When he's our age, he'll find out that he will still feel like he's only eighteen years old. Just because a person qualifies for a senior citizen discount doesn't mean life is over!"

"What's the name of your business? It has a name, doesn't it?" asked Taylor.

"Well, when we named it we decided that the name would have meaning—something to prove a point. We named it OLC, Inc. Who knew, huh?"

"Wait a minute. I got a scholarship from a company called OLC!" Taylor exclaimed.

"Yes, you did! I want you to know that you earned that scholarship. It wasn't just handed to you because you're my granddaughter!"

"Lucky for me! But I never knew what the business initials OLC stood for?"

"Old Ladies Club," laughed Regina. "Never underestimate the generations that came before you!"

During her visit, Regina tried to keep her mind off the situation at the Village and did pretty well until the morning they were awakened by the ringing telephone.

With a perplexed look, Taylor handed the phone to her grandmother.

"It's for you," she said.

"Hello? What? I'll meet you at the hospital!" Regina gasped and, turning to her granddaughter, asked for a ride to St. Michael's Hospital.

"I have to get there as quickly as possible! Bethany had a stroke!" she explained.

After they arrived and rushed through the automatic doors to the lobby, they met Donna and Cicely in the ER waiting room. Regina could sense that the tension between them was as thick as buttermilk but she was confident that her friends would be united in their concern for Bethany. Still, she observed, they were at least an arm's length from each other, which, under the circumstances, was highly unusual.

"What happened? Where's Bethany?" Regina frantically asked.

"They're still working with her," Donna told her, clasping her arm. "Stella's in there, too. They said she could stay because Bethany wouldn't let go of her hand." Donna gestured toward the two closed doors that marked the entrance to the Emergency Room.

Cicely stepped up, put her arm around Regina and suggested they all have a seat while they wait for word to come.

An hour later, Stella emerged from behind the closed doors. She was pasty white and seemed slightly unsteady on her feet. Her friends flew to her side.

"How is she? Is she alright?" they asked, speaking over each other.

"The doctor said it was close, but they were able to get to her in time. There is a chance she'll make it, but they can't be sure at this point. She goes in and out of consciousness, and when she's awake, she can't move her left side. Jack is with her now." Stella explained. She sank into a chair and the cold vinyl chilled her.

"I've never known anyone as long as I've known her. We're like family after all these years. She's the only family I have left!" Stella dropped her head into her hands and sobbed. Together, the friends huddled around a brokenhearted Stella and gave each other as much support as they could.

"She would want us to pray," reminded Donna as she reached for Regina's hand. Regina took it and held her other hand out to Cicely and Stella. Forming a circle, the group earnestly combined their voices in heartfelt prayer

Bethany made it through the night and continued to improve over the next few days. Within two weeks, she was well enough to be transferred to a rehabilitation center for head injuries and stroke patients. She regained the use of her vocal cords but her left side remained almost motionless. Stella stayed with her as much as possible and, when the time came, she broached the subject of having Bethany move into the assisted living wing of the Village.

"Are you sure it's the best thing for me?" the eighty year old woman asked weakly.

"Of course I'm sure! Jack suggested it, Bethany. You know you'll do anything for your boy, right?" Stella replied.

"Can I go back to my own apartment when I'm better?"

"Without a doubt. I've already talked to Larry Jr. about holding it for you. He wouldn't dare give it to someone else!" Stella asserted.

"But when I get there, who's going to turn me when I need it?" Bethany asked.

"I'll turn you, sweetheart."

"Who's going to shave my legs?"

"You don't shave your legs," Stella said flatly.

"What if I wanted my legs shaved, would you do it?"

"But you never have shaved your legs, Bethany."

"But what if I wanted to?" Bethany insisted.

"Ok, ok, I'll shave your legs!" promised Stella impatiently. "I'll shave your legs, and your armpits, and pluck those straggly whiskers under your chin! Are you happy now?"

"I'm just checking . . . ." Bethany said with a grin on the right side of her face.

"Good gawd, Bethany! Stop it!" said Stella with a pretense of annoyance. In her heart, she was relieved and gladdened that her friend's sense of humor was intact.

After the move and Bethany was settled in her new rooms nicely, many of her friends throughout the Village came to visit, including Tom Sanders. The first time he came, he was met with a defiant Stella at the door.

"I'm not sure what you think you're doing here," she told him.

"I just came to visit. Honestly, I want to say hello and tell her I hope she is getting better," explained Tom. "Come on. I'm not the bad guy you think I am. Please let me see Bethany." Tom's eyes pleaded with Stella's. Reluctantly, she stepped aside to let him enter. Going to the bedside, he made his presence known by picking up the frail woman's hand. Stella's dog, Camille, was lying on the bed at Bethany's side. His tail wagged hesitantly and his eyes wavered from Stella to Tom and back again as if silently questioning what he was expected to do.

"Hey Bethany," Tom said softly. "How are you doing? Everyone is so glad you're back," he assured her.

Bethany's eyes remained closed and she didn't acknowledge that she heard him. He took a seat next to the bed and an awkward silence hung thickly in the room. Neither Tom nor Stella spoke to each other. Fifteen minutes passed and finally Tom cleared his throat and rose to leave.

"Don't leave." The slurred words came from the woman on the bed. "I like holding your hand."

Surprised, Tom sat back down and took Bethany's hand once again. Stella glared at him before she leaned toward Bethany.

"I'm going to eat!" she snapped, and picked Camille up from the little nest he made on the bed, and left the room in a huff.

"Sometimes she just sucks all the air out of a room, doesn't she?" Bethany slurred. Tom coughed, trying to keep himself from exploding with laughter.

VII

ON THE MEND

Eventually, the time came for Regina to go home. Although she loved staying with Taylor, she was aware the young woman needed her space and privacy. In her heart, Regina knew that she would have to face whatever was waiting for her. The past, it seemed, was impossible to avoid.

"Taylor, I can't thank you enough for letting me stay here. You and the baby are so darling. I'm glad I got to spend time with both of you," she said when she told her granddaughter that she was leaving.

"We were glad to have you," Taylor smiled warmly. "I hope we can do this again sometime. You know you're welcome here. Gina . . . I . . . well, I love you." The young woman faltered.

"I love you, Taylor, and Penny too. Sounds like my taxi cab is here." Regina's eyes teared up and she wrapped her granddaughter in an affectionate embrace. The warm hug was cathartic for both of them. Regina took a deep breath, inhaling the scent that reminded her so much of her Renee'. Words couldn't describe how it felt to hold her sweet granddaughter in her arms once again.

"Come visit me soon."

"We will. Gina, I'm so glad we have each other," Taylor said with happy tears overflowing her eyes.

No sooner did Regina arrive back at the Village, Stella showed up at her door. Quite naturally, she let herself in, knowing she would be welcomed no matter the circumstances. In the time Regina was gone, a lot had happened. In addition, there were many unanswered questions.

"It's about time you got back. What is the matter with you anyway? What's the big deal taking off like that? Everybody has been a basket case for one reason or another since you have been gone, mostly because of Tom. And then Bethany's stroke . . ." Stella looked worried.

"Oh, I'm sorry. I'm terribly embarrassed because of the way Larry Jr. let Tom sneak in the back door, and hurt that he would do such a thing. Why, he has known Donna practically his whole life! I could not stay here and face that. I'm sorry if I upset anyone."

"You could have said so instead of running off like you did. I'd probably be embarrassed too if I was you," Stella said, not bothering to soften her words. "Anyway, Bethany is on the assisted living wing now and you'll never guess who came to visit her. Tom. Is he cheeky or what? I can't believe the nerve he had coming in here getting everyone upset. And can you believe Bethany wanted to hold his hand? I have *always* given her credit for being a good judge of character, but I guess this stroke did more damage than we thought. Do you think so? Can a stroke do that?"

The barrage of questions and updates on current events at the Village had Regina's nerves on edge. It took everything she had to maintain her composure during Stella's tirade.

"Is Bethany ok?" Regina asked quietly.

"I think she's coming along," Stella answered, beginning to calm down. "She isn't having much luck getting her left side to respond yet, but she is working with physical therapy every day. She's eighty, for gawd's sake. Who knows if she will ever get better? My little Camille has taken to staying right beside her in the bed. I can't get used to that. Do you remember hearing about that cat on the news who predicted someone was going to die by sitting on the bed? Then the person in that bed died. I wonder if it's like that. Maybe

Camille can sense something. Do you think a dog is capable of doing that?" Stella chattered, her hands twisting against each other nervously.

"No, no, darling. It's not like that. In fact, I think they figured out the cat thing was just a coincidence. Don't talk like that. Bethany is going to be alright, ok?"

Regina noticed that Stella's hands stopped their twisting and turning and she seemed comforted. Nobody could stand the thought of losing Bethany but she knew they had to prepare for the inevitable. Everybody has their time to go, not only Bethany. It could be any one of them and, Regina thought, the sooner they face it the better.

"Well, I'm glad you're back. It's been a real strain around here. Donna won't come out of her apartment and Cicely is spending an awful lot of time with her family instead of hanging around here. I've been cooking my meals in my apartment since you've been gone. Geez, I might as well move out!"

The news that Donna was staying closed up in her apartment was surprising. Maybe things were worse than she thought. After Stella's informative visit, Regina went to the apartment next to hers. Knocking on Donna's door sent butterflies to her churning stomach, but when Regina saw her friend's pale face, the butterflies inside her flew away, replaced with genuine concern.

"Donna, are you alright? I heard from Stella that you aren't getting out much. Are you still upset about Tom being here?" She asked.

"Oh Regina, I'm so glad you're back," she said, drawing her friend in by her arm. "I just didn't know what to do. Every time I think about leaving the apartment, I'm afraid I'm going to run into Tom. I just do not want to see him! Ever!"

"But you can't stay in here all the time," Regina told her. "Don't let him take that away from you! There is no reason to have anything to do with him. You can just ignore each other, can't you?"

"You've been gone, Stella's been with Bethany every minute, and Cicely won't come around. I've been all alone with no one I can talk to!" Donna dissolved into tears. "He left me! He took my heart, shredded it, and couldn't even tell me why! Now he thinks he has the right to live here? I can't take it! I'm going to have to move away from here."

"Wait a minute! No, no, no! You can't talk like that. Don't let him run you off. This is your home. Please Donna, you know we all love you. Don't say you're leaving. Where would you go? Could you live with Belinda? You're seventy-eight years old, how could you start over at this age?"

"We've still got plenty of rentals. All I would have to do is pick one. I could do it. Believe me, I could do it," Donna said assertively.

"But who would be there for you? You would be all alone. Stay here. Don't go. Don't even talk about it," Regina tried to convince her. "Ever since our children were little, we've planned to live in a place like this when we got older. They planned it! Your son, my daughter, both gone. Don't disrespect them by moving out. They wouldn't want that!"

She left Donna's apartment, shaken to her very core. When she got to her place, she wet a washcloth and put it to her face. Deep inside she knew the drama wasn't over yet. Perhaps the worst was yet to come.

By the next morning, perfect, sun-shiny weather did a lot to soothe the bundle of nerves threatening to ignite within Regina. Springtime was in full bloom and she decided to do a little gardening with the pots on her patio to distract her from the recent woes plaguing herself and her friends. While she stayed at her granddaughter's, her patio garden had been seriously neglected. She had several new plants that Taylor generously shared from her yard and they needed potting. Regina loved her patio area. It was peaceful, serene, and private. Situated in an alcove just off the living room, it was easily accessed from both bedrooms. It was sheltered from the wind and sun and harbored a courtyard atmosphere with a wrought iron fence and gate. Gardening was one of her passions and it was a healing balm to a wounded soul. The smell and feel of good rich soil in her hands had a calming effect on her. The different colors and textures of her plants were refreshing, and the return year after year of her perennials was a symbol of the continuation of life. Regina loved it all.

She was on her knees, up to her elbows in fresh potting soil, when the doorbell rang.

"Come in!" she called. Cicely slowly opened the door and popped her head into the apartment.

"Hey! I'm so glad to see you," Regina exclaimed. "Come on in here! Do you want some coffee?"

Cicely nodded her head and Regina washed the soil off her hands and prepared to make a pot of coffee.

"I heard you were back and I just . . . um . . . came by to . . . see how your visit was," Cicely hesitated. Then her words tumbled out as fast as the tears streaming down her face.

"I've missed you! I'm so glad you're back! I need someone to talk to because I'm so confused and hurt and everybody's upset and I feel like I've done something wrong but I haven't done anything wrong at least I didn't know I was doing anything wrong and Paul, or Tom or whatever his name is really hurt me with his lying and I'm afraid I hurt Donna and I just don't know what to do!" Cicely rattled as she collapsed into Regina's arms.

"Come on now, honey. Don't cry. You didn't do a thing wrong. Nobody blames you for any of this. You didn't know who Tom was. We all know that. Nobody is mad at you," Regina assured her friend. She took her hand, led her to a seat at the table, and poured two cups of coffee.

"I'm sorry to come apart like that, Regina. I've been holding it in for so long! I've been spending most of my time with one or the other of my kids but I know I can't keep hiding out with them. It's not easy to have someone else around all the time even if I am their mother. When I'm here, I feel as if I'm holding my breath waiting to run into Tom or Donna and I don't want to face either of them! I'm going to have to leave this place! It doesn't even feel like home anymore."

"Oh my good Lord, not you too!" Regina sighed. "Donna feels the same way! I've been doing my best to talk her out of moving away, too. But I have to admit, I've even thought about it myself."

"Why would you leave? You don't have anything to run from!"

"Well, you know, the tension around here has been pretty thick. That's why I went to my granddaughter's. I needed to get away for a little while. We all do now and then. I came back because you all mean so much to me. Look. We've been friends for years. We have the business. We can't just walk away from each other, can we?"

"No, I suppose you're right. What about Donna? Does she hate me?" Fresh tears began filling Cicely's eyes.

"Of course not! Donna couldn't hate you. She's upset with Tom but she could never hate you."

A knock on the door signaled another visitor had arrived. She left Cicely sitting in the kitchen as she went to answer the door, and when she returned, Tom was right behind her. When Cicely saw him, the color drained from her face and she looked like a deer caught in the headlights. She jumped up and headed for the door but Regina stopped her.

"Wait a minute, don't leave. Let's get this straightened out right here, right now," begged Regina. A doubtful looking Cicely sat down and Regina gestured toward a chair for Tom to sit in.

"Let's see what he has to say."

Tom began by earnestly apologizing to Cicely and trying to explain that he didn't plan for any of this to happen, much less, causing anyone to be hurt.

"Look," he said. "I needed a place to live and I knew I could come here. Before I could figure out how to explain it to Donna, I met you and I didn't want to take a chance that you wouldn't see me anymore. You are like a breath of fresh air to me. I just kept putting it off and putting it off until it was too late. I thought I could smooth things over with Donna once I explained it all to her but that's not how it worked out. I honestly didn't think she would be so upset with me being here."

Both Cicely and Regina stared at Tom, digesting his words, wondering if he was telling the truth.

"Please believe me," he pleaded.

The next morning Regina relayed all the details of Tom's visit to Donna.

"How can you believe him? What is all this about 'I had to find a place to live' crap? He's lying. I know he's lying!" Donna's defenses flared.

"Think about it, Donna. Something has to have wiped him out financially for him to resort to living here! Let me ask you something. Have you ever known Tom to lie? When you were together, did he ever lie to you?'

"Did he ever lie to me? Seriously? He walked out on me. He didn't hand me a packet of lies telling me why he was leaving. He just left. He left us hanging, wondering why. But, I guess he didn't actually lie, at least not that I know of. How can a person be sure? And what difference does it make anyway? He left whether he lied or not."

"I'm sorry, but the point I'm trying to make is that Tom wouldn't have shown up just to make your life miserable. He has to have had a reason for being here. I don't think he moved in just to intentionally hurt you."

After a few moments of silence, Donna quit studying her hands tightly knotted in her lap and nodded, affirming what she heard was probably true.

"You need to talk to him, Donna. Go, and get it over with. You need to find out what's going on before it tears us all apart. All of a sudden, everyone's talking about moving away from the Village! For what? Over this one thing? Please!"

"I already talked to him once, but I still can't get used to seeing him after all this time, especially here. We're not kids anymore, how can it still hurt like this? So many years have passed and I never got over him, Regina, because I never knew why he left. I mean there we were, a loving married couple, at least I thought so. Then boom, he was gone and the kids I were alone without a clue why."

"Please. Just one more time. Go talk to him."

Donna considered what was said to her, and finally acknowledged that, in order for this situation to be straightened out, she would have do what Regina asked and confront Tom one more time.

Before she could loose her courage, Donna immediately went to Tom's apartment. She held her breath when she knocked on his door. It took a few moments for him to answer and, when he did, the look on his face registered enormous surprise. For a split second, he paused before inviting her in.

"I'm sorry the place is a mess right now, but realistically speaking, I'm sure you couldn't care less," he offered, running his hand over the top of his graying hair.

"You would be right," she told him. "The only reason I'm here is to find out the truth about what is going on and why you are here."

"Fair enough," Tom sighed. "I'm sorry I didn't call you and talk to you before I moved in, but seriously, I didn't think you would mind. A lot of years have gone by, Donna."

"I'm well aware of that, but what happened between us is still unfinished business as far as I am concerned. It doesn't matter how long it's been. I still think you owe me an explanation about why you chose to move to the Village. I want to know what's going on. Something is wrong, isn't it?" she asked. She studied his lined face trying to detect at least one little hint of explanation, and wasn't surprised when Tom nodded his head.

"Have a seat, Donna. We'll talk." He accepted the fact that he was going to come clean at last.

They talked for several hours and when she left Tom's apartment, she appeared shaken and sad. Several bridges had been crossed and several boundaries were laid, one of them being that if he wanted to see Cicely, Donna wouldn't have a problem with it. However, if he broke her heart, there would be hell to pay. When they finished saying everything they had to say, she was determined to find Cicely and attempt to clear things up with her . . .

Cicely was sitting by herself in the pergola swing near the barbeque area by the time Donna found her. She was holding an open book as though actually reading, but the reality of it was that she read and reread the same words over and over. Her mind was too preoccupied for the words to register. She looked up in time to see Donna walking toward her, and nervously laid the book on the swing beside her.

"Do you mind if I join you?" Donna asked. Cicely shook her head and patted the seat beside her.

"Of course not but before you say anything, please believe me that I didn't know Tom was your ex-husband when I met him or I never . . ."

"It's ok, Cicely! Really, it's ok." Donna worked to keep her voice steady and calm. "I understand that and I don't hold it against you. I've already talked to Tom about it and told him I don't mind."

"You're ok with him being here?" Cicely's eyes widened.

"It looks like I have to be, doesn't it? He's here and he's not going anywhere. I don't know, Cicely. I didn't realize how much I still resent him for leaving us. I thought I was over it but when he suddenly appeared out of nowhere, all kinds of emotions broke loose from my soul and boiled out of me. I suppose I should have let that go a long time ago, but it hasn't been easy. I've been holding it in for all these years, not realizing how bitter I became. I don't want to be that way anymore. Living with that kind of resentment, whether a person shows it or not, is like being poisoned. I always said I wouldn't marry again because I'm Catholic and I don't believe in divorce but, really, that wasn't why. The truth is I didn't want to face the prospect of being hurt again. In my heart, I couldn't let go of Tom. Now, I can see that I stopped loving him a long time ago and it's time for me to lose the bitterness. I'm not going back to all the years I wasted hanging on, being resentful, and hiding the anger. I'm going to just look ahead, take everyday as it comes, and make it worthwhile. So, my friend, if you want to see Tom, it's ok with me."

Cicely hugged Donna for a long time before she said, "I don't know if I want to see him now. I don't like charades or a man that lies."

"Well, I learned something from Regina today. She pointed out that he didn't lie, but to be fair about it, he didn't tell the whole story," Donna wryly volunteered. Arm in arm, with their friendship restored, the women headed inside to the dining hall. Both of them were famished for the first time in days.

They joined Regina who was eating her lunch at their usual table. Donna wondered where Stella was, and Regina told her that she didn't feel comfortable leaving Bethany at the moment. The atmosphere became decidedly somber as these three passed knowing looks to one another. Nobody said aloud what they were all thinking.

Bethany's room on the assisted living wing was dark and quiet. The curtains were drawn and the head of the hospital bed was raised slightly. She was still and small under the sheets. Her breathing was slow and sounded a little raspy.

Stella felt so alone sitting in the room with her. Jack, as well as the doctors, had already talked to her and had given her a copy of Bethany's living will to prove that she didn't want any heroic measures taken should she stop breathing or her heart stop beating. It cut Stella to the core, but she knew the decision was a sound one. She, herself, had signed a living will identical to Bethany's. Her thoughts drifted back five years to the time when they signed the Advanced Directive papers after one of their crazy trips to Mexico. It was a sultry trip that prompted the group of women to swear they would never again trek to Mexico in the dead of summer, ocean breeze or not. Stella met an incredibly handsome Mexican man, at least 30 years her junior, who had a number of flashy tattoos. On one arm, he sported a high-stepping lady dancer decked out in colorful ruffled skirts and a sombrero beneath the words 'Madre Mia'. The opposite shoulder wore the words 'Ave Maria' above a rosary stretching from bicep to elbow. They spent the whole evening in a charming cantina where Stella taught him how to dance, and he taught her how to shoot tequila. When the young man saw Bethany staring at his tattoos, he told her in broken English "if you like, I can bring my hombre to make the same for you!" Bethany glanced at Stella whose laughing eyes dared her to take the man's offer.

"I don't think so, young fellow. The only tattoo I'm ever going to get is one right here," she pointed to her cleavage. "And it will be the outline of a heart with the words 'No CPR' tattooed inside."

The man looked at her in confusion, which made her friends laugh even harder. Bethany didn't get a tattoo that night, but Stella gave in and had a long stem rose tattooed on the outer part of her left thigh just above her knee.

"No need for you to get that tattoo, Bethany. It hurts like hell. When we get home, we're going to have some living wills drawn up so there won't be any question about what we want for our last days."

"I can NOT believe you got a tattoo at your age, Estelle!" Bethany admonished, wagging her finger in Stella's face.

"Age is just a number, Beth. They say that these days sixty is the new forty. I say, if that's right, then I'm only fifty! Besides, my tattoo is in a place no one is likely to see unless we're . . ." Stella pursed her lips and made little kissing noises.

"Hush your mouth, girl! I swear I'm never going anywhere with you again!" Bethany pretended to be flustered, but in her heart, she wasn't surprised at anything her dear friend would do. She knew her better than anyone and watched her hit her golden years kicking and screaming. The woman was not about to let life slip past her without stirring the waters and taking a big gulp of it.

Bethany didn't forget Stella's promise to have living wills drawn up and kept after her until they finally got the paper work done.

A whimper from a dreaming Camille, who was snuggled on the bed against Bethany's side, dragged Stella's thoughts to the present, and she pulled her chair closer to the head of bed. For hours, she sat by her side watching her breathing slow down and her body become as still as it could be. She felt as though she were going to choke before she began talking to Bethany in a hushed voice.

"Beth, we've been friends forever. You have been everything to me; mother, sister, teacher, friend, and lifesaver. I don't know how to tell you how much you mean to me." Stella kept her voice quiet. She wasn't at all sure that Bethany could hear her.

"You've always been the one who was there for me. When I was hardheaded and foolish, you were there, never judging, always supporting. Even when you didn't believe in what I was doing, you were still there for me. You did the one thing I couldn't do for myself. You found my little girl a good home when I couldn't give her one. You didn't want her to go, but you let her because that was my decision. My parents would have disowned me if they knew about her. You took care of that too. You never told. You've always been faithful. I'm here to say thank you, Bethany. Thank you for everything." She swallowed hard and sat quietly for what seemed like forever. Bethany didn't move except for the slow rise and fall of her thin, frail chest.

Finally, she began to speak again. "I have to accept that, even though I don't want you to leave, Bethany, I must respect your wishes. You can go, my friend. I won't hold you back. It's time for me to let you go. If you believe there's a heaven, go there. Don't stay here because of me. I'll be fine." She laid her head on the side of the bed and began to cry. Suddenly a movement on the bed startled her. Quickly, she raised her head and saw Bethany holding her arms straight out in front of her, struggling to a sitting position on the bed.

"What are you doing?" an incredulous Stella asked.

"I'm going," Bethany answered, her eyes still closed.

"Going where?" Stella was exasperated.

"Going to heaven! You said it was time to go, didn't you?"

"Not NOW, you dope! Oh my gawd! You're giving me a heart attack! You can't go till you DIE!"

"You mean I'm not dead yet?" the tiny woman asked, her eyes still closed and her arms still in the air.

"NO, I guess not, you are TALKING to me! Geez, how can you be so . . ." Stella's face was flushed and hot.

"Then stop acting like I am already and go call the doctor. I don't know if you noticed or not, but I can move my left side now," Bethany said with a weak laugh.

It took a moment for Stella to regain her composure. Then she started laughing. Bethany flopped back in the bed and snickered until the bed shook. They laughed so hard, tears streamed down their faces. Stella caught her breath when Bethany began tapping herself on the chest, gasping for air.

"Oh my gawd, are you alright? Can you breathe?" a frantic Stella grabbed her by the hand and tried to sit her up in the bed.

"I'm alright, I'm alright," Bethany waved Stella off as she worked to catch her breath. "I haven't laughed like that for so long!"

VIII

LOST AND FOUND

Jacques Bertrand III stepped off the curb to the street directly in front of the Louisiana Health Administration building in Baton Rouge, Louisiana. Just the day before, he was at his mother's bedside at St. Michael's in Ocean View, Florida. To have come so far, in such a short time, was exhausting. Bethany had sent him on an important errand. He was afraid it was her dying wish so it was his choice to forgo a bedside vigil in an effort to bring her peace of mind and make her last days, if they were her last days, happy ones. Jack was a devoted son. His father died knowing that he would see that his mom was well taken care of in her later years. It was a responsibility he treasured. His mother was a very special person and she set the bar very high in terms of being a wife and mother. He felt blessed, not only to have her as his mom, but also to have found a woman very much like her to fall deeply, head over heels, in love with. Of course, there had been some trying times. What marriage doesn't face problems occasionally? His Lisa Faye enjoyed walking in the very footsteps of his mother by her virtuosity and faith. "She's a Proverbs 31 woman, Jackie. You ought to marry that girl!" Bethany encouraged. It wasn't as if he needed to be pushed because Lisa Faye took his breath away the first time he saw her. She was standing in the show room window at Sears when he first caught sight of her.

Her elegance and porcelain beauty made his heart skip a beat. She was dressing the window, not like a sales clerk, but like a fashion artist, like someone who loved what she was doing. Jack could see right away that she was enjoying her work. When she noticed him staring at her through the window, she blushed. He winked, and she spontaneously blew him a kiss. The way her blush spread down her neck revealed how she had embarrassed herself, and she quickly stepped out of the show room window and back into the store. If Jack had not been on his way to classes at Florida State University, he would have gone inside to meet her. In his imagination, he had caught the kiss this golden haired beauty blew to him and wanted to exchange it for a real one. Day after day, he passed in front of the store on his way to classes, hoping to catch a glimpse of her, while she found herself watching to see if he would go by. One day, they finally met face to face at the drug store down the street. It was noon and every stool at the lunch counter was filled. The only available place to sit was a booth in by the window. He saw Lisa Faye slide across the bench seat and pick up a menu. With a few long-legged strides, he seized the opportunity to approach her and ask if he could share the table. It was obvious by the look on her face, how pleased she was to see him and she agreed to let him sit across from her. Both were shy at first but it didn't take long for the shyness to evaporate and an effortless admiration begin to take its place. The chance meeting at lunch was followed by a dinner date the next night. From there, the pair was practically inseparable. To no one's surprise, the friendship then blossomed into a deep and abiding love. They married shortly after he graduated law school and made their home close to his mother's. He couldn't have asked for anything better. Unfortunately, having children would not become a reality. Although she was heartbroken, Lisa Faye wouldn't let her sadness at being barren interrupt the very busy life she had planned. The way she dealt with being childless was to face the problem head on. She became a teacher. She wanted children in her life, and she would have them. Jack was proud to see his wife go to college and make her dreams a reality. Over the years, she became much more than a teacher to 'her' children. There were times when she was a protector too, as well as a provider, and a counselor. Her gift with children was undeniable and she gave it her all.

Carefully watching traffic, Jack was finally able to cross the street in front of a huge official building where the health records of every person born, died and immunized in Louisiana were housed. He had his cell phone open and dialed his home number. Lisa Faye answered with anticipation in her voice.

"Did you have any luck?" she asked.

"Yes, I did! I'm going to make the call when I get back to the hotel room. I think we found her," Jack sounded excited.

"Your mom will be so happy! I can't wait until you come home, honey. I love you for what you are doing," Lisa Faye told her husband. "Even after thirty years of marriage, you still amaze me. Oh, and by the way, Aunt Stella called and said your mom can move her left side quite a bit now. She was wondering why you haven't been by to visit. I told her that you had to go out of town on business and that your mom told you not to change your plans because of her. I didn't lie, did I?"

"It means a lot to her, babe. It might be the last thing I get to do for her. I don't know how Aunt Stella is going to take this, but it's what mom wants."

"Honey, Aunt Stella wants this as much as your mother does. She just doesn't know it yet. Be safe, sweetheart, come home soon. Love you." Lisa Faye hung up the phone with a glimmer of hope growing in her heart. The elder Mrs. Bertrand was completely loyal to her dearest friend over the years but never forgot about the baby girl she helped Stella relinquish. When Bethany told Jack and Lisa Faye about the baby, she did so with the utmost of respect for her friend, but explained she couldn't rest in peace until she could see Stella and her daughter reunited with her own eyes.

"Please, Jackie, go find her. It's the one thing I want most in the world. Having you was such a joy. I want my best friend to know what it feels like to touch and hold your own child. I have always known that she never got over giving the baby up even though she tried not to show it but I know her, and I know what is in her heart.

It haunts me to this day that I helped her give her child away." Bethany's voice, weak and quavering, spoke these words before she was moved to the assisted living wing of the Village after suffering her stroke. She made Jack and Lisa Faye promise not to tell anyone what she asked him to do. A secret that old deserved some respect.

Two days later, Jack headed home feeling satisfied that he did what his mother asked of him. When he stopped by the Village the night he returned from Louisiana, his news made Bethany's face light up and her eyes shine.

"She wasn't that hard to track down, Mama, because the nuns at the orphanage were a big help. They told me that the adoptive parents were from Louisiana. Thankfully, I called in some old favors and was able to find her."

Bethany kissed his hand and Jack's heart melted at the humbleness of his mother. Yes, he was a very fortunate man to have such a kind woman for a mother.

In a small south Louisiana town, fifty-eight year old Emma LeBlanc wondered how in the world she was going to deal with the fact that a friend of her biological mother wanted to meet her. Not her mother, but a friend of her mother. She always knew she was adopted because her parents were very open and never tried to hide it from her. As with most adopted children, she dreamed of the day when her biological mother or father would come looking for her. Her adoptive mother helped by giving her as much information as she could about the woman who gave her up. All they knew, she told Emma, was that her biological mother was very young and unwed at the time of her birth. The records were sealed but that didn't stop Emma from sending a letter to the convent responsible for arranging her adoption, stating that she would be open to any contact by her biological relatives. The letter was added to her adoption records should that remote possibility ever come to fruition. After many years, she stopped waiting and hoping, and accepted the fact that when her mother decided to give her up for adoption, it was because she never wanted to see her again. The surprise call from a man with information that his mom and her biological mother were best friends sent her into a tailspin. Only the best friend? Had her mother already passed away before she could meet her? The thought made Emma go weak in the knees and sent her emotions tumbling around her like parts of a jigsaw puzzle. If she met with this friend of her mother, would she be able to find the missing pieces of her life?

The first person Emma shared the news with was her husband. Marcel and Emma had always been a close couple for as long as their three children could remember. They weathered many storms in life, as most married couples do, but their relationship was special. They found common ground in that they both were adopted. Because of that, they dedicated themselves to providing for, and preserving, their own family. They married when they were both only twenty years old and were blessed with two sons and one daughter. Over time, their children presented them with six grandchildren who, from the moment they were born, were the absolute joy of their lives.

It took a moment for Marcel to process what his wife told him about the stranger's phone call earlier in the day. He had already found his biological mother and knew the perils of such a reunion. His mother, as it turned out, was a drug addict who didn't even know his father's name. After he found her and made the initial contact, she appeared to be thrilled to see him and vowed to make up for the lost years. Unfortunately for him, she asked to borrow money so many times, he began to understand the reason she said she wanted to be part of his life, and it wasn't because she regretted giving him up for adoption. Finally, when he closed his checkbook and refused to comply with her constant requests, she stopped calling. Emma was at his side for the whole ordeal and knew how crushed his heart was and how his hopes of having a relationship with his mother were shredded. Marcel prayed his wife wasn't headed in the same direction. The fact that it was her mother's friend, not her mother, who wanted to meet her, concerned him more than just a little.

"*Mais non*, Emma, do you think it's a good idea?" he questioned, his Cajun accent softening. He ran his fingers through her black hair sprinkled with bits of grey and pulled her closer, wrapping his arms around her waist.

Emma looked deeply into her husband's eyes and shrugged. Her hands rested on his broad shoulders and their bodies molded to one another.

"I don't know, Marcel. The one thing I do know for sure is if I don't meet this 'friend', I will always have questions. Ever since I was a little girl, I have wondered about my biological mother. Maybe now is the time for me to find out something—anything—about her."

"But, *cher*, what if what you find out isn't what you want? I couldn't stand it if you had to go through the same thing I did." Marcel's voice, thick with emotion, couldn't mask his concern.

"I won't," Emma insisted. "What we went through with your biological mother was the worst. Nothing could be as bad as that. If, for some reason, it is, I'll be prepared to walk away. I still have you, the kids, and the grandbabies. I could never want anything more." She kissed Marcel and loved the familiar feel of his warm, gentle arms around her. His embrace was strong, passionate, and a consistent reminder of how much a part of each other they were.

Emma returned Jack's phone call the next morning as promised, and assured him that yes indeed, she was ready to meet her mother's best friend. A tentative date and time for the meeting was proposed and Jack was very relieved to hear that Emma was available and willing to come in one week. His mother was over eighty years old and wasn't in good health, he told her, so postponing the meeting any longer might mean the elder woman's wish wouldn't have a chance to be fulfilled. Emma, overwhelmed with compassion, told Jack that she would pray that God would sustain and bless them, and strengthen all of them for this meeting.

"That's very kind of you," Jack said.

"Please tell your mother I am looking forward to meeting her," Emma told him before hanging up the phone.

The week passed very quickly for Emma and Marcel. Followed by the blessings of their children, the couple left for Florida before the sun rose on Friday morning. They took their time driving, prolonging their arrival and delaying the uncertain outcome that waited for them at their destination. By the time they checked into the motel where Jack made their reservations, the couple was exhausted but looking forward to the weekend's events. Marcel called the Bertrand's home to let them know they had checked in and the two couples arranged to meet in the hotel lobby at six p.m.

Florida and Louisiana had one thing in common for sure—seafood. The Bertrands took their guests to a locally owned restaurant that boasted of the finest, freshest seafood that could be found. The menu offered a plethora of fine seafood dishes; scallops, shrimp, many varieties of fish, and even alligator. Jack broke the tension both couples tried to hide by describing the details of his mother's life to the curious couple. He spoke of her with tenderness and respect, telling them how his parents met, how they raised him with a stern, but loving hand, how his mother pressed forward to raise him alone after his father passed away. He shook his head and his smiling eyes were moist when he described some of the jaunts his mother and her friends shared with each other. He didn't mention Stella. He couldn't. She still had no idea he'd made contact with the daughter she gave away fifty-eight years earlier. She wasn't aware that Bethany told Jack and Lisa Faye about that time in her young life. During the conversation, Jack was careful not to mention the name of his mother's friend and, not once, did he slip and identify Stella.

Arranging for the visit was simply a matter of gauging the moment when Stella and the others were away from Bethany's bedside. Jack figured that time would be during the breakfast hour. He knew how the group preferred to enjoy the meal together every morning and he didn't see that changing any time soon. He was correct in his theory. Promptly at eight o'clock a.m., Jack ushered Emma and Marcel through the front doors of the Village. They followed him down the central hallway to the assisted living wing. He asked the couple to wait outside Bethany's room so he could go in and prepare her for the visit and privately make sure that Stella wasn't with his mother at that particular moment. Minutes later, he indicated Emma could join him.

She entered Bethany's room slowly and hesitantly, having no idea what to expect and was surprised to see a tiny woman engulfed in a sea of vivid pink flannel sheets dressing a hospital bed. She had two long grey braids on either side of her thin face, and was wearing a lovely shell-pink peignoir set that highly complimented her mocha skin and green eyes. Their eyes locked and, without saying a word, Bethany opened her arms and welcomed Emma into them. Later, Emma remembered thinking how natural and effortless it was to hold and be held by her mother's best friend. By the time they let go, their emotions were unrestrained, making them struggle to find words for each other. Bethany broke through the awkwardness of the moment. Eager to know everything, she asked Emma what kind of life she had been blessed with. The question surprised the younger woman but gave her an opportunity to introduce her husband and proudly tell of their three children and six grandchildren.

"I'm so glad to know that. I always worried about whether you went to a good home or not, even though the nuns said they would be sure of it." Bethany confessed.

"You were there? You knew my mother that long ago?"

"Darling, I knew your mother when we both lived in New York and we were just children. We have known each other practically our whole lives. I used to baby sit your mother, can you believe that?"

Emma shook her head slightly and smiled.

"What kind of woman was she?" Emma asked.

"*Was* she? Girl, your mama is still alive. She's a wonderful person and a lot of fun; a little impulsive sometimes, but she's a good person. That's not the reason you agreed to meet with me, is it? You're wondering why you own mother hasn't called looking for you, aren't you?" Bethany asked.

Fresh tears blurred Emma's vision as she nodded her head.

"The truth is I haven't told her that I asked my son to find you. She has no idea at all. She doesn't realize you are even in this very state, much less standing at my bedside."

"I don't understand any of this, to be honest, Miss Bethany."

"I know. I'm sorry. I'll try to explain. You see, when your mother was only sixteen years old she came to me, pregnant, unwed, and scared to death to tell her parents. Here she was, a Jewish girl pregnant for an eighteen-year-old Protestant boy who skipped out on her. Times were different back then. Her parents would have never forgiven her. I had already married my Jacques and moved away from New York so it seemed best to let your mother come live with us. She never told her parents about you and decided to let you go for adoption. She was so young, sweetheart. She knew she couldn't raise you on her own. We tried to talk her into letting us have you, but she refused and said she wouldn't be able to face you if the truth that she was your mother ever saw the light of day. We understood but it broke our hearts. It cut your mother deeply too. She didn't think we noticed, but we saw how she grieved. She never did have another child. I never forgot you either. I can still see your tiny little hands and those big eyes. All these years, I've been waiting for the time we would meet again."

After relaying all of this information, it was clear that Bethany was beginning to tax herself physically. She was short of breath and found it hard to continue. Emma looked at Jack with alarm. Jack, acknowledging his mother's fatigue, suggested that perhaps the visit should come to a close until later.

"They can come back this evening, Mama. You need to rest, ok? All this excitement has you worn out now." Jack said.

"You're a good son, Jackie. Thank you so much for finding her."

"You don't have to thank me, Mama." he insisted.

Emma leaned over the side rail of the high bed and kissed Bethany on the brow.

"I'm glad we got to meet." She said with gladness in her heart.

"Me, too. I'll see you later, baby girl,"

Emma and Marcel left the room hand in hand, followed by Jack, who lingered just long enough to give his mother a hug and kiss goodbye.

"I can't believe my mother is still alive," she whispered in a shaky voice. "It's so strange to meet someone who actually knows her. A Jewish woman from New York? I never would have guessed. I grew up believing I came out of the swamp like daddy always told me," she nervously giggled. Marcel took her by the hand as they crossed the expansive rotunda toward the wide doors marking the exit of the building. They didn't notice the tall woman with salt and pepper shoulder length hair wearing a flowing caftan who was heading down the same hallway they just left. The woman's dark eyes looked puzzled as she watched Jack head out the door.

"I see Jack is back from his business trip. Who was that with him, clients or something?" Stella asked when she entered Bethany's room.

"No, he wanted me to meet some new friends."

"It was a quick visit, wasn't it?" She felt a strange, unsettled feeling come over her. It wasn't like Jack to come there and not look her up.

"Yes, I think because they could see how tired I am today. Bone tired, Stella. I'm just bone tired."

"Do you want me to stay with you while you take a nap? I was hoping to go shopping with the girls today but I'll stay if you want me to. You know the Memorial Day dance is coming up next weekend and I need something to wear. What do you think? Should I go?"

"Oh, go ahead and go shopping. I'll be all right. I need to rest."

Stella was hesitant about leaving Bethany but, for some reason, she suspected Bethany wanted to be alone.

"Ok, then. We will probably get something to eat as well so it may be late when I get back." Just as she was walking out the door, Bethany called out to her.

"See if you can find something new for me to wear too. I love a good dance!"

Laughing, Stella waved to her from the door. "You're crazy, old girl!"

Later that evening, Emma and Marcel returned for one more visit before the drive back to Louisiana. Bethany carefully explained why she hadn't told Emma's mother about her yet.

"Her name is Estelle. We call her Stella. I need a little time to prepare her before you meet her. This will come as quite a shock. I'd hate for her to stop speaking to me this late in the game!"

"I can wait," Emma promised.

"Come back soon, baby girl," Bethany said as Emma and Marcel left for home.

Regina, Donna, Stella, and Cicely loved to go to the mall. Of course, the one in Tallahassee was much larger than the one in Ocean View but it was plenty big enough for the ladies to shop around. It never failed during a mall trip that Cicely made all of her friends power walk at least one time in front of all the shops. At the end of the brisk walk, all the women, except Cicely, splayed themselves, huffing and puffing, across the benches strategically placed for the benefit and recovery of all mall-walkers. While her friends were trying to catch their breath, Cicely continued to pace back and forth in front of them.

"Ok Cicely, what's on your mind?" Regina panted.

"What? Why would you say that? We always mall walk."

"I know, but you've got more energy than usual so spill it—what's on your mind?"

"Well . . . Ya'll know about that dance coming up next Friday?" Cicely asked. Everyone nodded.

"I was wondering if it would be alright to ask Tom to join us." Cicely felt like she had just dropped a bomb. *Ok, there it is out in the open*, she thought.

"I don't see why not," answered Donna. Regina looked mildly surprised but agreed with her.

"Sure. Why not?"

"I'm just assuming that it would be easier for all of us if we could kind of break the ice with him and maybe become friends." Perhaps, she hadn't dropped a bomb, after all.

"I wouldn't go that far," Stella asserted. "But, I don't see why we can't invite him. Can he dance?"

"Come on, do you really think that's important?" Cicely sputtered.

"Well, of course I do! I want to know if he can dance! Don't you? What good is going to a dance if you can't dance? Hey, did I tell you that Bethany said to get her something to wear too? She wants to go! Can you imagine? It'll be like old times!"

"Not quite, but close enough," smiled Regina.

The Memorial Day dance was only a few days away and the whole Village was abuzz with excitement. Many of the residents invited family and friends, and the affair was becoming quite the event. The standard casual dress rule didn't apply to this dance. It was more like a 'Sunday dress' dance, maybe even a 'put on your very best clothes' dance. The little beauty shop at the Village had to stay open beyond regular hours to accommodate everyone requiring a new hairdo and, oddly enough, the little store was offering corsages and boutonnières in a variety of colors.

Cicely eagerly invited Tom. He was hesitant at first, but warmed up to the idea very quickly. Her enthusiasm was contagious and Tom was glad that her family was going to attend. He would have an opportunity to apologize face to face for the mistake he made by not admitting his true identity. He was glad everything was out in the open now and he no longer had a bitter taste in his mouth because of it.

His daughter, Belinda, and her husband decided to attend the dance as well. Tom and Donna agreed that the social atmosphere would go a long way in reducing the tension caused by the strained father/daughter relationship. Although Belinda spoke to her father a couple of times on the phone and saw him in person once she appeared cautious to invite him any closer, and it was clear that he understood why. He made some colossal mistakes in his life, and the one at the top of the list was leaving his children.

The day before the dance, the phone in Regina's apartment rang. Taylor was on the line.

"Hey Gina! Whatcha up to?" Taylor cheerfully asked.

"Hi darlin', I'm just trying to decide what to wear to the dance tomorrow night."

"Did Uncle Larry tell you I'm planning to be there?"

"No, he didn't. I haven't heard from him but I'm tickled to pieces you're coming. What about your cousins, are they coming too?"

"No, they aren't but I can't wait!"

"Honey, I'm not so sure you would have such a good time. It's just a bunch of retired folks getting together. You would be bored out of your mind, don't you think?"

"Gina, really . . . I'm looking forward to it. I even got a babysitter for Penny! I won't be bored. It'll be fun!"

Friday evening arrived and promptly at seven o'clock, Stella pushed Bethany's wheelchair toward Regina's apartment. On the way, Donna and Cicely joined her. By the time they arrived, the lights in the apartment were dimmed and Taylor was in the kitchen working over an impromptu bar set up. A large, deep, crystal bowl filled with crushed ice sat on one end of the counter top. Half a dozen crystal martini glasses were nested, stems up, in the ice. At the other end of the bar, Taylor was busy organizing an array of ingredients for various concoctions.

"I'm taking martini orders, ladies! We've got chocolate, apple, cranberry, and dirty martinis available! Made to order, girls, step right up!" she said enthusiastically.

"Chocolate martini? I'll have one of those!" Donna's face lit up.

"Oh, that sounds wonderful! Make mine chocolate too!" Cicely chimed in.

Taylor took a chilled stainless steel bar shaker and began to put ingredients together.

"Two ounces vodka, half an ounce of crème de cacao, a little ice. Shake, strain, and there you are!" Taylor said, handing the glass to Donna. She did the same for Cicely.

"Next?" Clearly, Taylor was enjoying herself.

"You can make another apple martini for me, darlin,'" Regina told her granddaughter. In a snap, Taylor had it in a fresh chilled glass.

"Ah yes, the martini glasses we got in Paris on our first trip. Isn't that right, Regina? These are the ones, aren't they? I'll never forget that trip! We all came home well versed in the art of cocktails, didn't we? I, myself, still prefer the usual Dirty Martini. Can you make one for me, dear? Dry please," Stella asked Taylor.

"Sure thing, Stella. Two ounces of gin, a smidge of vermouth, and what—two olives?"

"You know what you're doing!" Stella gratefully took the crystal glass from Taylor.

"What about you, Miss Bethany? What can I fix for you?"

"I'd like a virgin cranberry martini, if you don't mind," Bethany winked at Taylor with a sort of lopsided smile.

Once the cocktails had everyone warmed up, attention drifted toward what everyone was wearing. Cicely showed off her midnight blue dress. It had cap sleeves and a v-neckline from which a tiny bit of lace peeked. It had front and back darts that slimmed the look of Cicely's wide hips, as did the flair of the skirt at the hemline. Everyone could see that Cicely felt as beautiful as she looked.

"Very sexy!" Stella commented. "The 'girls' look pretty good too!"

Cicely's hands flew to her décolletage as if to cover the low cut neckline.

"Am I showing too much?" she asked, alarmed that perhaps too much skin was visible.

"Ha, made you look!" Stella teased. "No, it's not too much, honey. I was just picking at you. You look fabulous!"

"Oh, good. I was worried about these short sleeves and my arms. It's been a long time since I wore something with sleeves as short as this. I finally decided to stop hiding my arms. All that exercising I do . . . I feel like my arms look pretty good, even though I've used them for sixty-eight good years!"

"What about you, Miss Stella, huh? Look at your outfit! Don't you look grand in your pantsuit! I don't know if I could get used to seeing you in pants instead of one of those tent dresses you always wear!" Donna approached her friend and walked around her slowly. "Look at Miss Fancy Pants here! Darling, you look *mahhhvelous*!" Stella's face lit up and she obviously loved the attention her outfit commanded. A pair of wide-leg black velvet pants, a pearl white satin tank top, and a transparent black chiffon over-blouse flattered her long frame. Large, flashy, silver hoops dangled from her thin earlobes and chunky black and silver bracelets with a matching necklace completed the set. The ensemble complimented her black and silver hair perfectly.

"How about yourself, Miss Donna?" volleyed Stella. "Don't you look fine with yourself all done up now? That dress is the color of that silky smooth chocolate martini in your hand. What is that . . . a glazed donut stuck on the back of your head? No! I see. You've actually undone the braid and put your hair up in an elegant do and you call me fancy? I haven't seen you look this festive since Mardi gras in New Orleans in 2001. Do you remember that Ball? Of course, you do. Now *that* was a good time!"

Donna laughed at Stella's good-natured joking and as expected, everyone turned their attention toward Regina to admire her outfit. She chose a dress a little bit out of the ordinary from her usual tailored look; it was a deep burgundy empire-waist cocktail dress. It's soft, flowing fabric subtly gathered below the bust and dropped to mid-calf, giving the dress an elegance she could carry well. Regina was beautiful.

"Here, Taylor. Help me put this stuff on before we go," Regina asked. Taylor took the stunning garnet bracelet and necklace handed to her.

"Gina, these are beautiful! How come I've never seen them before?"

"I could probably count the times I've worn them on one hand. Big Larry gave them to me before he died. He sent them to me from Viet Nam. In the note that came with them, he wrote that he picked them up in Thailand because when he saw them, he knew they were meant for me. He told me about them on our last phone call, but I didn't actually get them until a couple of weeks after he died. They just about didn't make it out of customs. Now you can have them, Taylor. Well, after tonight, of course!" All was quiet for a moment as Taylor and Regina, mute with emotion, embraced each other. To everyone's relief, Stella took it upon herself to shift the atmosphere in the room from slightly morose to cheerful. She set her empty martini glass next to the sink and ushered everyone toward the door.

"Let's get this party rolling! Come on you two. No bawling tonight! Let's go have some fun. Ooh, I hope I can find someone to dance with me! I just *love* a good dance, don't you?" she prattled as she opened the door and led everyone up the hallway.

The Memorial Day event was held in the auditorium of the Village and when the ladies arrived, they were amazed at the transformation from a plain old auditorium to an elegant swinging nightclub. On the stage, a collection of various musical instruments reminiscent of the 1940's era could be seen as well as a few electric guitars sitting tall and upright in their stands. Chairs for the band members were organized in a semi-circle around a baby grand piano, which was positioned at center stage. The lights were low and the tables surrounding the dance floor were set with red, white, and blue linens. Centerpiece arrangements at every table were comprised of a trio of six-inch American flags surrounded by white flowers proudly arrayed in a short cobalt blue vase. Two bars were set up, one on each end of the auditorium. As a crowd steadily filed in, the ladies were able to find a table large enough for the six of them, and laid claim to the two smaller tables flanking either side as well, knowing they would need the space for family members. The whole room was a-buzz with low conversation and laughter as people greeted each other and found places to sit. Finally, just before the orchestra filed in to take their seats, Belinda and her husband, Sam joined her mother at the large table. Donna, happy that Belinda accepted the invitation, complimented her daughter on the white shoulder-less gown she was wearing.

"You too, Sam! You look so handsome!" Donna exclaimed, noticing that Belinda was scanning the room for her father.

The lights dimmed lower as a spotlight appeared from the ceiling and centered on a portly man suitably dressed in a tuxedo. He tapped his baton lightly on the microphone stand to get everyone's attention.

"Ladies and Gentlemen, We are proud to welcome you to the annual Memorial Day Dance at Heritage Memories Retirement Village! Tonight you will be transported back in time to the forties, the fifties, the sixties and so on. We're going to play selections from every decade! If you have a request, feel free to send it to us. If we know it, we'll play it! Have a good time, everyone!" With that, he turned toward the band, rapped his music stand, and enticed lively music to pour from the stage.

"Oh my gosh, isn't that beautiful?" Donna said, and everyone at the table agreed. Sam stood and offered Belinda a hand, leading her to the dance floor, which was already filling up with couples, young and old alike, swaying and stepping to the familiar tunes from the Glen Miller days.

A tall, older gentleman approached the table and surprised Stella with a corsage.

"I know you said you didn't want this to be a date, but I couldn't help getting you flowers. A beauty like you deserves flowers!" Ralph Watkins smiled warmly and presented the wrist corsage of dark velvety red roses and silver ribbon to Stella. She was speechless for once, and when she could, she stuttered her thanks. Ralph helped Stella from her chair, and with one hand around her waist, the other lightly holding her right hand, he gracefully maneuvered the awestruck woman onto the dance floor. They made a handsome couple; he, a regal three inches taller than his statuesque partner, and she, a beautiful woman caught off guard.

Taylor leaned into the table and commented, "I don't think I've ever seen Aunt Stella at a loss for words!"

"Well, I have. And it was right about the time her first husband swept her off her feet!" Bethany joked.

Donna felt a light tap on her shoulder and turned to face a very dapper looking Tom. He was dressed in black trousers, a white coat, and black bow tie. His face was clean-shaven and the cologne he wore was masculine and woody. His gray hair was neatly brushed straight back and if it weren't for the sparse red still in his eyebrows, one would never have guessed the nickname of his youth was 'Rusty'.

"May I join you?"

"Of course, Tom. Here, you can sit between Cicely and me. Wait a minute, that's a little weird, isn't it? You won't be uncomfortable, will you?"

"I'm ok if you are. You look lovely, haven't aged a day," Tom complimented and nodded a greeting to everyone else sitting at the table. He took note that Cicely turned her face away from him and was looking around as though she was hunting for the nearest route of escape. He graciously tried to put her at ease by telling her how charming she looked. She cast her eyes downward and blushed.

"You two should just go have a dance and loosen up! Enough of this awkwardness!" Donna suggested.

Glancing toward Tom for affirmation, Cicely accepted by shrugging her shoulders slightly. He rose from his chair and escorted her to the dance floor.

Regina, Donna, and Bethany remained sitting at the table but they didn't resent doing so. The music was wonderful, well rehearsed and well performed. The bandleader flashed his baton through the air while bobbing to the beat of past generations. It was the perfect time for the trio to give Taylor some insight about years past.

"Who said these were the golden years? *Those* were the golden years!" Regina said, referring to the legends of music from the forties. "I can still recall my parents turning on the radio, rolling the rug back in the living room, and dancing to the music!"

"We didn't have a radio when I was growing up," Bethany added, "but I remember lying in bed at night with the windows open so I could hear the radio at our neighbor's house. Oh, it was so sweet! I used to imagine the curtain was my dress when a breeze came through the window and made it flutter way out. We didn't dance at home, but, whoo boy, after I met my Jacques, we danced our shoes off! I never thought the day would come when I would listen to those old tunes without him. Here I am, eighty years old and wearing a damn diaper so I don't pee on my new dress! I can barely move my left side, and only half of my face smiles, but by golly, I don't feel a bit different in the inside as I did when my Jacques and I wore out the soles of our shoes!"

"Bethany! Did I just hear you swear?" Stella and Ralph returned from the dance floor and filled two empty seats at the table.

"You did indeed, so if anybody asks, you can tell them it's my way of living dangerously. Now, who wants to go get me a Shirley Temple," a feisty Bethany raised an empty glass questioningly.

"I'll get it for you, Mama."

"Jackie! Oh, I'm so glad you and Lisa Faye came! Did you bring your new friends? Are they coming?"

Lisa Faye bent down to give her mother-in-law a kiss on the forehead as Jack left to fill his mother's drink order.

"They'll be here in a few minutes, Mama Beth. They're parking their car."

"Wonderful! I can't wait to introduce them to everyone."

The band was playing the last bit of a slow, smooth melody that hypnotized the dancers to hold each other a little tighter while they still could. Cicely and Tom had been on the dance floor through several songs and were caught up in the romance the alluring music suggested. They were still in each other's arms when the bandleader announced that the next set would feature hits from the 1950's era, and would begin after a short break. As the crowd began to thin, Cicely and Tom reluctantly headed toward their table. He could barely tear himself away from the vulnerable look in Cicely's eyes when, suddenly, he bumped into someone. Looking up, he realized that he had led her directly into the path of his daughter and her husband.

"Hi, pumpkin, it's so good to see you," he said quietly and touched her hand. His heart dropped a little as she withdrew from him.

"I don't think we are at the 'pumpkin' stage yet. Slow, dad. I prefer to take it slow. I've gone years without seeing you and it's not easy to see you now." Belinda spoke candidly, as Sam stepped up to the two and put his arm around both of them.

"At least we've made it through the first step, right?" Sam happily and diplomatically commented while steering his wife toward their table.

As they left the dance floor, Tom guided his dance partner to the empty seat next to Donna but she hesitated, suggesting, instead, that they sit together at one of the adjoining tables. Less tension, Cicely explained, and he agreed.

Donna scooted her chair to the side so they could pass easily. She knew there was plenty of room at the next table, and they needed time to be alone. From the corner of her eye, she noticed Bethany's head was beginning to bob. She reached over and gently patted her hand to awaken her. Her head snapped up and she instantly looked confused. When she saw her son sitting across from her, her face lit up.

"Oh, look at you—so handsome! What a surprise! Come here and let Mama give you a hug!" the sleepyhead exclaimed.

Jack glanced around the table at his mother's friends who looked stunned by Bethany's momentary slip from reality. He hugged her and spoke to her gently, trying not to embarrass her in her confusion.

"It's good to see you too, Mama. Do you remember our friends, the LeBlancs, from Louisiana? They've just arrived. Aren't you glad they said they could join us tonight?"

Bethany's expression changed from joy at seeing her son, to bewilderment, and then dawned with the realization of time and place.

"Oh, of course I remember! I'm so glad you both are here," Bethany said brightly, her sense of awareness recovered.

As a round of introductions was made, Stella noticed Bethany's expression became quite animated and her energy level seemed to heighten. She studied her old friend's face and was puzzled at the unusual reaction. Her thoughts were interrupted when Bethany took her hand and held it tightly. Looking up, she found the LeBlancs standing in front of her.

"Emma, this is Stella."

"Oh! Stella . . . it's so nice to meet you," Emma's face seemed to pale.

"Emma, is it? It's a pleasure to meet you, too. I'm sorry, but I haven't heard Bethany mention you. You're friends of Jack and Lisa Faye?"

"Yes, we are. We recently met Bethany and we think she's adorable. The Bertrands are very proud of her."

"They certainly are," said Stella with a growing suspicion. "And how is it you know Jack and Lisa Faye?"

"We met through an old friend," Marcel answered for his wife.

"From Louisiana?"

"*Mais yeah*, from Louisiana."

"I see," but Stella seemed unconvinced. She didn't know why, but she had an uneasy feeling about these people.

"Emma, are you feeling alright? You do seem a little pale. Why don't you have a seat?" She pulled out the chair next to her and Emma nervously sank into it. *What's going on here*, Stella wondered to herself. She knew it was ridiculous to assume Jack and Lisa Faye didn't have any friends that she wouldn't know about, but normally when Bethany met someone, she mentioned it and, most likely, introduced them right away. These people looked as if they'd known Bethany, Jack and Lisa Faye all of their lives, and there seemed to be an air of intimacy about them that totally unnerved her. To make matters worse, engaging either of these mysterious new friends in conversation seemed to be next to impossible. Any question she asked would be answered in one or two words, and it seemed as though they would glance at Jack before they answered anything. Their attitude wasn't indifferent; it was more distant and cautious. She was uncomfortable that Emma seemed to stare at her, and even more uncomfortable by the questions she asked which didn't pertain to the present but were more about her past. Where was she from? Did she have any siblings? Sure, they were common questions, but she couldn't pinpoint why they left her feeling a bit unsettled. She trusted her instincts and right now, her instincts were telling her there was more to the story than these two were letting on. Visually assessing the couple, she saw they were clean cut, good looking, and appeared to be happily married. Good family? Background? That's what seemed to be lacking. She hadn't heard either of them mention family other than the three children and six grandchildren they had together. Stella didn't know why, but she felt there was a connection there somehow.

The lights in the auditorium dimmed three times signaling the band members back to their positions so the music could resume. The bandleader confirmed the next musical selections would be from the 1950's era. On the other side of Stella, Taylor's eyes lit up and her excitement was hard to miss.

"I love fifties music!" she exclaimed. Her excitement was obvious and Stella seized the opportunity to have the table to herself with the new guests by pointing Ralph into the young lady's direction. Astutely realizing her intention, he asked Taylor to join him on the dance floor.

"I'm not so sure if I can," she laughed. "I've never danced to this kind of music except for slow dancing but if you don't mind teaching me how to jitterbug, I'm you're girl!" She stood and let Ralph lead her away leaving Stella to concentrate on Emma and Marcel.

At the next table, Donna watched as Tom approached Belinda and asked her to join him on the dance floor. The young woman looked at her father as if he had lost his mind until he reminded her that he taught her the steps when she was a little girl by standing her on top of his feet and dancing around the room.

"Do you remember?" Donna heard Tom ask. Belinda nodded her head and rose to join him. When they got to the dance floor, the pair matched the tempo of the music perfectly as they began to jitterbug. Donna thought that when it came to dancing, they picked up where they left off as if no time had passed since father and daughter danced together. In spite of herself, it was clear that Belinda was enjoying the dance, and for that, Donna was grateful.

She watched them for a few minutes and then turned her attention to Taylor and Ralph on the dance floor. Apparently, Ralph was a good teacher and he had Taylor swinging through the moves as though she had been doing it all her life. When she did misstep, Ralph was there to steady her and send her in the right direction. Donna admired Taylor's quick adaptation and talent. The young lady was beautiful; no wonder Regina was so proud of her. Regina! Where was she? She and Regina hadn't made it to the dance floor yet. Heaven knows they danced together many times over the years. They did what they had to when male dance partners were scarce and the music was hopping. Donna spotted Regina across the table, caught her eye, and motioned to the dance floor. In a flash, she was up and they joined the crowd of arms and legs rhythmically punctuating the air. The two women easily blended in while enjoying the sounds of an era during which most of them came of age.

The set of music from the 1950's ended and Ralph returned Taylor to her seat. She wore a happy glow and gushed about how much fun learning to jitterbug was. Ralph stood beside her, nearly breathless, but proud of his quick study.

"Aunt Stella, did you see us? We sort of had a dance-off with Gina and Donna. It was wild!"

"Well Taylor, now you know how all of us kept our tiny waists back in the day! By the way, thanks for bringing my dance partner back!" Stella joked.

Donna and Regina returned to their table just as Larry Jr. was making the rounds as he was expected to in his administrative duties. He stiffly passed out hugs and handshakes in a smart, crisp fashion, and said he hoped everyone was having a good time. Then, just like that, he was gone. Everyone, including Tom, could see the embarrassment and disappointment in Regina's face.

"I don't remember him being so curt to you in the past," he quietly remarked to Regina. She blinked but didn't say anything. Donna, on the pretext of retrieving a napkin from the floor, gave him a gentle wack on the leg. Although startled, Tom got the message loud and clear. It was a shame, really, that Larry Jr. had gotten too important to socialize, or even be kind to his mother.

Taylor saw the exchange but discretely averted her eyes. She could spare her grandmother that much. Her newly close relationship with Regina was becoming more precious to her and she hated to see the way Larry Jr. carelessly hurt her. Taylor made a vow to herself that somehow, in some way, she would make it up to Regina for the way her uncle and his family treated her. She turned her attention to Belinda who had taken the seat next to her with compliments for her beautiful dress.

"Thank you, I'm glad you like it," she touched the shoulder of her dress. "I love this one bare shoulder style, and the color is my favorite. Your eyes are green, too and I bet it would look dynamite on you!"

"Maybe not, Taylor. Remember, I'm old enough to be your mother. I'm not so sure I would be comfortable wearing a dress with a slit up the side like that one! Sam might have something to say about it!" Belinda laughed.

"You knew my mom, didn't you?" Taylor changed the subject.

"Yes, I did. She was six years younger than me. Our parents were best friends and we were, too, when we got a little older. She was a beauty, your mom." Belinda found it easy to talk about Renee'. Even though it had been twenty-one years since her death, Belinda still missed her. Taylor sat on the edge of her seat, acutely attentive to Belinda's voice as she relayed memories of their childhood together. They didn't notice when the music started again, only that the atmosphere surrounding them was filled with people chattering and laughing, and that everyone was having an enormously good time. Taylor's thoughts about Uncle Larry and Belinda's thoughts about her father were as far away from them as the ocean was to the moon. They were lost in the moment; Belinda giving Taylor details of her mother's life and Taylor soaking it up like a sponge.

Across the table, Donna leaned forward to speak to Regina but noticed that her eyes were fixated on something at the next table.

Without saying anything, Donna followed her gaze. Taylor and her Belinda were laughing and eagerly chatting with one another. Immediately, Donna realized that seeing the two together must remind Regina what it might have been like if Taylor's mother would have lived. She looked away, feeling as though she was intruding on a very intimate and personal moment for her friend. Instinctively, she glanced to the side and caught Tom watching her, but couldn't quite interpret the expression on his face. He looked like he had seen a ghost. Just as she started to speak to him, his gaze shifted to Cicely sitting next to him. He spoke into her ear and they rose to make their way back to the dance floor.

Those left at the table had their attention suddenly diverted to Bethany who had once again fallen asleep and, unfortunately, began to snore. Suppressing his amusement, Jack suggested that perhaps it was time to tuck his mom into bed and head home as well. He gently nudged his mother and she awoke with a start.

"Mama, it's time to go now. Lisa Faye and I will take you back to your room. Are you ready? Did you have a good time?"

"Is the dance over?"

"No, Mama Beth, but everyone's getting tired and we want to beat the traffic," Lisa Faye told her.

"What about Emma? Is she leaving now too?"

Jack and Lisa Faye briefly glanced at each other and then looked questioningly at Emma and Marcel.

"We'll be leaving shortly, too, Miss Bethany. We'll come to see you tomorrow before we head back to Louisiana. Will that be alright?" answered Emma.

"Yes, of course, I'd like that. Ok, Jackie, I'm ready. Wheel away. I have to go wherever you push me anyway. Might as well go to bed." With a lighthearted wave of her hand, Bethany bade her friends good night.

"I'll get her ready for bed, Stella. You stay and enjoy yourself," offered Lisa Faye.

Stella, used to her role as Bethany's caregiver, took this news with a twinge of territorial intrusion, but she relented and nodded approval to Lisa Faye. As she watched them wheel Bethany's chair toward the door, she realized she had another chance to converse with the LeBlanc couple. Perhaps she would be able to get to the root of why she felt so strangely about the two of them.

"So how do you like living in Louisiana?" she asked them.

"We love it there. It's the only place we've ever lived, so it is home for us." Emma answered.

"What about your families? Are they originally from Louisiana? Do you get together often?"

"Well, we don't . . ." Emma hesitated before Marcel jumped in to rescue her.

"We haven't been in touch with our parents. It's been a long time since we've seen them." He explained.

"What a shame! Both of you? Why on earth not?" Stella asked rather pointedly.

"Oh, it's a long story. We married young, you know how it goes." Marcel said. "Sweetheart, I think it's time to go, *cher*. We have a long day ahead of us tomorrow." The LeBlancs rose to leave and Stella sensed the uneasy feeling her questions caused.

"I'm sorry, I didn't mean to pry. You are such a lovely couple and I'm glad you joined us here. Will we be seeing more of you?"

"I hope so, Miss Stella," Emma unexpectedly reached for her and hugged her warmly. "Good night everybody. It was such a pleasure meeting you all!" A chorus of goodnight and well wishes from their fellow partiers followed them as they headed for the door. With a puzzled look on her face, Stella watched them leave.

"Are you ok?" Regina asked when she saw the expression on Stella's face.

"I'm not sure. There is something different about them. I can't put my finger on it, but I've got a strange feeling about those two."

"Why do you say that? They seem like pretty normal people to me. If the Bertrands like them, then I'm sure they must be alright."

"But don't you think it's weird that all of a sudden they show up and are these great friends that traveled all the way from Louisiana, not once, but twice, just to visit? I've never heard their names mentioned before. Have you? It seems like Jack would have mentioned them at our business meetings if they were such great friends."

"Are you saying you think they have something to do with the business? Investors, maybe?"

"Geez, I don't know! Maybe they are and that's why I'm getting these weird feelings."

"Oh relax, Stella. If they had anything to do with the business, Jack would have said something. I'm sure Bethany would have said something. If anybody has a secret, it's not safe with Bethany, that's for sure! She doesn't believe in keeping secrets. If you don't want somebody to know something, do not tell Bethany. She just can't help it. Every bone in her body is honest and straightforward."

Stella's imagination was working overtime, but there was one thing she knew for certain. There is a difference between keeping a secret and being loyal. Bethany would walk on burning coals rather than give up Stella's secret. If Regina knew the width and depth of the secrets Bethany kept, she would be amazed. That was more than just keeping a secret. That was loyalty.

From her bed on the assisted living wing, Bethany tried to say her nightly prayers. She was having trouble closing her eyes as the night's events kept replaying in her mind, that is, the parts when she was awake. She decided it was too late to feel like a fool for falling asleep so easily. Such things were now a fact of life she had to deal with. It wasn't the end of the world, but she hoped that she didn't miss something important. Had she said something she shouldn't have? Did Stella realize she was face to face with her own daughter? Would she be mad at her? *'Dear Father in heaven, I hope I did the right thing. And if I didn't, please protect me from the wrath of that woman!'* she prayed.

IX

LOVE AT ANY AGE

Cicely tiptoed toward her apartment door, hoping nobody would see that she was just now getting home from the dance. It was six o'clock in the morning and because it was Saturday, she didn't expect to see very many people milling around. She knew that if she was caught still wearing the party dress she wore the night before, her embarrassment would be practically unbearable. She slowly and carefully slipped past Regina's, Donna's, and Stella's apartments and very nearly made it to her own door when a voice coming from behind made her freeze.

"Cicely? Are you alright?"

"Um, yes. Sure. I'm fine." Cicely turned around.

"Are you just now getting home?" Stella asked. She was standing in her doorway wearing a casual housedress. Ralph was standing just outside the door. He had the same suit on that he wore to the dance, minus the tie, with the jacket slung over his arm. He smiled weakly at Cicely, knowing he had been caught.

"As a matter of fact, I am just getting home. I went to a friend's last night and lost track of time. I don't know how it happened, but here I am."

"Oh I'm so sure! You spent the night with Tom, didn't you?" Stella had a sly smile on her face when she accused Cicely.

114

"Well good night, I mean, good morning. Hope you have a good day, Stella. Nice to see you, Ralph." Cicely chose to ignore Stella's remarks. "By the way, what are you doing here so early in the morning?" Knowing the answer, she waited to see what kind of story they would fabricate.

"I'm just bringing Stella the morning paper," Ralph hesitated.

"Yes, that's right! He's just bringing me the morning paper!" Stella's cynical smile spread wider across her face and she winked. A thoroughly embarrassed Ralph planted a kiss on her cheek, nodded in Cicely's direction and hustled up the hallway as quickly as he could.

"Careful there, Ralph!" Stella called after him. "Wouldn't want you to trip and break a hip!" Ralph's arm waved through the air to indicate he heard her, but he wasn't going to turn around to face Cicely again. He was embarrassed enough for one day.

"You stinker!" Cicely laughed.

"Me? You're the one sneaking around!"

The two women tried to suppress their giggles as they hugged briefly in the hallway before each retreated to her respective apartment.

As Cicely slipped through her door, she breathed a sigh of relief. She peeled her clothes off as she headed for the shower. Afterwards, while she was drying her hair, Tom consumed her thoughts. She hadn't been attracted to another man since Jim died although she had plenty of opportunity. Back then, if she did accept a date, she usually broke it before the suitor came to pick her up; she felt like she was cheating on Jim somehow. Tom was different. He wasn't anything like she thought Donna's ex-husband would be. He didn't seem like the kind of man who would abandon his family. She wasn't about to ask him why he did that, either. Cicely found herself very attracted to Tom, and last night was wonderful. She was surprised that he had been a perfect gentleman. It didn't matter what Stella thought they did. She and Tom talked until the dawn surprised both of them. They spent the night opening their souls to each other and talked about parts of their lives they had never spoken of with anybody before. They shared the most intimate thoughts hidden

115

inside, and they laughed at the silliest things, not just giggles, but deep belly laughs. She didn't know if it was because of the lack of sleep, the bottle of red wine he opened, or just the sheer pleasure of being that comfortable with another person, but whatever it was, she loved the feeling she had this morning.

She had butterflies in her stomach, and suddenly the room felt a little too warm. *'Good heavens! What am I doing? I'm sixty-eight years old. Tom is ten years older than me and I'm acting like a teenager!'* She found the thought amusing and was startled to realize that, perhaps, she was falling in love with Tom. She laughed to herself. She admired his tenderness and thoughtfulness, and he had many other qualities she found appealing. It had been a very long time since she had thought about making love; so long that once Stella told her to be sure to call the Fire Department if she thought she was going to have sex because it would be like rubbing two dry sticks together and they could start a fire. Cicely made a mental note to tell Stella she was pretty sure that she wouldn't need the Fire Department! She and Tom were taking their time and when the right time came, they would know.

Once she got the last touches of her makeup on, Cicely went to the dining room for breakfast. Chances were good that her friends would already be there so she mustarded the strength to keep a straight face. If Tom happened to show up, she hoped the sound of her pounding heart wouldn't give her away.

She need not have worried; Tom was still in his apartment. After Cicely left, he pulled out the bag he kept his medicine in and lined a handful of pills up in a row. He began swallowing them, one by one, with his coffee. When he got the last one down, he went to bed. This morning was one time he would break his routine. There would be no exercise in the gym today, or a breakfast drink either. He was exhausted but, oh, he was happy, too. Tom smiled when he thought of his sweet Cicely. Since he left Donna, finding someone to replace her had never been a priority. The fact was he hadn't been interested in ever being part of another relationship again. He didn't think he had the character to invest, and he never wanted to short-change another person again. Donna was . . . Well, at one time, she was his heart. He left her because he could no longer live up to the vows he made when he married her. Knowing that he'd hurt her tore a ragged gash in his heart too, but he did what he felt was the right thing. At the time, Tom thought living a lie was worse than pretending that he was a better person than he actually was so he walked away from his family, his friends, and his life. Then, out of the blue, Cicely came into his life. So many years had passed since he found someone whose company he actually enjoyed. He did enjoy her company! He nicknamed her 'Sugar' because she was so sweet. She was a breath of fresh air; happy and sincere. Such a tender heart, as well. His only hope was that he wouldn't break her heart, but considering his past, that was more of a probability than a possibility. He had some serious thinking to do.

X

Mind Your Business

The brass bell in Stella's hand didn't look like it would make as much noise as it did. Did it ever make a noise! It was loud enough to stop a train, which was why Stella bought it—not to stop a train, but to tame the loud din only a room full of women could produce in the boardroom of Jack Bertrand's law offices.

"Can I have your attention? ATTENTION PLEASE! Ok, ladies, it's time to get down to business." She vigorously clanged the bell.

"Stella! You don't have to go that far! You do that every time we have a business meeting. We aren't a bunch of children that you have to be so rude to, HONESTLY!" Bethany indignantly barked.

"I'm sorry, Madame, can I please have your attention if it's not too much trouble?" Stella reduced the tone of her voice to a low, sickeningly sweet tone. She squinted her eyes as she looked around the table at everyone gathered there. Still chattering, nobody even looked in her direction, and she glared back at Bethany. "See, that doesn't work. Nobody wants to stop talking." She picked up the bell and began to swing it back and forth again, finally bringing the room to silence and all eyes on her.

"Now, whose turn is it to chair this meeting?" she asked once she had everyone's attention.

"Stella, you do it." Regina said.

"No, let someone else do it this time," Bethany interjected.

A barrage of voices spattered back and forth. When Jack stood up and faced the group Stella picked up her bell and threatened to resume clanging it. The occupants of the room quickly hushed.

"Ladies, once again, as attorney for the group, I will assume the responsibility of chairing this meeting. Will you please come to order?" He had their undivided attention.

"Great. Can we have a summery of the last board meeting minutes?" His secretary, who was sitting at a small desk to the side of the board table, presented the minutes of the last meeting.

"Does anybody have anything to offer? No? Ok, we do have a bit of business to talk about today."

On the agenda to be discussed was the good news that their rent properties now totaled one hundred and twenty five and another eight were in the process of being renovated. Jack pushed the button on the intercom to the secretary's desk in the other room.

"Belinda, you can come in now," he instructed. Donna's daughter was the realtor for the business. Her presentation was simple enough; they had made quite a bit of money in the rent business. One hundred and twenty five rent houses were too much for the two-man maintenance crew they employed. A vote was called for and approved to hire two additional maintenance people to add to the crew.

Belinda presented a special case to the group concerning a young woman who had just been released from prison. She was incarcerated for shoplifting and spent the last six months in jail. It took that long for her case to be heard by a judge who, when she pled guilty, had mercy on her and sentenced her to six months in jail, with time served. She was released right away but had no place to live. At the present time, she was staying at a shelter. Her children were in foster care until she could prove her worth by getting a job and a decent place to live.

"She wants to turn her life around. I believe her," Belinda told the group. "I met her when she came to our real estate office to apply for a secretarial job. She seems sincere. I think she would be a good candidate for our special needs fund."

"But she's a shoplifter?" Regina asked.

"Yes, she did shoplift. She took food and diapers. She has been homeless and staying at shelters for quite a while. She was laid off her job about a year ago. With the economy as it is, she couldn't find work. No husband. When she came to the end of her money, her landlord evicted her and her two kids. I'd really like to give her a chance."

Following a brief discussion, the group unanimously agreed to offer the young woman a place to stay, complete with utilities, rent free until she found a job. Thereafter, her rent would be prorated according to her income and utilities would become her responsibility. They also agreed to give her a head start with five hundred dollars. Belinda was happy with the decision and said she believed that the woman wouldn't take advantage of their charity because she was desperate to have her children returned to her.

The rest of the meeting was comprised of business that required little attention from the partners, and a motion was made to end the meeting.

"Actually we do have one more order of business to discuss. Your partner, Bethany Bertrand, has something she would like to say. Mama?" Jack stepped to the side and all eyes focused on Bethany whose wheelchair was sitting to the left of Jack.

"As you all know sometimes I'm just not myself," she began. Several in the group tried to protest but Bethany waved them off and continued.

"Come on, you all know it and I know it. Now I am sorry to say it but that's the truth. I never realized that a person could get confused and know they are confused. It's the darnedest thing. I shift back and forth between reality and old memories at the drop of a hat. I never used to be like that. When my Jacques was alive, I never did that. Jacques was so good, always taking care of me. He was the sweetest person I ever met. Successful, too. Everyone said he was a fine doctor. Why, he would even take payments over time, or actually forgo his fee if one of his patients was real poor or had nothing to trade. That's how a person should be. It's what God wants, you know. God will always take care of you if you trust him. Just say 'Jesus, I trust in You'."

"Ahem," Jack cleared his throat. "Mama, can we get back to what you wanted to say?" he gently asked his mother.

"See? There I go again! Anyway, it proves my point. I need to resign from the board."

No one said a word. All anyone could do was helplessly stare at Bethany as she spoke in her soft pink housecoat and furry pink slippers. Her appearance was quite the opposite of her usual boardroom attire. In the past, Bethany wouldn't have dreamed of leaving her apartment in a housecoat. She prided herself in dressing with the kind of chic business attire she thought appropriate for a partner in an up and coming business. Everyone knew this day was coming; the day that one of them felt she could no longer manage being a part of the business. It was a dose of reality that came all too quickly. Jack stood to address the group.

"It is my mother's desire to ask this partnership to appoint someone to replace her."

The announcement set the room a-buzz again. Nobody wanted to replace Bethany. Nobody could replace Bethany. The other four partners looked at each other questioningly. Could she be serious?

"I insist," Bethany stated. "Since I am a full partner, I insist someone take my place."

"I suppose we could ask Lisa Faye to join since her husband is our attorney," offered Donna.

"I can tell you that Lisa Faye isn't at all interested in the job," Jack said. "Any other suggestions?"

"As far as my family goes, we already employ four of my kids in the business. I think they have their hands full, too. What about Tom?" Cicely pointed out.

"TOM? Look, I'm all for second chances, but I think making Tom a partner is taking things a little too far!" Stella's eyes were huge and the furrow between her brows deepened.

"I agree with Stella," Regina said. "I don't think it's Tom's place to get into our business. My own son doesn't even know about it. Asking Larry Jr. is out of the question anyway. He has his hands full with his practice and owning the Village. If we are looking at family members, what about Taylor?" Regina asked. "I think Taylor should be considered."

"Taylor is not old enough, Regina. She has school and a baby to take care of. As a business, we have funded several scholarships for Taylor so we may be talking conflict of interest or ethical breech if we appoint her. No offense, but I think we need someone else." Jack pointed out. "So my wife, Tom, and Taylor are ruled out. Anybody else?"

"I have a suggestion," Bethany injected. "I want Emma LeBlanc."

"Emma LeBlanc? Why on earth would you want to make her a board member? We don't even know her. She's not part of us. Emma LeBlanc?" The words exploded from an exasperated Stella.

"She's smart, that's why," Bethany challenged Stella. "I like her."

"But Bethany, dear, we don't really know Emma. How can we bring someone into the business we don't know?" Donna asked.

"I know her." Bethany firmly insisted.

"But we don't know if she has any business sense, or even if she would be interested." Regina said while Stella fumed with her arms crossed in front of her.

"She knows about business. She raised three children and is a grandmother to six. She's the center of a large happy family." Bethany's eyes flashed. "That's a big job, the hardest one in the world. If you want to measure success, take a look at the job she's done with her family. I'm sure she knows all about running a business."

"Beth, what on earth are you thinking? We can't replace you, especially with someone we have barely met!" Stella tried to reason with her stubborn friend.

Jack, aware of the extent of the furor his mother's opinion invoked, brought the meeting to order by assuring everyone that the decision needn't be made immediately and perhaps now would be the time to bring the meeting to a close so they could give the subject some thought before the next meeting. A motion was made, carried, and the meeting was over. Stella wasted no time storming out of the room leaving the other four partners behind. Jack took control of his mother's wheelchair and headed toward his car. It didn't take very long to load her up and put the chair in his trunk. In just a few moments, he was on his way to return Bethany to her room at the Village. Regina and Donna followed Cicely to her car where an anxious Stella was pacing back and forth. All of them were stunned by the last revelation of their board meeting. None of them quite knew what to make of it, although Stella was adamant that she was definitely not interested in bringing Emma LeBlanc into the business.

"My gawd, she lives in Louisiana! How can she do business from Louisiana? I mean it's not like she would want to live here where there is nothing but newly-weds and nearly-deads!"

"It can be done, Stella. It's not that far away, besides, there are faxes and computers," Cicely told her.

"Does anybody else feel uncomfortable with this but me?" Stella questioned.

"I think we all feel uncomfortable with the whole situation, but we really do have to consider what Bethany wants. She is still one of us and her word counts as much as ours does," Regina tried to explain. "But the thing is—I think we need to remember that so far we've managed to keep our business under the radar with the exception of our employees who are family members. There aren't many people who are aware of what we do. I hope we can keep it that way."

"Apparently Bethany doesn't feel that way about it," Stella claimed.

"Why are you so upset about this? Is it because Bethany isn't able to take as much of a part in the business as she used to? Or is it because you might be a little jealous of her relationship with someone you don't know?" Regina asked.

Stella, looking like she had just been slapped, whirled around to face her friend.

"Jealous? Why would I be jealous? I've never tried to keep her from having friends, and she's never said anything to me about my other friends. I know something is out of the ordinary about this Emma LeBlanc. I mean it! I know something is not right. Mark my words, you'll see!"

Nobody had the nerve to say anything else to Stella as she loaded herself into the front passenger side of the car and slammed the door. The ride back to the Village was quiet and seemed to take forever. Once they pulled into Cicely's parking space, Stella spoke out once again.

"I'm sorry. Maybe I am jealous, but I honestly don't think that could be what is bothering me. Maybe we should do a little background work on whomever we get to replace Bethany, *if* we are going to replace her. Maybe we can start by interviewing other potential board members. Surely, we can come up with someone else we could consider!"

"That makes sense. I think it's a good idea, don't you? We can call another board meeting to talk about it." Donna suggested.

"Just keep in mind that our endeavor is private. We made a lot of money, plenty enough to share. It is important to all of us that we help other people with the assets we have. It won't be private if we let the word out that we have this business and are on the hunt for a new board member," added Regina.

It took Tom several extra moments to answer the knock on his door and Cicely was surprised when he opened it looking haggard and pale.

"Tom, you look awful! How are you feeling?"

"Like death eatin' a cracker," he answered before standing aside to let his sweetheart enter.

"What?"

"Nothing. Never mind. It was a bad joke. Sorry." He led her to the kitchen where he put a pot of coffee on to brew. "I'm just a little under the weather today. But hey, it's so nice to see you, I feel better already!" Tom gave Cicely a little hug and pecked her on the cheek. She returned the kiss with concern in her eyes.

"Are you sure you're alright? Do you want me to take you to the doctor?"

"What, and miss grilling the best rib-eye you ever ate? Not a chance! I've been marinating a couple of steaks all day. When I tell you I can grill the best rib eye, I'm not kidding. Why, I've had people call me from all over the country asking for my marinade recipe," Tom teased. He went to the refrigerator and pulled out the gallon size plastic food storage bag he used to marinate the two choice steaks.

"Oh, Tom! You didn't have to do that, but I do love grilled steak! What can I make to go with it?" Cicely was happy with the notion of dining in with Tom.

"Not a thing, Sugar. I've taken care of everything. Don't laugh; I'm used to cooking for myself. We're going to have a nice salad and some red potatoes that I cooked in a little olive oil with onions and garlic. It's good; I think you'll like it." He led her through the sliding glass doors opening up to the small patio. He lit the gas grill and invited her to have a seat while he fixed them each a glass of wine. She sat gratefully, still slightly undone from the board meeting earlier in the day. She ached to talk to Tom about it but knew better than open that can of worms. Her friends probably wouldn't take it well if she told him about their business. After all, not even Regina's son knew about it and she could certainly understand that, given the fact that Larry Jr. had grown into such a snotty man. Even Bethany said so and she seldom had a derogatory remark to say about another person.

Tom returned to the patio with their wine and a platter with the marinating steaks on it. It only took a minute for him to slap the rib eyes on the barbeque and grill them to perfection. Cicely was impressed. They had a great evening telling stories to each other and laughing about adventures they each had throughout the years. Tom was tickled when Cicely told him about her first trip to Jamaica. He said the thought of her and her four friends smoking pot on the beach was hysterical. It was hard to imagine, he said, that his ex-wife would do anything like that.

"Well, she did! If it hadn't been for Stella, none of us would have even thought about doing that. You know, Bethany did say she was kind of a hippie when she was younger. Don't you know our kids would just die if they knew about that?"

"So Stella was the one who instigated the pot smoking?" Tom asked.

"Yes, of course, Stella's the one who instigates everything!"

"Does she do it only in Jamaica, or does she smoke pot here too?

"Actually, I know that she has smoked in places other than Jamaica, but I don't think she's done it here. She's kind of out grown smoking pot, if you know what I mean. None of us are spring chickens anymore," Cicely stated. "Why?"

"Oh, no reason. I was just wondering." Tom smiled at Cicely and she warmly returned his smile.

"Hey, how about a little dessert over at my place?"

"Let's go," Tom answered.

XI

RISKY BUSINESS

Donna had the phone to her ear and her mouth dropped open in surprise.

"You want me to do *what*? You must be out of your mind! Tom, I can't do that for you. It was ok in Jamaica, but not here. And how could I ask Stella to get it without telling her why?"

The man on the other end of the line held the phone in his hand with a grip so tight, his knuckles looked white and pearly like the inside of a clam shell.

"I'm sorry, Donna. I shouldn't have asked. I know it would be taking a chance. I was just hoping." His voice sounded broken with resignation.

"Ok, Tom," she relented. "I can't promise anything, but I'll see what I can do."

Later that afternoon, when Donna put the question to Stella, nearly everyone in the dining room heard her response:

"You want what? Are you crazy?"

"Shhhh! Do you want everybody to hear you? I just asked that's all!" Donna pulled Stella's elbow, drawing her friend closer to her so she could whisper without anyone overhearing her words. "I know you still have contacts, Stella. I'm only asking for a little bit, anyway. It's not as if I want to sell the stuff. Good grief—get real!"

Stella whispered harshly back, "You want me to get real? You get real! It would be my ass on the line if I was caught with it, not yours! For gawd's sake, I'm seventy-five years old! Oh yeah, I can see the headlines now: Senior Citizen Gets Busted In Drug Take Down At Old Folk's Home! No, Donna, I don't think so. That's not going to be my fifteen minutes of fame!"

"You don't have to get sarcastic about it, Stella! I'm just saying that because you're seventy-five and you live in a retirement village, who would suspect you had a little pot? I thought it would be easy for you, that's all. Don't worry about it, if you can't do it, you can't do it. I guess everybody has to grow up sometime."

"Oh, I can do it, alright. It's just been a long time. I won't have any trouble getting my hands on some. Let me ask you this: Why? What on earth do you want with marijuana? You don't even smoke cigarettes and I practically had to force you to smoke pot on our trips to Jamaica. What's going on here?" Stella's eyes narrowed and she slapped her hands flat down on the tabletop.

Donna looked around to see if anyone was listening.

"It's not for me," she whispered. "It's for somebody I know."

"Who?"

"I can't tell you."

"You mean you *won't* tell me."

"Yes, that's right. I won't tell you."

"Is it somebody who lives here?"

"Yes. And this person needs it for medicinal reasons."

"Oh. That changes everything. I have always thought they should make pot legal in Florida by prescription. Sure, I can get it and don't even worry about the cost. If your friend needs it to feel better, it will be my pleasure to provide it! Do I know this person?"

Donna made a face and pretended she was smacking herself on the forehead.

"Ok, ok! I was just asking. I'll let you know something later."

The next day, just before lunch, Cicely dialed Tom's phone number from her apartment. No answer. Half an hour later, she dialed again. He still didn't answer. Now feeling a bit worried, she decided that perhaps she needed to go check on Tom. It wasn't like him not to answer the phone and he did look a little peaked yesterday. What if he was sick and couldn't get to the phone? She left her apartment and headed for his. Just before getting there, she stopped dead in her tracks, hoping her eyes were playing tricks on her. Surely, that wasn't Donna coming out of Tom's apartment. She was wearing a large floppy straw hat and kept her eyes focused on the floor as she quietly slipped into the hallway. Cicely made a hasty retreat around the corner praying that Donna didn't see her. '*What's going on here,*' she wondered. Why would Donna be sneaking out of his place? For that matter, why didn't he answer the phone when she called just moments ago? She managed to keep herself out of Donna's line of vision but the sight of her friend scurrying down the hallway multiplied the questions flooding her mind. Once Donna was far enough away, Cicely tiptoed to Tom's apartment. She knocked on his door. It opened a small crack and she saw Tom peeking out.

"Oh, it's you," he said, opening the door wider beckoning her to come in. She saw that Tom was wearing nothing more than a pair of cotton pajama bottoms.

"That's ok; I can see you're not ready for visitors. I'll check with you later," she told him. Tom looked down at himself and realizing how disheveled he appeared, he nodded his head.

"I guess you're right, Sugar. I—I've been taking a nap. I'll give you a call later, ok?"

"That'll be fine, but only if you feel like it. You don't look like you're in the mood for company anyhow. Did someone come to check on you?" she asked. Tom's face began to redden.

"Who, me? No, nobody's supposed to be here. I've been taking a nap." He swallowed, knowing there was no truth to his words, and they left a bitter taste in his mouth.

Her heart sank. The man she trusted with it had just lied to her.

"Look, I've got a lot of things to do today; that's what I was coming to tell you. So don't call me, I'll call you." She snatched at Tom's doorknob and slammed it shut. Tears began filling her eyes as she fled down the hallway. She heard his door open behind her, heard him step out, and heard him call her name. She didn't answer. She had no idea what was going on, and there were a lot of unanswered questions she wasn't sure she had the stomach to hear. Certainly, she could understand that Donna and Tom could have a friendship, but there was no need to hide it. So why would they bother sneaking around and lying?

On the way back to her apartment, she ran into Stella. Seeing that her friend was obviously upset, Stella caught her by the arm.

"Where's the fire, honey? Oh shit, you're upset! What happened?"

"I don't know what's wrong. I can't believe what my eyes are telling me. Oh Stella, something is going on and I don't know what it is. It doesn't make sense to me. I think Tom is lying to me. I just saw Donna coming out of his room. She was sneaking around like she didn't want to be caught there." Cicely's voice was quavering.

"Wait a minute, slow down, and tell me what happened. You're not making much sense. Donna sneaking out of her ex's room? Really?"

"Ok, just listen to me for a minute, Stella." Cicely was wringing her hands. "It's true. I was worried about Tom because he wasn't answering his phone so I went to check on him. That's when I saw Donna sneaking out of his room. I waited until she was gone and then I knocked on his door and he answered it wearing only his pajama pants. Then, he lied to me by saying he had been alone taking a nap. He lied to me!"

"Don't worry. We will sort it out. Cicely, I know that Donna wouldn't do anything to hurt you and you know that too. There has to be a reasonable explanation for everything. I'll find out what is going on and let you know later." Suddenly, Stella knew what Donna was doing at Tom's apartment and it had nothing to do with Cicely's suspicions.

The dining room was fairly empty with the exception of a few residents who opted for companionship rather than having a solo lunch in their own apartment. Stella popped her head in the door and spotted Donna and Regina at their usual table. Both of her friends looked up just in time to catch her about to leave so she mouthed the words 'I'll be right back' to them. They nodded, indicating they understood, and went back to enjoying their lunch and each other's company. Neither had a clue that Stella had something up her sleeve, which suited her just fine. She left and followed the hall to the west wing and Tom's apartment. She had to knock three times before she heard his voice on the other side of the door.

"Who is it?"

"It's Stella. I need to talk to you."

"Can it wait? I'm kind of busy," he hesitated.

"No. Open the door, Tom. Now. I have to talk to you."

When he opened the door, Stella instantly recognized the faint odor wafting into the hallway from his apartment.

"I know what you're doing. Let me in." Tom's blood shot eyes widened and he opened the door enough for Stella to pass through. Once in his apartment Stella whirled around to face him. He stood there in his pajama pants looking pale and helpless.

"So you're the one Donna is trying to help out with the pot," she started.

"What are you talking about?"

"Look Tom, you don't have to lie to me. I wasn't crazy about the way you dropped into the picture, but I figured you had as much right to live here as anybody. I sure as hell didn't appreciate the fact that you tried to hide your identity at first but I can understand that you wanted to tell Donna yourself instead of letting her find out through someone else. Now, Cicely is falling for you hard and you're sneaking around behind her back. She knows Donna was here this morning. She doesn't know about the pot, so she thinks you've been lying to her. And I do have a big problem with that."

"Donna and I—we're not—you know, she was only doing me a favor. How could Cicely think that? I would never do that to her. Stella, I love her."

"The only thing I can tell you, Tom, is you better get your stories straight with the woman you love or you might just get your pecker knocked to your watch pocket! Believe me when I tell you that! I love her too. I don't like to see my friends hurt or misled and you've done both. You're on shaky ground with me, Sir."

"Stella, I'm sorry. Everything is such a mess. I thought moving here would be the right thing to do, but I've messed everything up. I'll get with Cicely and tell her why Donna was here and I'll make it right, I promise."

"So why did you ask Donna to get the pot for you?"

"I don't want to go into that right now, Stella. It's personal and I'm not ready to talk about it."

Stella looked at Tom long and hard while processing what he said. Finally, she nodded her head.

"You're entitled to your privacy. Let me know if I can help."

With a grateful look, he extended his hand to her. She took it and they shook over the secret they shared. She felt a new and unfamiliar compassion for Tom and he, in turn, viewed her with new respect.

Donna sat on a worn, red vinyl-clad dinette chair and watched as Stella leaned over the laminated red and chrome table to refill her cup of coffee. She was very comfortable in Stella's apartment and, although it wasn't exactly her taste, she admired the retro style that Stella loved. Their apartments were basically identical in layout but the décor was entirely individualized. Regina filled hers with family heirlooms and treasured pieces. Her passion for flowers and gardening was obvious by the way she utilized her patio space. Cicely's style included big plush furniture, sturdy enough for grandchildren to crawl all over and play under. She surrounded herself with rich bold colors—a red sectional sofa, zebra rug, rich sapphire blue bedding. Donna preferred the traditional early American style with maple wood and earth tone hues with the occasional splash of burnt orange or avocado green. And Stella—Stella's taste clearly leaned toward the 1940's. She collected vintage furniture, fabric, lamps, and anything that reminded her of that period. The style was bohemian and it suited her.

Donna accepted the cream and sugar passed her way and then acknowledged to Stella that yes, indeed, Tom was the mystery person.

"But I can't go into it with you because that would be breaching a confidence," Donna confessed. She hated not being able to share what she knew about Tom, but he swore her to secrecy, and although it was reasonable to expect she didn't owe him a thing, she could at least give him that.

Stella understandingly nodded her head. She stood up and motioned Donna to follow her to the patio where they could resume their conversation while sitting in the warm sun and fresh air.

"I don't know, Donna, I'm not crazy about a man who tries to deceive, but I can see that, in his case, there are circumstances that call for compassion, not blame. I suppose there is a reason behind what he thought to accomplish by showing up here, and I guess that maybe the thing with Cicely was an unexpected complication. At any rate, I'm willing to try to be a little more understanding. Gawd, you're his ex-wife so if you can do it, I can. By the way, did I tell you I've ordered a hot tub?" Stella grinned, happy to have taken her friend by surprise with her news.

"What? Are you serious? Where are you going to put a hot tub? Are they even going to let you have a hot tub here?"

"Right here, smarty, on my patio. It will be great, you'll see. It seats eight people! I don't garden, so there is nothing to have to take up and move out of the way. I will still have enough room to sit in the sun if I want to. I can keep the water tepid in the summer and warm in the winter, even though it doesn't get very cold here. It will be so lovely. I've got plenty of room and, for your information," Stella's eyebrows arched higher and her lipstick-ed smile spread across her face, "I've already run it by Larry Jr. He said he didn't have a problem with it. Of course, I'm not sure he even heard what I asked him, but I'm going to do it anyway. Ha! Can you imagine? All of us can sit in the hot tub and not have to worry about who has been in it, how sanitary it is, or if there are any unknown foreign objects floating in the water. Come on, you know you'll love it!"

"It does sound wonderful, Stella, especially the part about not having to worry about what's in the water! Ok, now I'm excited! So, when are you getting this hot tub?"

"Tomorrow morning. By this time tomorrow evening, we can all have our old butts in the bubbling caldron getting more wrinkle-y by the minute!"

"I was looking forward to it until you gave me that visual, my friend," Donna chuckled.

"Yeah, well don't mention it. I want it to be a surprise for Bethany. Won't it be fun? You gotta get your kicks where you can, I always say"

Early the next morning, a crew arrived to do the honors of installing the massive hot tub. Luckily, they were able to get it into position without too much of a problem by removing the back section of the privacy fence. Donna was there to watch it being installed. To find a safe place to observe from she had to navigated her way through the jumble of patio furniture they shoved aside to make room for the tub. Stella's enthusiasm for her new toy was contagious and so was the happiness in her voice.

"I can't wait to show it to Bethany! She is going to love this! The poor thing, she gets so uncomfortable sometimes from her arthritis." Stella's eyes were bright as she spoke and her excitement was contagious.

"We all dread those visits from our dear friend Arthur Itis," Donna reminded her.

"Yeah, I guess so. Personally, I never thought it would afflict me, but it has. It still amazes me that I made it past seventy-five."

"Do you have any regrets about your life? Sometimes I wonder if I would have done anything differently. I have had a good life, Stella. More good than bad."

"Regrets? Maybe. If I had a do-over, there are some things I would do differently. Like after my Herman died. That was awful. Within two years, I had two different husbands and two divorces. I kept trying to replace him. Once I discovered that nobody could take his place, I stopped trying. I don't really regret that. Nope, the only real regret I have was for something that happened long before I married Herman. And I will always have that regret for as long as I live." She turned her face away as she wiped a tear that was sliding down her once smooth-as-marble cheek. Donna respectfully pretended not to notice.

"Let's go eat while we are waiting for the water to warm up!" Quick as a wink, she headed for the door and Donna followed closely behind.

Bethany loved a good surprise. When Stella suggested that she come to her apartment for a visit, Bethany could tell a big one was coming. By the time her wheelchair crossed the threshold of Stella's apartment, the octogenarian was giddy with excitement and could barely sit still. Then, when she saw the hot tub sitting out on the patio under a night sky filled with stars, Bethany could hardly contain herself.

"I love it!" she squealed, but then she looked concerned. "How am I going to get in it?"

"Don't worry, Beth, I've taken care of that. Ralph is coming over to help us. I'm thinking between us, we can handle you. What do you think? Are you up for it?" The look on Bethany's face was all the answer Stella needed. "First you have to go pee. Can't be having an accident in my hot tub! I have your swimsuit here, too. Shoo, let's go get you ready." A few minutes later, Ralph, and Tom arrived and, in no time at all, the three of them were able to slide Bethany from her wheelchair to the side of the over-sized ocean blue hot tub where she could then be shifted into the swirling, bubbling water. She was so tiny it took very little effort. Stella got into the tub as well and handed her two long, narrow floating foam tubes.

"What are these?" Bethany asked, obviously delighted with the bright pink and yellow.

"Noodles, my dear," Stella informed her. "We're going to have noodles of fun. Here, I'll show you how."

By the next morning, all of the staff and most of the residents knew about Stella's hot tub. The administrative office was swamped with requests from at least a dozen residents who wanted the same on their patios, prompting Larry Jr. to pay a visit to Stella.

"You said I could have it."

"I didn't know a 'tub with jets' meant a hot tub on the patio! Miss Stella, please! I thought you were talking about replacing the tub in your bathroom." Larry Jr.'s face was red with exasperation.

"That's what you get for only half listening to me. I told you I wanted a hot tub with jets on my patio. We talked about it, you and I, so don't tell me I did something wrong. Why can't we have one as long as we pay for it?"

"Insurance, for one thing! Do you realize how this could affect our insurance premiums? It would be astronomical. In addition, safety. Don't get me started on that. Can you imagine what would happen if a resident slips and falls in a hot tub? Really, Miss Stella, I have to insist that you have the company come back and pick it up."

"I don't think so, Junior."

As soon as the very angry Larry Jr. left, she was on the phone with Regina telling her about the disturbing conversation.

"Really, Regina, he said that! Can you imagine? Why would he tell me I could have one then tell me to take it back? I mean, I paid for the damn thing, there's no need for him to get his drawers all twisted up."

"You know Larry Jr.," Regina sighed. "He doesn't like to have his chain pulled. He probably wasn't paying any attention to what you were saying when you asked him for permission to have one installed. Don't say anything else about it and maybe it will blow over. If it doesn't, I'll talk to him."

That evening, Stella was lounging in the now infamous hot tub when she heard her phone ring. It was Cicely asking if it was a convenient time to come over and try out her hot tub.

"Come on over now, girl. You're going to love it!"

A few minutes later, there was a knock on her door. Thinking it was Cicely, Stella called out from the patio for the visitor to come in, but the door didn't open. Finally, she climbed out of the hot tub, and after throwing a robe on over her bathing suit, flung open the door to find Tom standing there with a bottle of wine in his hand. Stella cocked her head questioningly.

"I wanted to bring a gift to thank you for that little favor you did for me." Tom handed the wine to Stella.

"Did you bring your swim trunks?" she asked. When he sheepishly nodded, she laughed and invited him in. After pointing him in the direction of the patio, she made a detour to the kitchen for some wine glasses. Just as she began to pour, she heard Cicely let herself into the apartment.

"Hello? Stella? Are you here?" Cicely called out.

"Yep, right here," Stella answered as she stepped out of the kitchen. In one hand, she carried a cluster of crystal glasses by their stems, and her other hand clutched the neck of the wine bottle. With a nod to the French doors, Stella led her friend to the patio.

"We already started the party," she said. "Come on in, I'm sure the water's fine." She paused, waiting for her friend to notice that they were not alone. The dismayed look on Cicely's face as she spotted Tom was no surprise to Stella. She expected it and instinctively knew Cicely would think that she and Tom were intentionally alone. However, the hopeful look registered on Tom's face told her she had done the right thing by allowing the two to bump into each other at her place.

"Let's all have a glass of wine, shall we? Tom brought it because of a little something I did for him. Now, come, get in the hot tub. It'll help us all relax a bit." She pushed a full glass into Cicely's hand and ushered her toward the water.

"Only if I'm not interrupting anything." Cicely's frosty eyes were focused on Tom.

Stella sank into the hot tub across from both of her obviously uncomfortable friends. *'Well, shit. This is going to be an early night,'* she thought.

By the time her feet hit the floor the next morning, Stella knew the hot tub would bring more trouble than it was worth. A memo from Larry Jr. had been slipped under her door. After the usual letterhead and pleasantries, it read:

"Most of you know that one of our residents recently had a hot tub installed on her patio. As administrator and owner of Heritage Memories Retirement Village, I must inform all tenants that, in the interest of resident safety, there are now rules in place that prohibit hot tubs, or any other addition, unless approved by me. Failure to abide by these rules, even if said addition would be paid for privately, could possibly result in eviction. I'm sure I can count on your full cooperation."

XII

A Son's Wrath

Regina read the memo slipped under her door and instantly knew the extent of the trouble that was brewing. Because of her son's coolness toward her, she normally avoided any type of confrontation with him. Now Larry Jr. had crossed the line. In essence, he was threatening to evict her friend Stella. Regina was prepared to go to war for that. Her friends were more than family to her. She couldn't help but wonder what on earth was causing him to behave so stubbornly. She decided to go to his office and confront him personally. Before she asked Cicely if she could borrow her car, she called and made an appointment so he wouldn't have an excuse to cut her off. She was going to meet him on terms he understood. She was going to pay for his time.

When her name was called, Regina stepped into her son's office. The look on his face was a cross between annoyance and surprise.

"Mother, what are you doing here?"

"Larry, I felt that I had to talk to you in person and the only way I could do that was to come to your office. I want to talk to you about Stella and her hot tub."

"Do you, now? I don't see that there is anything left to talk about. I stated my position in the memo I sent to all the residents of the Village. Didn't you get yours?"

"Yes, I got it. I just don't agree with it. You told Stella that she could have the hot tub. You gave your permission."

"Miss Stella tricked me into agreeing to install a hot tub and I won't have that. You know, Mother, I have put up with a lot from you and your friends. You all act as if the Village is some sort of country club or something."

"You mean it isn't? That's funny. I was under the impression it was a retirement village," Regina responded acidly. "At least, that's what it was supposed to be. That's what you and Chad planned. What is the matter with you, Larry? For years now, I've seen you go from being a loving son to someone I hardly know!"

"What's the matter with me? How dare you bring Chad's name into it? He was my best friend for many years, and you can thank him that you even have a home to stay in."

"What are you talking about? It was both of you who decided to build the Village. Donna and I never asked you to do it. It was a childhood dream of the two of you boys."

"Some dream, Mother. I'm not the one who really wanted to build the Village. That was all Chad. The only reason I haven't sold it since he died is that now I have you and all your old crony friends living there. If I didn't own the place, you all would be out on your asses! Chad and I made another promise to each other. If one of us died, the other would take care of our parents. Do you even know how hard it is to run a place like the Village? Oh, but you probably don't care as long as you and your friends get to do what you want!"

"Son, I don't even know this side of you! Where is all this coming from? For years, I have felt that you resented me for something. Is this what it is? Do you feel like my friends and I are a burden to you? Is that it?"

"Are you serious? Do you really think that the only reason I would resent you is that you're a burden? That's not even half of it!"

"What is it then? I have to know. Why do you hate me so much?"

"I don't hate you, Mother, but I don't know how you can live with yourself."

"What are you talking about?" Her back stiffened and her brows pinched together.

"I'm talking about what happened as soon as Dad left for Viet Nam. I'm talking about you not wasting any time replacing him with a lover. I'm talking about you and Tom Sanders!" Regina's hand flew her mouth and she was too stunned to say a word.

"Oh yes, I know about Tom! Chad and I both knew! We saw you two together one day when we got out of school early. You were in the bedroom, the bedroom you shared with my father, the war hero. The one who was shot down defending our country. He was brave enough to die serving the American people, even for lousy cheats like you. When we saw you, I cried like a baby but Chad didn't. He was the one who said not to overreact. I don't think I did, Mother. I've kept your secret all this time. Therefore, before you come in my office telling me what to do, you had better think about this; without me, you have nothing. Because Chad's mother is your best friend, you wouldn't have a pot to piss in. None of you have enough Social Security to pay for an apartment like you have in the Village, much less to be able to do all that traveling and shopping that you all are so fond of."

Regina stood to leave. Her legs felt like rubber and she could feel her heartbeat pounding in her throat. Anger boiled beneath the surface of her skin and behind her eyes. She didn't say a word as she turned to leave. She knew what she would have to do. In her mind, she was setting the wheels in place to call an emergency business meeting. Then she had to talk to Donna.

"Oh, and before you leave, Mother, please tell your good friends that there will be no more pot parties at the Village or I will call the police. Is that understood?"

Regina wasted no time finding Stella to inform her about most of the conversation with Larry Jr., at least the parts that concerned. Predictably, Stella was furious.

"That smart ass! Sorry, I know he's your son, but who else does he think he is? All of that just because I wanted a hot tub?"

"There is a little more to it, but it's kind of personal and I can't go into it right now. Even that doesn't change the fact that he is being so harsh. That man is not the son I remember!"

"So what are you going to do?"

"If you would have been in my place listening to him go on and on about how, if it weren't for him, we wouldn't have a pot to piss in, you would know what I'm going to do. That's why I am calling for an emergency business meeting. I don't know about you, but I am going to get out of here. God knows I would hate to be a burden! It's a good thing I never let anyone in my family know about our business except Taylor. Thank God we have that!"

"I'm with you. If we all move out, that will give that smug son of a bitch—no offense—something to think about! I am sorry I brought all of this down on you, Regina. If I had known that hot tub would cause so much misery, I would not have bought it. I was really thinking about Bethany and how much benefit she would get out of it."

"Stella, darling, it wasn't the hot tub that did it. Apparently, this has been brewing for a long time over reasons I can't discuss at the moment. Know this; I'm glad to finally find out why he has long treated me with so much disrespect. He will never get the chance to do it again, I promise that. I have already talked to Jack and the only time he has available for our business meeting is a week from today. Put it on your calendar and I'll tell everyone else."

Bethany was the next person Regina sought out. To her relief, she was having a good day and had no trouble understanding the argument that took place with Larry Jr. concerning Stella's hot tub. Her mind was clear when she was informed of the meeting but she surprised Regina by telling her that she wanted Emma Bertrand in attendance.

"Bethany, what on earth for? We haven't yet voted about replacing you with anyone. Emma's not part of the business so why should we ask her to join us?"

"Because, as the one retiring from the board, I want her to replace me. If the floor is going to be open for business at that meeting, I want her there to prove to everyone that she is the right person to replace me on the board."

"Did you tell her about the business?"

"Yes, I did and she wasn't a bit surprised. She said she was proud of us especially because of all the good works we do with the profits. She said that kind of endeavor is something she has always wanted to be part of. She doesn't know, yet, that I want her to take my place. I've saved that part for later, but I hope with all of my heart that she can. I'd love to see Taylor come into the business, but there is that little thing about conflict of interest since we awarded her with those scholarships."

"I know, and I hate that for her. Who would have known that we weren't doing the right thing by helping her out with her education? She does have a good head on her shoulders, which is something I will not give Larry Jr. the credit for."

"Boy, oh boy! Is he going to get the shock of his life when he finds out the Old Ladies Club isn't as dependent on him as he thinks we are!" Bethany knew she was making perfect sense and it pleased her.

During the week preceding the business meeting, Regina could see that everyone seemed to be walking on eggshells, and she was the one designated to listen to all of their troubles. Cicely told her she was still confused about Tom. Donna was indignant about Larry Jr.'s attitude and Regina had to talk fast to keep her from side swiping him with a piece of her mind. Poor Stella. When she was told that Bethany invited Emma to the meeting, she looked at Regina as if she had her head on backwards. By the time the week was over, Regina felt like every nerve she had was shredded.

The board meeting was on a stormy Monday morning. From the floor-to-ceiling windows in Jack's boardroom, one could see just how harsh the weather was. Clanging cymbals of thunder and lightening were muffled by the slapping sound of the rain on the thick glass. The OLC business group assembled with the addition of Emma LeBlanc who looked slightly confused as to why her presence was requested. The thick tension permeating the room was as stifling as the humidity outside. A hot, late summer storm in Florida, combined with the sweat of anxiety and anticipation, left everyone in the room wilted and uncomfortable. This was not going to be an easy meeting to get through.

After the previous meeting's minutes were read, Jack opened the floor to discussion. As expected, Regina began by citing the memo all of the Village residents received from Larry Jr. She confessed how upset and disappointed she was with his decision and the manner with which he delivered it. She recounted word for word what Larry Jr. said about them not having a pot to piss in if it wasn't for him, but she didn't reveal the most consequential reason he gave for his lack of respect. She concluded her carefully worded statement by informing her business partners that she never wanted to be a burden to anyone. Even if they, as a group, didn't have the very prosperous business they did, she would still want to move out of the Village.

"If we didn't have this business and I was poor as a church mouse, I would still move and I hope you all can understand why." When she was finished speaking, she nervously studied the faces around the table and was surprised to see tears in everyone's eyes. A few seconds passed in silence before the commotion began. They validated her decision and, one by one, confirmed that the feelings she had were mutual. Her nervousness vanished, and in its place, she felt loved, comforted, and anything but alone.

Following a short discussion, the consensus was unanimous. They were going to strike out on their own. For years they all made their home at the Village because of who built it and why. The added convenience of being neighbors with their best friends was very important to them, and it was a blessing that they didn't have to worry about maintenance or grounds keeping. However, at this point there seemed to be no room for sentimentality. The amenities were excellent, and the question was asked whether or not they wanted to seek a place with the same perks, or could they live without them?

"Oh for gawd's sake!" Stella declared. "Any of that can be replaced! All we have to do is drive a little, or take a bus or a cab to get to the store, or get our hair done, or whatever," she sputtered.

Cicely, ever the practical one, put an idea before the group.

"What if we build our own place?" A discussion followed, but after a few minutes, the general opinion was that construction would take too long. Regina especially wanted out as quickly as possible and Stella was equally as eager to leave.

"May I say something?" The question came from Emma, who was sitting alone at the opposite end of the board table. Everyone stopped talking and looked at her expectantly.

"Let the minutes note that the board recognizes Emma LeBlanc," Jack told his secretary and motioned for Emma to begin.

"I'm not trying to butt into your business, but you might want to think about buying a place that is already built. Maybe all you would have to do would be some remodeling and that wouldn't take very long, would it?" Poor Emma had been afraid to interrupt anyone since the meeting was clearly based on a personal matter. She was hesitant to offer any ideas but felt this one could be to everybody's benefit.

"That's a great idea!" Cicely offered. "We can have our real estate manager look into that very easily."

"That's all well and good," Stella impatiently stated, "but, where would we find such a place? I don't want to live just anywhere. We have to think about which section of town, how much we can afford to spend, accommodations, funding remodeling, and lots and lots of other stuff."

"Excuse me," Emma's hand raised again. "The last couple of times Marcel and I came to visit, we stayed at the sweetest place on the beach. It's called the Tropical Inn and it has a restaurant and dining room, an indoor pool, a workout room and more. I noticed when I arrived yesterday that it has a for sale sign in front of it. Moreover, there is a full staff already working there that I'm sure don't want to loose their jobs. With a little remodeling, it could be exactly what you all need."

Nobody spoke as Emma's words were absorbed and considered.

"Well, we already know we now how to orchestrate renovations, don't we? So, what do you think the asking price would be? No wait, do we know if we can we afford such a big place? That's the question!" Donna said.

"Now do you see? That is why I wanted Emma here! She has a brain and can think on her feet," Bethany offered.

"What?" Emma looked surprised.

"We'll get to that later," Jack quickly took over. "Ladies, I can tell you that I'm certain you can afford to buy a hotel. The downfall of the economy has worked in your favor. Not only did you, as a business, come up with a sound plan to control your interests, it has paid off very, very well."

"How much are we worth, Jack?" asked a stunned Regina.

"I can't give you the exact numbers until I get with our CPA's but I can tell you this: millions. Over the years, OLC has made a net profit of millions. We have put the money here and there and used a lot of it for good works. There are still a lot of liquid assets we can pull from. The OLC is quiet well off."

Everyone in the room began talking at once. Regina looked from face to face with tears causing her eye make-up to puddle under her eyes and run in rivulets through the hills and valleys of her soft skin. She didn't care. It was good to know that she had her friend's support and that they were more than financially solvent.

"May I speak now?" Bethany raised her hand once more. "I think now is a good time to nominate Emma to take my place on the board."

Emma's mouth fell open. "Miss Bethany, you don't mean . . . Is that why you asked me to come to this meeting?" Emma's voice mirrored her distress.

"I have a lot of faith in Emma," Bethany began, ignoring the question. "I think she is good for the company and she's at least ten years younger than the youngest one of us. I'd prefer to think my predecessor would likely live longer then we will, don't you? Now with the grand news we just heard about our financial situation, I think it's a good idea to have someone on the board that can help manage the company in the best interest of our families."

"I second that nomination!" Cicely's head bobbed up and down in agreement.

"Is this something you would be open to?" Jack asked Emma.

"Well, sure. I guess so." Then more confidently, she said, "Yes. I would like to be on the board. I'm sure I could do whatever you asked of me. In fact, it would be an honor." Her Irish green eyes swept across the room and crashed into Stella's puzzling dark glare.

Jack hesitated at first, and cleared his throat. With a strong voice he stated that Bethany's nomination was heard, seconded, and would be put to a vote at the next month's business meeting. Due to the palpable tension in the room, that was the best he could do.

"I declare this board meeting of OLC, Inc. has come to a close. The next meeting will be in two weeks, September 1st, 2008. Meeting adjourned."

When the doors opened, the room's occupants spilled out, eager to begin planning their new adventure. Within seconds the only three left in the room were Jack, Stella, and Emma. The two women stared at one another, their eyes taking inventory of every hair, every wrinkle, and every mole. Skin color was examined and physical proportions were visually estimated. Stella made the first move and stood in front of an emotional Emma. With Jack as a witness, she asked,

"Are you my baby?"

XIII

CONFESSIONS

O n the ride back to the Village, Regina was quiet, but Donna and Cicely were happily chattering about the meeting and the outcome of their financial report. Jack offered to take his mother home and, oddly enough, Stella preferred to hitch a ride with Emma. The passengers in Cicely's car were curious, but were too excited with the prospect of a potentially huge project in the near future to worry why Stella chose to ride back with the woman she was having so much difficulty accepting. She was, without a doubt, opposed to Emma becoming a part of their business, so time alone for the two women was quite unexpected.

Neither Cicely nor Donna was aware that the third party in their car was quiet. Way too quiet. The truth was, Regina's heart was skipping around her chest and her sweaty hands trembled. She knew what was to come and she did not relish the job of telling Donna what happened after her beloved Larry left for Viet Nam. Regina dreaded telling the truth, not only to Donna, but also to her friends and family as well. She knew they would be furious with her for what she had to confess, to say nothing of the fact that she had kept the secret for so many years. She wondered how Cicely would react to the news that she once had an affair with Tom. The truth would hurt Cicely too, she feared. After the short ride back to the

Village, she decided her next move would be to talk to Taylor before saying anything to Donna. Taylor was the one person in her family whose opinion mattered the most to her. In her heart, she knew that it would be easier for Taylor to forgive her than it would be for her best friends. Explaining that she wanted to visit her granddaughter, Cicely happily gave permission to borrow her car. After a quick phone call to Taylor, she was on her way.

Three hours later, Regina returned Cicely's car keys and went to her apartment without saying a word to anyone. Once she got there, the only thing she wanted to do was lay on her bed. Her confession to her granddaughter had not gone well. It ended with a sobbing Taylor slamming the door to the bathroom and refusing to come out. Regina knew better than to try to reason with her. It would be quite some time before their torn relationship could mend. Her arms and legs felt like lead weights but she had no time for her guilt to weigh her down just yet. There was more to do, more soul to bare. She knew the hardest part would be talking to Donna. Her head pounded and she was emotionally and physically exhausted. Her eyes were red and swollen and her heart thumped erratically in her chest. She needed to rest. She simply had to. The dreaded meeting with Donna would have to wait until tomorrow.

On the assisted living wing, a napping Bethany stirred, then suddenly jolted awake when, out of the corner of her eye, she saw someone lurking near her bed. At first, she thought it was a robber or someone who meant to do her harm. The intruder's face, it seemed, was dark and scowling. She tried to pull the blanket over her head but the stranger wouldn't allow it. In scarcely a moment, the half-asleep woman recognized that the person in her room was no stranger at all. It was Stella, her sweet Stella. Wait, something was wrong. This Stella was not so sweet; she was frowning and unhappy.

"How dare you!" the formerly sweet Stella growled.

Taken aback, Bethany blinked her eyes several times and shook her head. Had she been dreaming? No, Stella was standing at her bedside with her arms now crossed in front of her chest. She looked like a wild animal backed into a corner, holding herself to keep her feet from running away. Bethany was alarmed.

"What? What is it? Is something wrong?"

"Bethany, how could you do this to me? How could you go behind my back like that? What made you think I wanted to be in her life?"

"Oh, it'll be alright, dear. Don't you worry. Bethany will fix everything," she said with a now vacant look in her eyes. She began to move her hands through the air as though she was folding invisible clothes.

"Didn't you hear me? Bethany, put your hands down and tell me why you brought my daughter here!"

"I'll have time to play with you in a little while, baby girl. You just give Bethany a chance to get these clothes folded. Before you know it, your mama and daddy will be here to pick you up and take you home! They love you, sweetheart, we all do. You're such a good little girl."

Stella stared at the small woman in the bed who was lost in a sea of sheets and blankets and confusion. Clearly, the body was there but the mind was not.

The next morning, the sun rose just as it did every other day, but Regina was surprised to see it because, to her, nothing in the world would ever be normal again. She was sad that at this late stage in life she was about to turn several lives upside down. How had she let this happen? She had been a loving wife to Larry. She did everything she could possibly do for her children. She loved her family so much and when Larry died, she thought she would too. After what she did, her guilt kept her from ever loving another man. It was with an unspeakable dread that she dressed herself and phoned Donna to let her know that she would be there shortly. When she put the phone down, she sat at her writing desk and dropped her head into her hands.

O Holy Father, she prayed, *I have asked You many times to forgive me for my infidelity and deceit and I believe that through Jesus Christ,*

You have. Now I am begging you to give me the strength to do what I have to do. Amen.

Donna's smile disappeared when she saw Regina's face. After her friend told her she needed to talk to her about something serious, the first thing she did was put on a pot of coffee.

"Don't worry, what ever it is, we'll figure out what to do over a good cup of coffee."

The aroma of the fresh brew had a calming effect on Regina as she took a seat in the kitchen and prepared herself for what she was about to say.

"Donna, I'm not sure even a pot of coffee is going to help this time. I made a huge mistake a long time ago and I have kept it to myself all these years. Something Larry Jr. said when we were arguing about Stella's hot tub convinced me that I'm going to have to tell you what happened." Her voice was burdened with pain and she kept her head down as she spoke.

"I knew there was something more to the story than just Stella's hot tub. Tell me. What did he say to you?" Donna would have gladly come to her defense.

"It's not just what he said. It's what I did after Larry left for Viet Nam." She hesitated. Pink color appeared on Donna's cheeks and her eyes seemed to glaze momentarily while searching her memory for those long ago days. Finally, she focused on Regina again.

"Are you talking about the affair you had with Tom?" she asked quietly.

"What? You knew about that? You never said a word! Does that mean you've already forgiven me? Donna, I'm so sorry!" Regina's heart was pounding.

"I suspected it right from the beginning, but I didn't want to admit it because I didn't want my perfect little world to break apart. Chad confirmed it for me later. He told me that he and Larry Jr. always knew. Didn't you know that was what Chad and Larry Jr. fought about in college?"

"You mean my mistake was what ended their friendship? Oh my dear God, please tell me it isn't so!" Regina covered her face with her hands.

"Oh, I doubt that was what finally broke up the friendship. I think that ended when Larry Jr. married Sherry. Chad always thought he and Larry Jr. would end up together, after all, Larry Jr. knew he was gay but they were still best friends. Unfortunately, Chad thought that meant Larry Jr. loved him. No, Regina, your actions didn't end that relationship. But I have often wondered if the affair might be the reason Tom left me." Donna pulled two coffee cups from the cabinet, filled them with the rich hot brew, and brought them to the table. "I could never bring myself to ask you about it."

"So you've known all this time that Renee' is Tom's daughter?" Regina had relief written all over her face.

Gold-rimmed porcelain cups and saucers slipped from Donna's hands, crashed to the table and from there, to the kitchen floor. Coffee splashed on the tablecloth and splattered the clothes of both women before streaming down the table legs into a puddle beneath. Donna froze, except for the quivering of her hands, after her best friend in the world bluntly delivered the worst news any woman could possibly hear.

XIV

To Have and To Let Go

Nothing could have prepared Stella for the kind of week she was having. Not only did she have to endure a great deal of dissention from Larry Jr., but also she was now faced with the fact that the baby she gave up for adoption fifty-eight years ago was under her nose for weeks, and she had been unaware the whole time. *How could Bethany do that to me,* she wondered. As if that drama wasn't enough, Regina delivered a bombshell by revealing that none other than Tom Sanders himself fathered her daughter. Stella's head reeled and she worried about all the changes that took place in such a short time. She could see very well that Bethany had not weathered the stress well. Ever since the day Stella confronted her, Bethany wasn't herself. Her trips into the real world were becoming fewer and farther apart.

All Stella wanted these days was to be quiet and find some way to put the pieces of her life back together and carve out some peace in the chaos that her life had become. She missed her hot tub too. After Larry Jr.'s memo threatening eviction, Stella arranged to have the thing picked up and moved to Taylor's house. The young lady was delighted to receive the gift and promised that she would take good care of it.

Stella packed little Camille, into a large, red striped vinyl beach bag before she went to breakfast in the dining room. She always hid him in some sort of large purse so no one could say anything about bringing her dog into a space where food was served. Although nobody was fooled, not one person ever said anything to her about it. These days, she tried extra hard to conceal the Yorkshire terrier's presence considering how far down on the list she was in relation to the powers that be, namely Larry Jr. This morning, she thought it would be just her and Camille for breakfast until Cicely came through the door of the dining room. The younger woman didn't look as cheerful as she usually did and Stella steeled herself to hear what new drama might be taking place now.

In the serving line, Cicely added a bowl of cinnamon oatmeal and a tangerine to the tray beside her morning cup of tea. Stella waited for her friend to join her before she continued with her breakfast. Eating alone wasn't good, she thought, even if the company was in a bad mood.

As soon as Cicely sat down, she honed in on Tom as if he were the nastiest man she had ever encountered.

"Has *everybody* slept with him? I swear I don't know what I saw in that man. I am mortified. Mortified, do you hear me? I should have stayed away from him from the very beginning. My Jimmy spoiled me against other men. There never will be another man as good as he was. I should have known . . ."

"Cicely, take it easy. Tom is not that bad. Really. I think he's a good guy and you know he's crazy about you."

"Oh yeah, right! That's why I saw Donna sneaking out of his room and managed to interrupt your hot tub date with him. Now, Regina says . . ."

"Wait a minute . . . *My* date with him? I've never dated him! Good gawd, Cicely! What is the matter with you? He just came over to give me a bottle of wine because I did him a favor. I asked him if he wanted to get in the hot tub because I already knew you were coming over. Can't you see I was trying to get you guys back together again?"

"You were?"

"Yes. Do you have air pockets in your brain, or something? All of a sudden, you don't trust your best friends? Come on!"

"Stella, I'm sorry! You would have thought the same thing, too, if you were in my shoes. It doesn't matter anyway. Oh, I don't know what to think any more. I just want everything to go back the way it was."

"Well, listen to me for a second," Stella parked her clenched hands on her hips. "I have been in your shoes and I didn't like it either. Right now, you can't scrape me up off the floor with a spatula so please don't make me feel worse with all that woe-is-me crap you are dealing with. It is all in your mind anyway. Tom loves you. He told me so. I believe he is sick. Not sick like 'perverted' sick—sick like 'illness' sick. I think that is why you saw Donna with him. She was delivering marijuana to him. Pot that *I* got for him. Donna told me he needed it for medical purposes and that's why he brought me a bottle of wine, not because he wanted to date me."

Cicely looked as if she had been slapped in the face. Her eyes widened and filled with tears. She drew one hand to the neck of her frilly white blouse and held the other to her pale cheek.

"Do you really think he's sick? What's wrong with him?" Panic elevated the pitch of her voice.

"I don't know. Why don't you go ask him," Stella said with resignation. *Why doesn't anybody ever care enough to ask about what I'm going through?* She thought. After Cicely picked up her tray and left, Stella reached under her chair with a bit of a biscuit for the hiding Camille. The big handbag was empty. She scanned the immediate area for Camille. *Great. That's all I need,* she muttered to herself. She looked under the tables surrounding hers, but still no sign of Camille. She stood up and took her tray to the counter. Again, no Camille. One of the servers behind the salad bar caught her eye and pointed to the open doorway. Stella acknowledged her with a nod of her head and set out to search for her pet. She scoured the hallway for any sign of him and asked passersby if they had seen him. Nobody had. Finally, she decided that Camille probably would have gone back to the apartment, but when she got there, the little dog was not waiting at the door. She made her way to the assisted living wing and when she entered Bethany's room, she spotted Camille curled up on the bed beside Bethany.

"There you are! Bad dog! You gave me quite a scare, didn't you? Come on, let's go back to our own room and leave Beth alone to so she can rest," she coaxed.

She reached for the dog, but he answered with a faint low growl before laying his head firmly against Bethany's leg. Stella laughed and told Bethany how funny it was that Camille didn't want to leave her. Bethany didn't answer.

"Bethany?" Stella nudged her friend. She didn't move. Stella reached for her hand and found it cold and lifeless. Bethany was gone. She died in her sleep, alone, with no one to see her off on the journey except for Camille, a shaggy little dog.

Stella felt her world crash down around her, and the wail that came from her throat pierced her soul. She crawled in bed beside the one person she loved more than anyone in the world, glad that nobody else was around so she could express her grief in her own way. In the pain of her loss, Stella placed her hand over her heart and ripping her caftan, she began to recite a traditional Jewish prayer.

"Baruch Ata Adonai . . ."

The memorial service was simple, just as Bethany designated when she made her pre-funeral arrangements years before. It was her desire to be cremated as soon as possible after her death, which was very hard on her friends, especially Stella. She believed according to Jewish law, that cremation was desecration of the body. However, she respected the fact that Bethany was Baptist and in her faith, cremation was acceptable. Bethany had long ago declared that she absolutely did not want to go to the ground in a coffin. She requested, instead, to have her ashes released to the natural elements so that, in death, she would become one with the earth. Her remains would add to the earth, not take up space unnecessarily. She didn't want a grave for someone to visit, mourn over, and then in time, forget. It didn't seem right to her that there were graveyards full of old neglected graves with only the occasional grief-stricken person visiting, partly because they couldn't let go of the physical aspect of this world, and partly because they felt guilty if they didn't, as though their deceased loved one could tell. Death was final. In Bethany's words, she wanted her loved ones to 'keep the memories alive, but let the body go back to the place from whence it came'. Ashes to ashes and dust to dust.

For the memorial service, the entire Village chapel choir offered their best vocals to the stirring hymns they knew Bethany loved most. Her friend, Reverend Early, provided a tender eulogy and a passionate sermon. He spoke of the footprint a person leaves behind in this world and how one is not only remembered for the good they did, but also for the mistakes they made. The mistakes were not the most important things, he explained. The most important thing was how a person grew from them, and how willing she was to admit, repent, and accept forgiveness.

"A man writes his own obituary with every step he takes. Miss Bethany's steps were solid, sure, and always on the right path. Ladies and Gentlemen," his beautiful, melodious South African accent thickened with emotion. "I would like to conclude with this: Today we stand on this side of the shore and watch as her sail glides across the great sea toward the horizon, getting smaller and smaller. With much grief we say 'oh no, there she goes'. On the other side of the horizon, a host of angels stands on their shore watching as her sail drifts toward them, growing larger and larger. With great joy they say '*Ah yes! Here she comes!*'"

When Reverend Early took his seat, Larry Jr. stood to offer words of comfort to Bethany's family and friends. His wife Sherry and both daughters sat on the row behind Jack, Lisa Faye, and Bethany's four best friends. Though he didn't make eye contact with any of them, his words were filled with compassion.

"I've known Miss Bethany for a long time, even before she came to live at the Village and I can honestly say to you that she had more integrity than any person I have ever known. She lived a good life and she shared it with everyone. Many, many people loved her. I would hope we could all be so lucky. May she rest in peace."

The memorial service ended with a special rendition of Bethany's favorite hymn, Rock of Ages. Tom arranged the music with the choir as background and himself the lead singer with a guitar. The music was beautiful, but when Tom got to the last verse, his voice broke and he ended the song in tears.

> *While I draw this fleeting breath*
> *When my eyes shall close in death,*
> *When I soar to worlds unknown,*
> *See thee on thy judgment throne,*
> *Rock of Ages, cleft for me,*
> *Let me hide myself in thee.*[2]

He had not known Bethany for as long a time as the others had, but they did have a special bond with each other. She saw the goodness in him that many refused to see, and he acknowledged her unconditional love for everyone she met.

Because he knew Stella had such a deep love for her friend, Ralph expected she would be sitting Shiva for Bethany and he was right. Stella made no effort to change the torn clothing she had on when the funeral home personnel came to take the body away. She covered the mirrors in her apartment and spent her days sitting in Bethany's old rocking chair, motionless, with a book of prayers in her lap. It worried him that she stayed there for a full seven days after her death and the only time she left her apartment was for the memorial service. To his credit, Ralph stayed by her side as she mourned. Knowing the importance the traditions of her faith were to her, he wanted to show support for her in any way that he could. He loved Stella and was almost sure that she loved him too.

On the first day, Regina paid a Shiva call to Stella's apartment, bringing a traditional Jewish mourning meal of eggs and bread on a round platter. She stayed with her with her until night fell and witnessed her mourning prayers. The next day, Donna took her place by Stella's side. Following that, Cicely came, then Jack and Lisa Faye. Tom solemnly paid his dues as well. By this time, Stella was so weary and so spent with grief that she welcomed the comforts her friends provided. They brought food for her and saw to it that Camille was fed and walked. When they didn't know what to say, they held her hand, and stroked her hair. Although all of them grieved Bethany's passing, Stella was determined to make a lasting tribute to Bethany in the only way she could; by her faith. Finally, on the seventh day, Emma and Marcel came to Stella's side. She accepted their kindness without speaking, and although they stayed only four hours, she was aware of the effort it must have taken for them to come. The whole time they were with her, she was listening to an inner voice, one that sounded remarkably like Bethany's, telling her that it was time to make amends. It was time to open her heart to the daughter who, for her entire life, longed to know her; the daughter who was in the here and now, waiting to be accepted or rejected. This was no curse. It was a blessing. It was time to make, and live, in peace.

XV

CONSENSUS

Donna was already reeling from the bomb Regina dropped on her before Bethany died. The loss of one of their own was a harder blow to take but somehow she managed to hold herself together. Several times, she wondered how it was possible. She loved her best friends dearly and could barely fathom how she could be so deeply wounded by two of them at the same time. Of course, Bethany wasn't at fault for dying, but the loss was nothing less than ripping out a piece of Donna's heart. Then, there was the matter of Regina and her confession. Why she hadn't figured out years earlier that Renee'was actually Tom's child was beyond her. She remembered watching Regina stare at Taylor and Belinda at the Memorial Day dance. She realized that, at the time, she thought Regina was missing Renee' when, actually, she was probably studying the similarities between Renee''s daughter and Belinda. *How could I have not seen it before?* Donna thought.

Tom was equally distressed to discover that Donna knew the truth about the affair he had with Regina. Just one week after Bethany's memorial service, Donna confronted him. He knew it was coming. Cicely had already confirmed what Regina confessed to Donna. No matter how well informed he was nothing could prepare him for the pain he saw in his ex-wife's eyes that day. *My God,* he thought, *it's been forty years! For forty years, I have tried to keep from hurting her with the truth and after all this time, she finally knows.* Not only had the truth crushed her, it had damaged his relationship with Cicely as well. He was dreadfully sorry that he had hurt both of them with his actions. Now, he realized, running away from the truth for so many years could not stop the deep shame that choked his heart.

Cicely's reaction to both Bethany's death and Regina's secret was typical for a woman who had become independent out of the need to. She made herself very busy and seldom stopped long enough to ponder the reality that Bethany was gone and Tom was a scoundrel. She directed her attention to OLC, Inc. and filled her days with details of ongoing renovations and lists of benefaction projects needing attention. She was like the ostrich that stuck her head in the sand; what she didn't see, couldn't hurt her. The time was coming soon that all four remaining board members of OLC, Inc. would have to face each other. There was business to attend to, and their partnership was still intact despite the newly created vacancy and the huge fissure dividing their friendships.

One month after Bethany's memorial service, her son Jack called for a board meeting. He was still mourning his mother, but honored his mother's life-long attitude that life goes on. She would be the last one to neglect any business, and she wouldn't have wanted them to either. He opened the meeting by saying how proud his mother was of their accomplishments and how she was certain that they were all as close as any family could be. Jack was oblivious to the recently surfaced problems and revelations, but was quite aware of the tension heavily permeating the room. The women glanced sideways at each other, none willing to break the news to Jack that something besides his mother's death had, indeed, fractured this family.

"We need to address the unfinished business nominated and seconded at the last meeting," he said. "It's a matter of record that my mother stated she was resigning as a board member and wanted Emma LeBlanc to replace her. Cicely, I believe, seconded that nomination. Today, we need to accept any other nominations and vote on that issue. Does anybody have anything to say?" Jack looked directly at Stella. She slowly shook her head and averted her eyes.

"I'll be abstaining from the vote," she said, surprising everyone.

"Let the minutes show that Estelle Taub excuses herself from voting on the issue of replacing board member Bethany Bertrand. Will everyone in favor of adding Emma LeBlanc to the board of OLC, Inc. please raise your hand?" He scoured the room and saw two hands raised.

"Anyone not in favor?"

Regina timidly raised her hand.

"Due to the fact that one board member has abstained from voting, the vote is two for and one against. The vote to induct Emma LeBlanc as an official and functioning board member is carried," Jack declared. "Ladies, if you all will agree, I would like to close the meeting at this time and defer any business pending to next month's meeting."

"What about buying that commercial piece of property Emma talked about, the one we can renovate into a new place for us to live?" Cicely asked.

"I'm not so sure I want to move just yet," Stella stated. "I need a little more time to get used to Beth not being here. Making plans like that right now is more than I can bear."

"I agree," Donna added.

"I do, too," Regina acknowledged.

Cicely looked from one person to another and observed that no one was making eye contact.

"Yes, I guess it is a bit too soon. Do you think we can schedule it for next month's meeting?"

"If that is the consensus of the board, we can," Jack said. "Does everyone agree?" All of the women nodded approval.

After the meeting ended, Jack gave Regina and Stella a lift back to the Village, and Cicely and Donna rode together. Keeping his ears and eyes open, Jack wondered what could have caused the very obvious rift between the women, but he was clueless. At first, he thought the awkward silence was because Stella and her long lost daughter were reunited, but he realized that not a word was mentioned about it. Apparently, Stella had not yet brought the rest of the group up to date.

By the end of the week, Emma LeBlanc received confirmation that OLC, Inc. appointed her the newest board member and she accepted the news with mixed emotions. She had grown to love Bethany and knew in her heart that she could never take her place. In the short time they knew each other, they were more like mother and daughter than mere acquaintances. An odd feeling, Emma thought, considering her biological mother was present, yet unavailable. When the truth of her parentage was revealed, she didn't expect the reaction she got. She had hoped that open arms would receive her, but it wasn't to be. Instead, Stella rejected her and refused to acknowledge that the young woman meant anything to her, and then she served a sullen attitude to Bethany as though the woman betrayed their friendship and sideswiped her with a broken confidence. The day Stella confronted her about her identity, she did so bluntly, and coldly admitted that she had never set eyes on her before Bethany found her. Emma's heart sank with the knowledge that her own mother had not known what color her hair was or who she looked like. With a great deal of effort, she managed to suppress the burning tears threatening to fall when Stella revealed she had never wanted to see her baby because if she did, she would have never been able to give her up. The stoic woman's voice was void of any emotion when she said she doubted they would ever be able to have any kind of relationship.

Emma heard the words, but could plainly see that Stella was only fooling herself. It was just a matter of time before the wall so carefully erected between them would come tumbling down. Her mother couldn't possibly know that she had seen beyond the façade and understood that there wouldn't have been so much pain unless there had first been love. She was willing to wait.

She folded the letter from the OLC and dropped it on the table before searching out Marcel to share her bittersweet news. From this moment on, she had to make a determined effort to ready herself for the business world. It no longer mattered that Stella was her long lost mother. For now, they were business partners only.

Back at the Village, there was no denying the splintering camaraderie and the strain it laid on everyone. In a few weeks, they would have another business meeting to welcome Emma as an official board member and begin planning for the purchase of an establishment to convert to a new home for them. That is, if anyone still wanted to. Nobody discussed it outside of the last board meeting so anyone's point of view was a mystery.

XVI

HOPE

It was a fabulously sunny Saturday morning early in September when Tom decided he'd had enough of dragging his tail behind himself. He was sick and tired of staying in his apartment trying to avoid crossing paths with his ex-wife or any of her friends. He was feeling like hell. His color was changing as he expected it would, and his doctor had increased his pain medicine to help him get through the days and additional sleep medicine to help him get through nights. This existence, this feeling of alienation and isolation from the world, was not how he had planned living out the rest of his life. It may be that he would never enjoy the warmth another person could offer him but he would be damned if he would go down without enjoying *something*. He needed to see people and have some form of human contact. At this late date, he needed to believe his life mattered and the only solution for that was to do something positive with it. It was time. Therefore, the first thing Monday morning, Tom was on the phone with an old pal whose grandson was an administrator at Ocean View Hospital. It was his intention to volunteer his services, hopefully in an area he would be able to physically navigate. At this point in his life, it was very important that he make an attempt to right the wrongs committed in his youth and becoming a volunteer might be the way to accomplish that. There seemed to be no going back to the relationships he had, or ever hoped for. The phone call to his old friend led to another and then another, until finally he was in touch with the director of the hospital auxiliary, a crew of volunteers who made their various services available for almost any need a patient or visitor might have. Comprised of mostly female volunteers, the members of the auxiliary were more than happy to take whatever time and talent he had to offer. It wasn't very often a man called to volunteer, and they were thrilled.

He started his orientation early the following Monday morning. The class was six hours long with a thirty-minute lunch break. Although he was tired at the end of the day, the fact that he now felt useful put a little bounce in his step. This was the first time since he sold his business up north that he felt like a working man and it was a good feeling. He hadn't realized how much he missed being an integral part of the outside world. He hoped he could maintain his stamina for a while longer, at least until he was able to exorcise those demons sitting on his shoulder whispering in his ear that the harm he'd done to the people he loved would render him useless forevermore. Finally, he was looking forward to tomorrow.

As luck would have it, Tom's first assignment was at the welcome desk, easy enough but a little boring at first. It wasn't long, however, before a handful of older gals, each wearing a red hospital auxiliary jacket, was hanging on his every word. His face flushed and he found himself flattered that his mere presence would garner such attention. Over the next several days, he monitored the welcome desk and enjoyed every minute of it. By the end of his first month, his two favorite rotations were the welcome desk and pediatrics. The children's ward touched him and opened places in his heart he had forgotten were there. He loved delivering mail, passing out coloring books, colors, puzzles, and whatever trinkets were on hand for the sick little ones. He especially enjoyed seeing the delight on their faces when he was able to bring stuffed animals or toys to the children. Tom believed this was exactly the place he should be to do penance for the way he had walked out on his own children.

His least favorite rotations were the cancer ward and ICU. Both areas caused him to shudder in remembrance of the trials he had been through with his own health. He averted his eyes from the faces of the patients there. If he saw what they were going through, if he witnessed their pain, he would be subjecting himself to a preview of things to come and he wasn't ready to face that just yet.

Despite Tom's mission of adding some worth to his life, as well as one of reparation, he looked forward to each and every day he volunteered at the hospital. The crew of the auxiliary was giving him something he hadn't had in a long time; friendship and a sense of belonging. Life was beginning to look up but when he returned home in the evenings, the happy glow faded every time he caught a glimpse of Cicely. He missed her. He still loved her.

When the new rotation schedule was posted, Tom stopped by the office to check on the location of his duties for the next week. He walked in on a cluster of ladies huddled around the desk as they were laughing and cackling like a brood of hens. As soon as they saw him, the commotion ceased. When he asked what was going on, several woman burst into laughter. It was obvious they were sharing some kind of joke.

"Come on, ladies! You know you can tell me!" Tom coaxed.

"Ok, if you insist," snorted a woman named Sarah.

"No, Sarah, don't! I'll be so embarrassed!" one member of the group exclaimed.

"Oh, get over it! Hey Tom, do you know how to tell when a guy becomes an old man?"

"Other than look in the mirror, how?" he asked, knowing the punch line would be aimed directly at his gut.

"Well . . . First, the hair on his head starts thinning out but his eyebrows get thicker. Then his nose gets bigger and turns red. His ears get longer and stick out to the side like the back doors of a taxi cab!" Everyone laughed before Sarah continued.

"Then his shoulders kind of slump, his chest caves in, his belly pops out like a beach ball and his butt gets flat as a pancake. But you *really* know he's an old man when his sack floats in the tub!" Howls of laughter deafened the room and Tom could feel hot color rise from under the neck of his shirt and shoot up to the roots of his hair. Even though the joke was on him, he couldn't help but laugh. *Oh yes*, he thought to himself, *laughter is the best medicine of all!*

He was still chuckling on the way to the elevators. All things considered, it looked like it would be a good day. As he rounded a corner, he almost ran into a transport orderly pushing a wheelchair and struggling to control it, as well as an IV pole. A young woman was in the chair holding a sleeping baby. Tom helped clear the way for them to get through and, as they wheeled past, she happened to look up and meet Tom's eyes. Her startled expression surprised him and he could see that her blue eyes mirrored his. Because the secret of his affair with Regina was revealed, there could be no hiding the truth now. Taylor was his granddaughter, and her baby was his great grandchild. As he stood beside her wheelchair, the very idea made him weak in the knees. He longed to pick the darling baby up in his arms and hold her for the first time. The orderly kept going, not realizing that this moment, the one he pushed through, was a pivotal moment in the lives of these three people. Tom watched them roll down the hallway until he saw Taylor turn around for a last look before they reached their room. He went to the unit's desk and busied himself with minor tasks until he saw a nurse exit the room where Taylor and Penny had disappeared.

"Hey, nurse? I was wondering—I saw you come out of that room—Taylor Stracener's? Can you tell me what's wrong with the baby?" he asked. The nurse looked at him, took note of his hospital auxiliary uniform, and shrugged.

"I guess since you're a volunteer, I can tell you. The baby has pneumonia. She's been pretty sick for a while, but she's on the mend now," the nurse answered in a low, barely audible.

"Really? How long has she been here?"

The nurse narrowed her eyes as she thought.

"I think it's been over a week now. Why don't you go down to see her? I'm sure they could use the company. As far as I know, nobody has been here to visit them at all since the baby was admitted."

"Thanks, Nurse. I'll do that," Tom said. He started toward the room but before he could reach it, the door flung open and Taylor shot out, head down, and ran straight into him. She struggled to keep from dropping the baby's bottle in her hand and regain her balance. He reached out to steady her.

"Taylor? Hey, how are you? Is the baby sick?" he stammered.

"Hi, Tom. Excuse me, I need to get a fresh bottle," Taylor said as she brushed past him.

His disappointed eyes followed her as she took a few steps down the hall before she reluctantly turned around and came back to the spot where he stood.

"I'm sorry. You didn't deserve that. I'll be back in a moment if you don't mind waiting."

"Oh sure, sure. I'll be right here. Do you mind if I go in and have a seat? Is Penny ok?"

"She's in her crib waiting for her bottle. Could you wait until I get back before you go in? I don't want her to be afraid. She doesn't really know you."

"Yeah, I guess you're right. Go ahead. I won't move," Tom said with a hopeful voice.

"I'll be back in a sec." Taylor hesitated briefly before she went to the patient canteen.

Moments later, she returned with a fresh bottle. She opened the door to the room and led Tom inside. His face flushed as he neared the baby standing in her crib and surprising tears began to sting his eyes. Penny cautiously eyed this stranger up and down then she saw the bottle in her mother's hand and started jumping up and down. Her pudgy-baby hands reached through the rails of the metal crib and she loudly expressed her desire for the bottle.

"Come on, sweetie," Taylor said as she lifted Penny. Stepping back, she managed to juggle the wriggling baby, her blanket, and the bottle of milk until they were all safely deposited in the rocking chair positioned between the window and the crib. She motioned for Tom to have a seat on the small blue sofa next to her.

"What's going on? Is the baby ok?" Tom asked. He hesitated to take the seat she indicated.

"She is now, but we were very worried about her for several days. She has pneumonia." Taylor informed him. "What are you doing here? You joined the hospital auxiliary? I can't imagine that," Taylor said with humor in her voice.

"Yeah, I did. I figured with the way things are going around the Village, I needed to get out and find something to do. Having a few new friends doesn't hurt either."

"I guess you and Gina stirred up quite a hornet's nest, didn't you?"

"Well," he hung his head, "You could say that, I'm not sure we should talk about it. It was a long time ago and not something I was ever proud of."

"Tom, don't you think we need to talk about it? I mean, after all, you are my grandfather, or so I hear."

"Ok, Taylor," he said with a resigned voice. "You're right and I shouldn't try to keep anything from you or anybody else. Ask anything you want, and I will tell you the honest truth. I have spent so many years keeping it to myself. It will be refreshing not to hide it anymore. I'm seventy-eight years old. The time for charades is long over."

Taylor didn't speak for a moment. She kept her face turned away from Tom so he couldn't see the pain registered there. Penny suckled her bottle, and keeping eye contact with her mother, reached up with her chubby little hand to grab a wisp of the blonde hair dangling in front of her face. Taylor winced as Penny gave it a good tug. She carefully freed the strands of her hair from the baby's playful grip.

Finally, she faced Tom again knowing she would be facing the truth as well.

"I'd like to know what happened," she told him as she looked squarely into his eyes. "Please, have a seat."

Your grandmother hasn't told you anything yet?"

"Yes, she told me her side, but I'd like to hear yours. This is weird, you know, thinking you are pretty much alone, and then all of a sudden a grandfather shows up. If she lied to everybody about that, what else has she lied about?" Taylor steadied her gaze toward Tom and set her chin defiantly.

"Wait a minute there! Your grandmother is one of the finest women I've ever known." Tom sat down and faced Taylor squarely.

"I should have known you'd take up for her," she said defiantly.

"Maybe so, but I can tell you this: Regina kept what happened between us from everyone because she knew it was wrong and she loved her family. She loved my family just as much. She and I were never in love. It happened because she loved her husband so much that when he went to Viet Nam, she went to pieces. She was devastated and distraught almost as if she knew she would never see him again. We were all so close. Donna and I, we did our best to calm Regina down."

"Apparently."

"No, come on. It wasn't like that. It was one time, one weak moment for both of us. I swear we were together only once. Donna was headed out the door for some garden club meeting or something and she asked me to go over to check on Regina because she was running late and couldn't stop over herself. When I got there, Regina was in the bedroom, still in bed. In fact, she had begun staying in bed all day while Larry Jr. was at school. I tried to cheer her up but the next thing I knew . . . both of us, we could have just died. We were so ashamed of ourselves. We swore that it would never happen again. Believe me, it didn't. Then, a couple of months later, Donna tells me that Regina is pregnant! Thank God, she didn't know what we had done so she believed the pregnancy happened before Big Larry left for Viet Nam. Regina let everybody think that. I knew that baby was mine and so did she. I told her we needed to tell the truth, but Regina couldn't do that to Big Larry while he was at war and, frankly, I didn't want to loose Donna." Tom paused in disbelief that he was actually getting the burden this secret off his chest.

"Go on, Tom. Tell me the rest. What happened?" Taylor urged, her voice and her eyes growing softer.

"It was hard to stand by and do nothing but watch Regina grow in her pregnancy. She was beautiful too. Donna was always there for her. She was with her every day because Regina was a wreck worrying about Big Larry, and I'm sure what we did made matters worse. Then one evening, she got a phone call that the Air Force was sending someone over and she needed to stay at home and wait for them. She called us to come over, and together, we got the news that

Big Larry was shot down and killed. She collapsed and twenty-four hours later, your mother was born. The poor thing was a couple of months early so she was scrawny and red and only weighed about four pounds, but there she was. She had red hair standing up all over her head and when she cried, everyone was amazed at how such a tiny little thing could throw a voice so big!" Tom tried to disguise the pride in his voice. "Anyway, Regina let everyone believe she was a full term baby and said the doctor told her the reason she was so tiny was because of all the anxiety she had with Big Larry in the war and all that." Tom paused again.

"So my mother never knew you were her father?" By this time, Taylor had tears streaming down her face.

"Not that I'm aware of. I don't believe Regina ever told Renee'."

"Is that why you left?"

"I tried to stick it out, honestly, I did. It was excruciating to see this perfect little baby who was born because her mother and I cheated on the two most important people in our lives. The baby was a constant reminder of the kind of person I was. Donna was falling in love with her, too, not knowing that the baby was mine. Regina still depended on Donna so much! She was so fragile, your grandmother was. After a while, I knew I was either going to have to confess or I was going to have to leave. I chose to leave. I knew that I had already destroyed my family and couldn't destroy hers, too. I couldn't face them with the truth. I was so ashamed; I took the coward's way out. I thought it would be better for everyone if I took myself out of the picture rather than crush them with my sins."

"Nobody knew? You just left without saying why?" Taylor stopped crying.

"I did. They were better off without me."

"Good heavens, Tom. How could you possibly think that? You had a wife and two kids. Didn't you ever think about what would happen to them?" She stared incredulously at him.

"Like I said, they were better off without me. But I always made sure they would never have to do without."

"So why did you come back? Why now?"

"Well, that's not something I want to talk about. Let me ask you something. Does anybody else know Penny is in the hospital? Or are you still not speaking to your grandmother because the last time I saw her she didn't mention that Penny was sick and I'm pretty sure she would have. She's crazy about the two of you, you know."

Taylor looked down and shook her head.

"I shouldn't have blown up like I did but I couldn't help it. I know I've hurt her by not speaking to her. It has been hard not to call her, especially when Penny was admitted to the hospital. I guess I felt like I needed to prove we could make it on our own."

"Listen, Taylor. Don't make the same mistake I did. Don't throw away your family. It would be the worst mistake you will ever make in your life."

Twenty minutes later, Tom was at the nurse's station making a phone call. He told a surprised Regina that Penny was in the hospital and her granddaughter was too proud to call her.

"The baby's getting better but Taylor is another story. She needs you. She looks completely worn out. Oh, and by the way Regina, I've told her everything." After replacing the handset to its cradle, Tom stood to leave but became so dizzy that he had to steady himself by holding onto the desk. His stomach churned and rolled like an alligator with a death grip. Fiercely painful, his gut felt like it was exploding. The next thing he knew, he felt like he was floating through a sea of blackness. He barely heard the emergency code being called over the hospital intercom.

XVII

ABSOLUTION

As soon as Regina got off the phone with Tom, she called the cab company to arrange for a ride to the hospital. She was assured that she would be picked up quickly so she ran a comb through her hair and smeared some lipstick across her mouth. As she was about to leave her apartment, her phone rang again. Impatiently, she answered it and, as it turned out, was glad that she did.

"Gina, its Taylor. I know Tom was going to call you, and I'm assuming he did, but you need to get the others and get to the hospital now. Tom collapsed and he is in the emergency room. It doesn't look good."

"Taylor, are you alright? Is Penny?" Regina heart was pounding and she was on the very edge of panic.

"Yes, we're ok, just, please, come to see about Tom. When I heard that one of the volunteers collapsed I went to the nurse's station to see if it was him and it was. They said he was throwing up blood and blacked out."

Regina hung up the phone with the promise that she would be there as soon as possible. She quickly dialed Donna's number and wasn't at all surprised that the phone was answered by a guarded, hesitant voice.

"Donna, I'm sorry to bother you. Taylor just called from the hospital and said Tom collapsed. She said he was throwing up blood and he is in the emergency room! I have a cab coming to pick me up. If you want to come with me, you can."

"What? Oh my Lord, of course, I'll go with you! She was already at the hospital when she called? Why?" Donna's voice was now very concerned.

"Penny has pneumonia. I just found out because Tom called to tell me. Then Taylor called to tell me about him. I'll fill you in on the rest on the way."

Donna scrambled to get herself ready before Regina's cab arrived. At the last minute, she thought to call Cicely. She knew their relationship was strained, but nobody could deny the fact that Cicely was miserable without Tom. She had to let her know.

Cicely was alarmed at the news and didn't hesitate to say she would join them at the hospital as soon as she could get ready.

"I'll call Stella, too," assured Cicely.

When Donna joined her in the cab, Regina reached over and took her hand.

"Donna, I'm sorry. I can't tell you that enough." The two had not spoken since the day she broke the news that Tom had fathered her child.

"Let's not go there right now," Donna said, withdrawing her hand. "I don't think I can take it. Now can you please tell me why Tom was at the hospital in the first place?"

The ride was short and filled with tension between the two women. Regina carefully filled Donna in on all the missing facts about Tom's phone call concerning Penny's pneumonia. Then she explained the call she got from Taylor concerning Tom.

"Apparently, he's been volunteering at the hospital." Regina informed her.

"I guess that's a good thing because he couldn't have been in a better place if he was going to collapse." Donna added.

When they arrived at the emergency room, to their dismay, the staff would not give them any information on Tom's condition.

"But I'm his ex-wife!" Donna exclaimed.

"I'm sorry, Ms. Thompson, we can only discuss his condition with a family member. Ex-wives don't count as family. We have called his daughter already and when she gets here I'm sure she will give you all the details." The nurse was quite firm but her voice and eyes were soft. "Actually, I'm glad you are here. Your daughter might need you."

Barely a minute later, Belinda barreled through the entrance, white as a sheet and anxiously looking for her mother.

"What happened to Dad? Is he alright?" Belinda's voice was shaking.

"We don't know yet, honey! They won't let us see him or tell us anything about him because we're not immediate family members." Donna held Belinda's hand as she spoke, trying to ease some of the panic in her eyes.

"Are you Mr. Sanders' daughter?" asked a nurse who came to the door.

"Yes, that's me," Belinda said. "Can you tell me what's going on with my father?"

"Come this way," the nurse answered while leading her to the emergency department, leaving the others behind.

Regina heard someone speak her name and, looking up, she saw that Taylor joined them. The young girl was pale and shivering in the bright light of the chilly waiting room.

"Oh Taylor, are you alright? Is Penny ok?" She threw her arms around her granddaughter and held her tightly.

"She's okay. I left her on pediatrics with one of the aides watching her. I'm sorry for the way I spoke to you before, Gina," Taylor offered, turning away to shield the emotions registered there.

"No, no, I'm the one who's sorry, so very sorry. We'll talk about it later, ok?" She answered, stroking her granddaughter's hair.

The heavy waiting room door flung open and an ashen Belinda stumbled through. Her face was red and puffy and she was struggling to maintain her composure.

"It's not good," she said. "He has liver cancer." Her expression indicated that she was about to lose what little composure she had left.

"I know, darling. It will be all right. Come here, let me hold you." Donna reached for her daughter.

"You knew?" Belinda sobbed.

"I did, Baby, but he made me swear I wouldn't tell anyone, not even you." Belinda buried her face in Donna's neck and freely wept while everyone else stood around them in stunned silence.

Much later, Tom was stabilized and moved to the intensive care unit. Belinda gave the staff permission to include her mother and their friends on the list of visitors allowed to see him. Taylor had to go back to her daughter's room, but the others were able to take turns to see him and they found it difficult to get past the sterile smell of alcohol and betadine that assaulted their senses in the intensive care unit. It was a painful reminder of Bethany's stay there.

Belinda asked Donna to come with her the first time they were allowed to see Tom and he seemed relieved to see both of them. His room was small with a glass door and windows facing the nurse's station and the atmosphere was quiet except for the steady beep of the heart monitor. There was a column behind the head of the bed that was host to heart monitors, oxygen, a suction set up, and various other pieces of equipment. An oxygen mask covered Tom's face and he had a tube coming out of his nose that was draining dark coffee ground looking fluids from his stomach into a canister. His dry lips were blue tinged and his body seemed small and frail surrounded by the cold chrome-colored bed rails. When he spoke, his voice was weak but he tried to smile reassuringly.

"It's okay," he said. "I'll be alright. It is this dang ulcer, not the cancer this time. I've been taking so much medicine, I guess I just got a big ol' hole in my stomach," he tried to joke.

Donna and Belinda stayed until it was time to allow another visitor in. When they returned to the waiting room, Regina and Cicely looked at each other questioningly. Cicely motioned for

Regina to go in ahead of her. She obviously needed a few more moments to collect herself before seeing him.

Regina navigated herself around the unit until she found Tom's room and when she entered, he looked like he was sound asleep. At his bedside, she bowed her head and closed her eyes to pray silently. Sensing her presence, he opened his eyes, startling her when he spoke.

"Hello, Regina."

"Hi, Tom." She reached over the bed rail and patted his arm. "Are you okay? Taylor told us what happened and Belinda gave us the rest of the details. You really have cancer and you didn't tell us?"

"Yes, I'm afraid so. It is nothing new. I've known about it for a while, but I didn't think it would catch up with me this fast."

"So this is the reason you came to live at the Village? It wasn't to antagonize anyone?"

"That's a fair question, but you should know I wouldn't do something like that. Basically, I knew I had to get some place where I wouldn't be alone when things get worse," he admitted.

"How have you been treated for it? What are they doing? Can you be treated?" Regina asked the questions rapidly, hoping for some good answers.

"I had chemo and radiation last year. The tumor did shrink, but it doesn't look like it is going away. It's growing again. I never figured this was how I was going to check out!" Again, he tried to joke.

"About what happened . . ." hesitated Regina.

"No worries . . . let it go, Regina. I'm glad it's not a secret anymore."

"I'm so sorry. You were right; we should have told the truth a long time ago."

"Keeping the secret is finally over. Everything will work out, you'll see. It has to; we've gotten too damn old for it not to!"

When it was Stella's turn to see him, she entered Tom's room in her typical semi-abrasive style.

"So I guess that's not really a tan?" Her long scarlet tipped finger pointed to the exposed skin on his arms and face, indicating the yellow hue. She held her breath hoping Tom would see the humor in the question. Tom stared at her wordlessly until she began to fear that perhaps her sarcasm might have crossed the line this time. Finally, his eyes crinkled up, his pale lips curled and he laughed, shaking the whole bed and all of the various tubes entering and exiting his body.

At last, it was Cicely's turn to visit Tom. After greeting each other, they slipped into an awkward silence. Finally, Tom spoke.

"Sugar, I never meant to hurt you."

"I understand. What happened with you and Regina was a long time ago and I have realized that I can't hold that against either of you," she assured him. "But what I don't get is why you tried to cover the fact that you have liver cancer. Why wouldn't you tell me that? Didn't it occur to you that I had a right to know?" Cicely's eyes were pleading with him.

Tom could barely stand the look on her face. She was pasty white and had dark circles under her eyes. Her fingers fidgeted with the gold cross on her necklace.

"The truth is I didn't want anybody to know until I was ready to tell. I didn't know how I was going to be received at the Village when I moved there. I wasn't sure if there would be any objections to me being there. If it didn't work out I could leave without letting anyone know about the big C. No sense in opening a can of worms if you don't have to."

"But why? Why wouldn't you want anyone to know?"

"Because I didn't want that to be the first thing a person would see when they looked at me. I can hear it now: *'Yeah, that's him, the guy with cancer. Doesn't he look awful?'* I don't want that. But I didn't count on the kind of acceptance I received and I sure didn't count on falling in love with you!"

"Do you love me, Tom?" Cicely held her breath.

"Yes, I do. But I hate to burden you will all of this," he confessed.

"I love you too, and you should let me decide how much of a burden you are." Cicely pushed her way through the tangle of IV tubes and the oxygen mask to give Tom a gentle kiss, barely touching his lips.

When she rejoined her friends, every eye was trained on her face looking for any possible clue of how well the visit went. Cicely offered a tentative smile and felt as if everyone in the room collectively took a deep breath and sighed in unison. The tension in the atmosphere had lessened considerably, and she knew in her heart that the Old Ladies Club would make it through this crisis all together and in one piece. Times like this prove who a person's friends really are. These women in the waiting room knew without a doubt that they could count on each other, no matter what.

A week passed before Tom was well enough to be moved to a private room. He didn't lack for visitors there, for sure. Many of the auxiliary members came to visit him and kept him supplied with fresh flowers and an endless supply of silly, sometimes off-color cards. Cicely stayed with him most of the day, but went home before nightfall at Tom's insistence.

As soon as Penny was discharged from the hospital and settled at home, Taylor returned to the hospital to visit her newly minted grandfather, bringing with her a large vase of fall spider lilies tucked among twigs sporting newly turned orange, yellow, and red leaves. It was a grand autumn bouquet that Taylor proudly gathered from her own back yard, and it was perfectly suited for a man. The appreciation in Tom's eyes confirmed that.

"Hey!" Tom greeted her with a smile. "Where's Penny? Is she well yet?"

"Hey, yourself. Yeah, she's well now. I left her with Gina. You know how grandmothers love taking care of babies."

"That's what I hear," Tom answered.

"So . . . they tell me you're dying." Taylor wasted no time getting to the point.

"Let's skip the subtleties, why don't we," Tom wryly laughed.

"I'm sorry! I—I don't really know what to say, I mean, I don't really know you but you are supposed to be my mother's father. It's weird."

"I am her father, Taylor. Yes, it is weird. I'm sorry the truth didn't come out before now. It would have saved everyone a lot of heartache." Tom's eyes were apologetic and wet.

"What about this liver cancer thing? Are you really dying?"

"I guess so," he explained. "They've done everything they could for me even though all the tests confirm that it hasn't spread to any other parts of my body yet. My liver is just giving out. The chemo and radiation I took was very difficult to live through. I don't want to go through that again. So, it looks like I'm a goner." Tom's feeble attempt at humor fell flat.

"What about a transplant?" Taylor questioned.

"A transplant? Yes, we talked about that but my blood type is unusual and there aren't that many organ donors with my blood type. You're just a kid, how did you know about transplants, anyway?"

"I studied it in school. You've got type AB blood, right?"

Tom nodded.

"You can be matched with type O blood. It's universal." Taylor explained.

"I know, but at what risk? I mean, suppose an organ donation didn't come soon enough. Who would be willing to donate their liver to an old man?"

"My father was type O and I've got type O blood. I could give you part of my liver."

Tom looked at her in stunned silence. When he spoke, his voice grew stronger.

"No!" He clasped his boney, parchment colored hands around her young soft hands and took a deep breath to calm himself. "I can't let you do that, Taylor. I mean, that's very sweet of you, but look, honey, I am way too old for that kind of stuff. It's not your problem."

"Technically, you're my grandfather. That kind of makes it my problem, doesn't it?" Taylor tilted her head and arched her eyebrows, challenging him to deny it.

"But I would never, ever let you do such a thing," Tom emphatically stated. His mouth formed a straight line across an angry determined expression.

"You think you've got the last word on that, don't you? Well, I just found you and I'm not about to give you up so easily." She spoke tenderly.

Neither of them noticed Belinda standing in the doorway. She hadn't intended to eavesdrop but when she arrived and found her father in such a weighty conversation with Taylor, she couldn't bring herself to interrupt. As she mulled over what she heard, it occurred to her that, although he had abandoned his family, he still had that solid strength about him that she missed so often over the years. She could fault him for what he had done, but she couldn't ignore the fact that he was still her father. Maybe he regretted leaving them. Maybe this illness was forcing him to take stock of his life and come to terms with how he had lived it. Maybe he was a good person, after all.

"I think I would be a better match for you, Dad," Belinda said, startling both Tom and Taylor. "After all, you are my father."

Tom welcomed her into the room with a smile and a look of concern. The fact that she came to visit him meant a lot, but offering to save his life was quite unexpected.

"Pumpkin, I can't let you do that. I'm a very old man. You have the rest of your life to live. I won't jeopardize that in any way."

"She'll only have to give part of her liver, Tom. It will actually regenerate itself. What she has left and the part you get will both grow," Taylor interjected. "Besides, you are still active and even after suffering with cancer this long, you still don't look your age. You look like a man twenty years younger."

"But you don't understand. I've already made her life hell," he told Taylor. "And I'll never be able to make up for it. What if something goes wrong? She doesn't deserve that. I just won't take the chance."

Not taking her eyes off her father, Belinda heard what he had to say and with mischievously sparkling eyes, she added:

"Ok then, I'll just let you have a little piece!"

XVIII

In the Beginning

Once Tom appeared to be somewhat stable, everyone felt reasonably certain they could return to their normal lives. For Stella, it was a futile attempt. She could not remember a time when she felt as lonely and miserable as she was now. In fact, the last time she had been anywhere this close to miserable was when she was pregnant with Emma. Back then, she was convinced she would never see her baby and spent years trying to recover from the emotionally devastating effects of it. When they were young, Bethany always took it upon herself to see that she was taken care of, but her biggest supporter was no longer around, and had left behind a mess that Stella wasn't sure she could handle. Her own parents died without knowing that they had a granddaughter in this world. When she gave herself any time to think about that at all, a small niggling doubt would creep into her soul and torture her by playing a condemning game of berating self-criticism. She was ashamed, but she would have preferred death rather than bring disgrace to her father's name. Bearing an illegitimate child for an Irish Catholic boy was not something taken lightly by a Jewish family in 1950's New York. *Gees,* she thought, *when was the last time I thought about Matthew O'Neal?* While the course of fifty-eight years took the edge off the pain that stabbed her heart when he abandoned her, it never occurred to her that she had every right to be angry. In those days, the girl was almost always considered at fault should an unexpected pregnancy manifest prior to marriage. No respectable family would allow such a thing to occur. Stella never learned to forgive herself. Throughout the years, she wore her guilt draped around her shoulders like an old sweater. It grew to be a familiar feeling, this cloak of shame, one that kept her searching for absolution through nearly every aspect of her life.

These thoughts played repeatedly in Stella's mind as she sat in Bethany's old chair and rocked back and forth, her rhythm steady and slow. The action itself, this rocking chair scenario, was becoming a habit in the evenings. She enjoyed it because it brought her closer to a sense of Bethany's presence and she was comfortable with that. She missed her old friend and was consumed by a mixture of betrayal and relief at the same time. She could honestly say that it never occurred to her that Bethany would try to bridge the empty space in her heart scarred by never coming to terms with what she had done. It seemed foolish to her, over the years, to even think about it, or hope for it. She forged through her life trying to ignore the trapped feelings beneath the surface and she eventually became skilled at packaging them into a tightly wrapped box set aside in her heart and very seldom opened. Surprising as it was, Bethany was the one who loosened the bits of old string tying her box of memories shut. Given the tiniest opportunity, every secret and every hidden moment cried out to be emancipated. At the first taste of freedom, her secret refused to remain stored out of sight, clamoring for the possibility of awareness while deeply, fully breathing the air of acknowledgement. It was time for Stella to face her past.

She leaned her head against the cushion Bethany had sewn many years ago to soften the hard wooden rails of the rocker's backrest. The present, the here and now, was gone for the moment. She couldn't think of Tom's illness, the deception between Regina and Donna, Cicely's heartbreak, or Bethany's death. Even life at Heritage Memories Retirement Village was no longer visible in her mind's eye. Instead, she let herself wander into the past, determined to make peace once and for all. The running was over. Stella wept over the memories of her baby's birth, allowing herself to feel, for the first time in many years, the ache in her heart that lived there since the day she relinquished her parental rights. She wept remembering the tears Bethany tried to hide from her all those years ago, knowing that her heart was aching as well.

Stella exhausted herself but knew this journey into the past was necessary and she allowed memories of Herman Taub to surface. Her Herman. How she loved that wonderful, compassionate man! They met shortly after that time in her life when she thought she would never be happy again. She was helping Bethany in the store when he came in looking for something he promptly forgot about as soon as he saw young Stella. He was in his early twenties, a strapping navy man, drawn to her by her statuesque beauty and her shy demeanor. She was taller than him by at least four inches, a big woman, not fat, but solid. She noticed him looking at her, but she turned her back to him until Bethany insisted she help him find what he was after. When he couldn't remember what he came for, Herman made up a story about looking for a nice gift to send to his mother in New York. The coincidence of both of them being from New York opened an avenue for the two to make conversation, and their relationship began as easy as that. Her parents approved of Herman, proud that she found such a nice Jewish man although she was so far from home. Any disappointment they had about her deciding to stay in Florida dissipated under the unexpected declaration of her happiness. Herman was a blessing and Stella married him in a traditional ceremony planned by both families in New York. While not willing to leave their home or the family business, the Morgensterns visited their daughter and new son-in-law often at their home in Florida.

Before they married, Stella was sure to tell Herman about the baby she gave up for adoption. Rightfully so, she didn't want to enter into the marriage with any secrets. Herman was heartbroken, not because of what she did, but because she had to endure it. He thanked Bethany and Jacques for taking her in when they did and giving her the support he knew she must have needed. He made a promise that as long as he lived he would see to it that she would never want for anything, and that her secret would remain untold. He was a man of his word. After his stint in the navy was over, Herman opened a Chevrolet car dealership in Ocean View, the first of its kind in the little town. He was a good salesman in a business he loved so it didn't take long for success to find him. His sharp business sense directed him toward other ventures as well; a mechanic shop, a car parts store and a gas station. He was smart enough early on to take the money he earned and invest it into businesses that would support each other. It was a wise move that gave the Taubs a very secure future and good economic growth for the town. *"He keeps me in high heels and new cars,"* Stella would often joke, her eyes sparkling in the direction of her doting husband.

They had sixteen happy years together before Herman passed away. He died six months into a battle with leukemia and for the second time in her life, Stella was devastated. She grieved privately because she didn't want Bethany to worry about her but when her friend objected to her avoidance of the grieving process, she thought it was best to move back to New York. Using her parent's advanced age as her excuse, she packed her bags and left. The truth was she couldn't face the fact that Herman was gone. Instead, she ran headlong in the opposite direction.

Shortly after she settled into her parent's home, her father had a stroke, and while he was in the hospital, she attracted the eye of his doctor. Even after Mr. Morgenstern's death, Dr. Harry Stein persistently pursued her for a solid six weeks before she surrendered herself to him. Not long afterward, they were married. It was a marriage that was unhappy and short-lived owning to the fact that there was no love on her part for this new life. When she left her brokenhearted husband, she apologized for marrying him because in her heart she knew Herman was the love of her life, and she had not gotten over him yet.

Caring for her mother consumed her days until, only a few months later, the elderly woman died in her sleep. Every one of their friends knew Mrs. Morgenstern wouldn't last long after her husband's death and Stella was left wondering why, when a husband and wife shared such an inseparable love, she was still breathing after Herman's death. She managed her parent's estate with the keen business sense taught to her by her beloved Herman and was able to easily tie up all of the remaining loose ends. It was a sad day when she sold her parents home but, at the same time, a relief because she knew that she needed to return to Florida, to Bethany, and the family waiting there for her. She felt as though she had lived a lifetime within the space of only six months.

When Stella returned to Ocean View, Bethany knew immediately that she had changed. Knowing her friend as well as she did, she feared what her next step would be and with good reason. Stella seemed to throw caution to the wind and spent her evenings going out with a partying crowd. She barely slept and had taken up the habit of smoking and drinking excessively. Quite a few men came calling for her and when Bethany voiced her concerns, Stella threatened to move into a place of her own. For no other reason than to keep an eye on her, Bethany came to the conclusion she had no choice but to back down and keep her opinions of this new life style between herself and her husband.

Close to a year after Stella's return to Florida, she met a very interesting man by the name of John Powell, who claimed to be a descendent of the famous Seminole chief, Osceola. He was dark and handsome and he taught Stella many things, including how long to hold her breath when she inhaled smoke from a marijuana joint he seemed to always have available. He was charming and charismatic and appeared to be quite well educated. It didn't matter to Stella that he never shared anything more about his background other than his legendary Native American relative. He was fun to be around and made it easy for Stella to anesthetize herself from any feelings of loss or sadness. Although she knew she was not in love with him, she accepted his proposal and, to everyone's great disappointment, they eloped. Bethany tried on several occasions to warn her about her mysterious man, but Stella had begun to hope for a new life that included a baby and a home in which she could be happy. Her hopes dried up and blew away like the seeds of a dandelion riding a gust of wind by the time she realized that John Powell had an aversion to holding down an honest job. Her greatest disappointment was that he had no reservations about living off her inheritance. One morning Stella woke up determined to put an end to the nonsense and she confronted her husband, pressing him to find a job. She informed him that their days of partying and smoking pot were about to come to a close and that her influx of funding would no longer be available. His answer was to beat her within an inch of her life. She remembered the first blow, but thankfully, not the rest. When she regained consciousness, she was in a hospital, aware she was in dire straits and confused because she could hear someone talking about the baby she no longer had.

"How did you know about my baby?" she asked struggling to get through the fogginess enveloping her.

"Mrs. Powell, do you remember what happened?" they asked. She shook her head.

"You've had a miscarriage, honey. Your husband has been arrested and taken to jail. He won't hurt you anymore."

"But I'm not pregnant," she answered groggily.

"I'm sorry, ma'am," a calm voice answered. "You were in the early stages of pregnancy, but apparently you miscarried. You have been hemorrhaging and we have to take you to surgery. Do you have any next of kin? Is there someone we can call?"

Once again, Bethany was there for her and Stella vowed not to let anyone come between them ever again. It was a hard lesson for the misguided young woman to learn. She had a new appreciation for the stability and love Bethany perpetually offered.

Although physically spent, she garnered enough strength to endure her husband's trial for attempted murder and to arrange an immediate divorce. To her surprise, she found that John Powell had a long history of scamming women out of their money and she was no exception, although she was the only one he married. *Lucky me*, she thought dryly. During her recovery, she did a complete inventory of her heart and soul and realized that Herman's death left her feeling lost, and she tried to compensate that loss any way she could, leading to decisions that ultimately resulted in disaster. After the second divorce, she returned to her married name of Taub.

It seemed the right thing to do because, after all, Herman was her one true love.

Some weeks later, Stella told Bethany that she wanted to go to work and busy herself to take her mind off the troubles of the last couple of years. It was a good decision, as it turned out, because her quest for a job landed her in the offices of the telephone company where she trained as a long distance operator opposite a young woman named Regina Whitmore. The two became fast friends right away and before long, their work relationship wasn't nearly as important to them as their personal one was.

The early memories of Regina brought Stella back to the present. She dried her tears and stopped the incessant rocking back and forth of Bethany's old chair. There was a knock at the door and it slowly opened wide enough for Ralph to poke his head through. Seeing her in such a state alarmed him and he immediately came to her side and knelt next to the rocker.

"Stella, my darling, what's wrong? Are you alright?" he anxiously asked. His concern touched her heart and she could see that Ralph was sincere and looked at her with love in his eyes. He was a good and honest man, so much like her Herman was. Stella put her arms around him and answered him with her heart.

"I am now. Ralph, I want to tell you about my baby girl."

XIX

ONE YEAR LATER

The stars in the night sky bowed to the first morning light, leaving the pale moon alone to make a final curtsy before stepping aside to welcome the brilliant sunrise. A bit of gold peeked over the Jamaican horizon, painting the sky with new colors of warm pink and soft yellow. Four lovely women stood barefoot in the sand watching and waiting for the sunrise before beginning their solemn ceremony. They all wore pure white clothing in various forms according to their individual personalities. Regina; white silk pants rolled up to mid-calf and a short sleeve jacket. Donna; a simple but lovely sundress in a white cotton-polyester blend fabric. Cicely; cropped white linen pants and matching sleeveless top. Finally Stella, in a gauzy white caftan that she delicately held up off the sand with one hand. She was the only person in the small group who wore any jewelry.

"That's not fair! We said we were going to dress all in white and here you are decorated up like a Christmas tree!" Cicely complained.

"We never said anything about accessories," Stella said, fingering the strand of large red beads hanging from her neck. "I think Bethany would have wanted me to wear these," she said, tossing her head back to jingle the matching drop earrings she wore. "She gave them to me."

"Ok, come on girls. Let's circle up as we planned, and do this thing. It's been too long already." Regina spoke with authority as she unscrewed the top of a cobalt blue ginger jar she carried and set it in the sand. Newborn sunshine illuminated the container causing it to sparkle as it reflected the images surrounding it.

The women formed a circle around the ornate jar a few yards away from the water's edge and stood silently as they contemplated its contents. Finally, Regina cleared her throat and picked up the jar.

"Bethany, you were a good friend and a beautiful spirit," she said as she walked to the edge of the water and poured some of its contents out. Returning to the circle, she set the blue container back on the sand.

Then everyone looked at Donna, whose voice trembled as she spoke.

"Bethany, every time I heard you sing, I felt closer to God." She picked up the jar and walked through the damp sand toward the water. She, too, poured out some of the contents. She carefully placed the jar on the sand in front of Cicely.

"Bethany, your faith has inspired me and I am grateful." Cicely went to the water's edge and repeated the ritual. After she returned the jar to the circle, everyone held their breath, waiting for Stella to pick it up.

She stood silently with her eyes closed for several moments before she spoke.

"Bethany, you taught me what unconditional love is. And thank you for finding my baby girl." There wasn't a dry eye among them as Stella tiptoed through the sand with the jar in one hand and the tail of her caftan in the other. Seeing that the attempt to keep her dress dry was futile, she dropped the hem into the wet sand and emptied the ginger jar of the rest of its contents. She stood by the ashes and waited for the waves to come in. The other three women moved away to give her a few moments of privacy.

"What the hell is she doing?" Regina's voice startled everyone and they whirled around to look at her. To their surprise, Stella was stomping up and down the beach, waving the sleeves and hem of her caftan wildly about. At first, no one said a word to her, they just watched silently as though they were witnessing some quirky, antiquated, native ceremony. Finally, Regina broke the silence:

"Stella, what are you doing?" she called with exasperation.

"I'm shooing," Stella answered, continuing to prance up and down the beach.

"What?" Regina asked.

"I'm shooing the birds away! I don't want any one of those damn things to pick at Bethany's remains. No telling where she might end up. One of those damn birds could get a piece of Bethany in its beak and fly to Cuba or somewhere and then what? She would be all over the place, that's what! Nope, she loved Jamaica so I am shooing the birds away until the tide comes in and takes her. Her remains will rest here!"

Regina and Donna looked at each other with worry in their eyes but Cicely laughed gleefully and, without hesitation, ran to Stella on the beach. Together they stomped up and down the beach, waving their hands about and laughing.

"No way! We're not going to . . ." Donna asked Regina.

"Yes, we are! We are the Old Ladies' Club, and we old ladies stick together!" she laughed as she took Donna by the hand and trotted through the sand toward the others.

Anyone, tourist, native, or otherwise, passing the beach from a distance might think that a group of children playing near the ocean's edge was having the time of their lives. Upon closer inspection, they would see that the children were, in fact, much older women who wouldn't compromise on life. The way they saw it, a person didn't have to trade maturity for happiness. The two walked hand in hand. Their philosophy was that it didn't matter how old they grew, they still felt the same inside as they did when they were young.

EPILOGUE

The OLC, Inc. continues to prosper, giving the Club financial security and enabling them to purchase the motel south of town with the intent to convert it into a new apartment complex. The end result turned out beautifully and they were much happier there than they were under the dispensation of Dr. Larry Whitmore, Jr. Although Regina and her son finally made peace after he learned that his mother's past was no longer a secret, moving out of the Heritage Memories Retirement Village was a cathartic event for Regina. When he got wind that she was moving and taking her friends with her, he challenged her to stay financially stable without the home he provided for her. The smug look on his face melted and he nearly fell to the floor when he learned of the business his mother and her friends started.

"You never did give me much credit for intelligence," the mother told the son. "But as it turns out I'm not so bad after all, am I?"

Donna forgave Regina and Tom for their indiscretion years ago, and eventually forgave them for keeping the secret about Renee' for so many years. She and Regina resumed their close relationship. She decided to write a list of things she wants to do and see before she dies. Learning to play the piano was the first thing on her list.

Cicely married Tom in a huge celebration hosted by her children. Every one of them had a part in the wedding, ranging from singing wedding songs to serving cake. The happy couple honeymooned in Paris where they fell in love all over again, and made good use of the wedding gift Stella presented them—a case of Ben-Gay.

Tom (*AKA—Paul*) had a successful liver transplant and both he and Belinda recovered nicely from their surgeries. He is feeling better than he has in years and, as a happy groom, has a certain spring in his step.

Stella fell in love with Ralph Watkins, despite her best efforts not to. She and Emma have become as close as any mother and daughter could. Although, it's been a year, Stella is still trying to get used to being a grandmother, to say nothing of the adjustment to being a great grandmother. She is thoroughly enjoying the process.

Emma LeBlanc assumed the position of the newest board member of OLC, Inc., as well as daughter to Stella, with ease and confidence. Getting to know her biological mother has tied up a lot of loose ends in her life and she is grateful they have become close. She and her husband, Marcel, moved to Florida and bought a sprawling beachfront home large enough to accommodate frequent visits from their children and grandchildren.

Taylor graduated college with honors and is looking forward to working on her doctorate in psychology. She is raising Penny with lots of love and joy. Her relationship with Regina has grown and she makes every effort to spend as much time with her grandmother as she can.

Jack and Lisa Faye decided to sell their home and move into the new complex the OLC, Inc. built. They thoroughly enjoy their beautiful new apartment and all the amenities available to them. Jack continues to represent the OLC and Lisa Faye works by his side on the newly formed Bethany Bertrand Memorial Outreach Committee. Together, they work to help disadvantaged families get back on their feet.

Camille, the Yorkshire terrier, misses Bethany something terrible, but he still lets Stella believe she owns him. He really likes Ralph and will be relieved when Stella decides she is ready to marry again. He is a dog who does not believe in living in sin.

ENDNOTES

1. **"Fever"**—a song written by Eddie Cooley and "John Davenport" (Otis Blackwell)
2. **"How Great Thou Art"**—a Christian hymn based on a Swedish poem written by Carl Gustav Boberg in 1885
3. **"Rock Of Ages"**—a Christian hymn by Reverend Augustus Montague Toplady written in 1763